Eve Houston is a pseudonym for the author, Evelyn Hood.
e
years, turning her talents to plays, short stories, children's
musicals and the novels that have earned her widespread
acclaim and an ever-increasing readership. *Scandal in Prior's
Ford* is her fourth novel writing under the name Eve
Houston. For more information about the author and her
books, visit www.evehouston.co.uk and www.evelynhood.co.uk

D0272953

Also by Eve Houston

Secrets in Prior's Ford
Drama Comes to Prior's Ford
Trouble in Prior's Ford

Writing as Evelyn Hood

A Matter of Mischief
The Silken Thread
The Damask Days
This Time Next Year
A Handful of Happiness
A Stranger to the Town
McAdam's Women
Pebbles on the Beach
Another Day
Birds in the Spring
The Dancing Stone
Time and Again
A Procession of One
The Shimmer of the Herring
Staying On
Looking After Your Own
A Sparkle of Salt
Knowing Me
A Certain Freedom
Voices From the Sea

SCANDAL IN PRIOR'S FORD

Evelyn Hood writing as
Eve Houston

sphere

SPHERE

First published in Great Britain as a paperback original in 2011 by Sphere

Copyright © Eve Houston 2011

The moral right of the author has been asserted.

*All characters and events in this publication, other than
those clearly in the public domain, are fictitious
and any resemblance to real persons,
living or dead, is purely coincidental.*

All rights reserved.
No part of this publication may be reproduced,
stored in a retrieval system, or transmitted, in any
form or by any means, without the prior
permission in writing of the publisher, nor be
otherwise circulated in any form of binding or
cover other than that in which it is published and
without a similar condition including this
condition being imposed on the subsequent purchaser.

A CIP catalogue record for this book
is available from the British Library.

ISBN 978-0-7515-4221-9

Typeset in Bembo by Palimpsest Book Production Limited,
Falkirk, Stirlingshire
Printed and bound in Great Britain by Clays Ltd, St Ives plc

Papers used by Sphere are natural, renewable and recyclable
products sourced from well-managed forests and certified
in accordance with the rules of the Forest Stewardship Council.

Mixed Sources
Product group from well-managed
forests and other controlled sources
www.fsc.org Cert no. SGS-COC-004081
© 1996 Forest Stewardship Council
FSC

Sphere
An imprint of
Little, Brown Book Group
100 Victoria Embankment
London EC4Y 0DY

An Hachette UK Company
www.hachette.co.uk

www.littlebrown.co.uk

This book is dedicated to
Simon and Stefan with my love,
and to the memory of Jimmy and Alastair,
who both left far too soon.

Acknowledgements

My thanks and my gratitude go to the following people for their generous assistance during the writing of this book.

The Reverend Alison Burnside, who throughout the series has patiently answered my questions regarding the work of one of my favourite characters, the Reverend Naomi Hennessey; Charlotte Peck, landscape architect, who provided invaluable advice on the restoration of the Linn Hall estate, and my friends Beryl Shaw, who offered to proofread each chapter as it was written and kept me on the right lines, Steve O'Brien, who was generous with advice on police procedures and Angus Livingstone, who, amazingly, discovered the word 'cruciverbalist' just when I was able to make use of it. If you want to know what it means, you will have to read this book.

I would like to take this opportunity to say that the members of Prior's Ford WRI are all my own fictitious characters and not based in any way on real WRI members. For those who don't know what a Daffodil Tea is, it is a very worthy annual event to raise funds in aid of Marie Curie Cancer Care, one of the UK's largest charities.

Finally, I would like to thank all the readers who have taken the trouble to email or write to tell me how much they have enjoyed the series. Writing is a lonely occupation and hearing from readers is a writer's lifeline.

Main Characters

The Ralston-Kerrs – **Hector Ralston-Kerr** is the Laird of Prior's Ford and lives with his wife **Fliss** and their son **Lewis** in ramshackle Linn Hall. Lewis is engaged to **Molly Ewing**, the mother of his baby daughter, **Rowena Chloe**. Fliss wonders, secretly, if Lewis is really Rowena Chloe's father, and if flighty Molly is the right person to take over the reins of Linn Hall.

Ginny (Genevieve) Whitelaw – Is helping to restore the Linn Hall estate, which Lewis hopes to open to the public to raise much-needed income.

The Fishers – **Joe** and **Gracie Fisher** are the landlord and landlady of the local pub, the Neurotic Cuckoo. They live on the premises with their widowed daughter **Alison Greenlees** and her young son **Jamie**.

Jenny and Andrew Forsyth – Live in the private housing estate, River Walk, with their young son, **Calum**, and **Maggie Cameron**, Jenny's teenage stepdaughter.

Helen and Duncan Campbell – Live on the local council housing estate. Helen records village news for the local newspaper and is also, secretly, the newspaper's agony aunt columnist. Duncan is the gardener at Linn Hall. They have four children.

Ingrid and Peter MacKenzie – Live in River Walk with their daughters **Freya** and **Ella**. Ingrid is Norwegian and runs the local craft shop, the Gift Horse, with the assistance of Jenny Forsyth.

Clarissa Ramsay – Lives in Willow Cottage. A retired teacher and a widow.

Alastair Marshall – An artist, lives in a small farm cottage on the outskirts of the village. Although Clarissa Ramsay is some twenty years his senior, Alastair has strong feelings for her.

Sam Brennan and Marcy Copleton – Live in Rowan Cottage and run the local village store together.

The Reverend Naomi Hennessey – The local Church of Scotland minister, part Jamaican, part English. Lives in the manse with her godson, **Ethan Baptiste**, Jamaican.

The McNairs of Tarbethill Farm – **Bert** and **Jess McNair** are struggling to keep the family farm going with the help of their younger son **Ewan**, who is in love with the local publican's daughter, Alison Greenlees. Bert has fallen out with his older son, **Victor**, who has deserted the farm for a life in the nearby town of Kirkcudbright. Victor, engaged to a town girl, persuaded his father to sign one of the fields over to him to use as a caravan park. When his plans fell through he broke the promise made to his parents, and sold the field to a builder.

Jinty and Tom McDonald – Live with their large family on the village's council housing estate. Jinty is a willing helper at Linn Hall, and also cleans the village hall and the school, while Tom is keen on gambling and frequenting the Neurotic Cuckoo.

SCANDAL IN
PRIOR'S FORD

1

Normally the Prior's Ford branch of the Women's Rural Institute meetings were relaxed and friendly occasions, but on the day Alma Parr was voted in as the new president the village hall was more like a nest of angry wasps than a Rural meeting.

'I demand a recount,' thundered Moira Melrose, the only other nominee.

'I'm quite sure the count was fair,' Iris Waldron, the outgoing president, insisted, but as Moira and her supporters began to argue loudly with her, she swiftly capitulated. 'Very well, since you feel so strongly about it, but can we *please* have a moment's silence in which to regain our composure before we vote again?'

'There's nothing wrong with my composure!' Moira snapped.

'Then I'd hate to see you losing it,' one of Alma's friends fired back at her.

'Enough!' Iris banged the president's gavel on the desk and said into the sudden hush, 'Let's all count silently to one hundred – all right, then, to twenty,' she amended as a twitter of protest began to arise, 'very slowly. I shall lead by counting aloud. Then we shall have another show of hands.'

'Who did Doris Thatcher vote for?' Ivy McGowan asked Gracie Fisher, landlady of the Neurotic Cuckoo, in a loud stage whisper as the counting began.

'Moira – sshh!' Gracie muttered, while Iris droned, '. . . and – five – and – *quiet* – and – seven . . .'

'Then I'll plump for Alma.'

'One more word and we'll start over again. And – ten – and . . .' Iris intoned, grateful to be at the end of her own stint as president.

The second show of hands resulted in a drawn vote, which puzzled everyone until they discovered the three ladies on tea duty had gone off to the kitchen, not realising their absence would make a difference.

'While we're having our tea,' Iris announced after a swift discussion with her committee, 'you'll each be given a piece of paper on which to write the name of your choice of president. The papers will be collected and counted and the result' – she ran a stern gaze over each and every face – 'will be final.'

'You would think,' said Cissie Kavanagh, her left hand whirling about the growing ball of wool held in her right hand, 'that grown women would have more sense.'

'Mmm,' her husband Robert murmured, his eyes fixed on the television set to the left of his wife's busy arm. A cookery programme flickered on the screen; Robert had no interest whatsoever in cooking, only in eating the results, but he had discovered that watching Cissie create a ball of wool at top speed tended to make him feel dizzy. He had hoped by now to be enjoying a pre-dinner pint in the Neurotic Cuckoo but Cissie had caught him on his way to the street door.

'I mean, it's only the presidency of the Prior's Ford Rural, not the United States,' she prattled on as the skein of pink wool holding her husband's wrists captive as firmly as metal handcuffs began to shrink, 'but Alma and Moira managed to turn it into another War of the Roses. You should have seen Moira's face when Alma got it by one vote. She was livid. You know how people say that someone's nostrils flared? I could never understand what that would look like. I didn't think it was possible, but today in the village hall I saw Moira Melrose's nostrils flaring. Not a pretty sight. You could have cut the air with a blunt knife!'

For some reason, probably because the television chef was dismembering a cooked lobster and Robert detested all forms of shellfish, his wife's final sentence caught his attention. 'Why would anyone want to cut air with a blunt knife?' he asked, confused.

'Nobody would. I'm just saying that when Alma was voted president of the Rural over Moira by one vote there was such tension in the village hall you could have cut the atmosphere with a blunt knife.'

'You make it sound more like a champion snooker match than a Rural meeting.'

'Anything,' Cissie said, the ball of wool growing fast, 'is more exciting than a champion snooker match, if you ask me. I don't know – it's bad enough with this feud between Ivy McGowan and Doris Thatcher without another starting between Moira and Alma. I really don't see why Moira should get a third crack at being president just because she's local born and bred. Alma's a go-ahead woman with a lot of good ideas, and there's nothing wrong with a fresh outlook, is there?'

'What's this about a quarrel between Ivy and Doris?' Ivy McGowan and the Kavanaghs were neighbours, living as they did in the row of houses that had once been the village almshouse before being turned into six neat little dwellings with a shared back garden. 'When did that start?'

3

'Oh, a lifetime ago as far as I know. Something about them both falling for the same man – Jinty McDonald's father, I've been told.'

'So who got him?'

'If either of them had got him, Robert, she'd have been Jinty's mother and grandmother to that brood of hers. He married someone else entirely, but Ivy and Doris never got over the loss for all that they both married after he did. And now it looks as though the Rural's going to have a rocky time ahead. Mark my words, Robert, Moira might well have the touch of an angel when it comes to choux pastry, but she's not the type of woman to take failure kindly. I can see trouble ahe—'

The phone rang and without thinking Robert reached out to pick up the receiver. What was left of the unwound wool slipped off his other hand and the almost completed ball of wool was twitched from Cissie's fingers to roll across the floor. Monty, the kitten Robert had given his wife the previous Christmas, appeared from nowhere and went dashing after it.

'Robert – Monty. Naughty cat!' Cissie made a dive for the ball, but Monty neatly batted it to one side from beneath his owner's fingertips.

'Robert!'

'I'm on the phone,' Robert said, beating a hasty retreat to the kitchen with the cordless phone.

It seemed to him that dangerous things such as helping wives wind balls of wool should be on a list given to men considering marriage, not sprung on them when it was too late to change their minds.

2

'I am not going to have a blow-up Father Christmas on the roof, or a bunch of reindeer pulling a sled across the front wall of the house,' Andrew Forsyth said firmly.

'Are you telling me that I'm going to have to cancel the order at this late stage?'

'Jenny, you haven't!'

'Of course I haven't, don't be such a goose! When I said I wanted to make this Christmas the most special ever, I meant inside the house. Lots of decorations – tasteful decorations,' Jenny added hurriedly as her husband screwed his nose up, 'and a full Christmas dinner and lots of presents and friends round for drinks, and all the trimmings. I'm celebrating!' She threw her arms wide. 'Celebrating you getting over cancer and Maggie beginning to settle in and us being a proper two parent, two children family with a future before us. Call me a sentimental fool—'

'You're a sentimental fool, but on the other hand, I can see what you mean. Let's push the boat out.'

'Let's! Remember that guinea pig Calum said he wanted for

Christmas? We should get it for him, and a good keyboard for Maggie. She ought to get back to her music lessons, and you can get keyboards with headphones so only the musician can hear what's being played,' she added as Andrew frowned slightly. 'I've checked. And that kitten she mentioned as well. It would be nice to have a kitten.'

'Don't blame me if the kitten eats the guinea pig and Maggie starts playing horrible rubbishy pop music on her keyboard,' Andrew grumbled, but she could tell by the slight lift to the corners of his mouth that he was willing to go along with her plans.

'It won't and she won't, and everything will be lovely,' she assured him, 'you wait and see!'

She hugged him hard. The past two years had been difficult. Maggie, Jenny's teenage stepdaughter from a disastrous early marriage, had come to live with them, and had found it hard to settle down in Prior's Ford; Jenny, Andrew and their young son Calum had suffered considerably from her teenage sulks and tantrums. Then to make things even worse, Andrew had been diagnosed with bowel cancer and had had to undergo chemotherapy, radiotherapy and finally an operation. He had recently been told he was cancer-free, though he would be monitored for the next five years. He was due to return to work in the new year.

As it happened, this new crisis had forced Maggie to think of others instead of herself and, as a result, she was finally beginning to settle into the family, though there was still some way to go.

Jenny was right, Andrew thought as his wife bustled off to the kitchen, singing a Christmas carol even though it was still November. They had a lot to celebrate this Christmas.

★　　★　　★

Cissie Kavanagh's prediction about unrest in the WRI began to come true in early December. When she, Gracie Fisher and Clarissa Ramsay met in the Neurotic Cuckoo the Rural was the main discussion point. The Kavanaghs had gone there for lunch, as had Clarissa, who had had a busy morning turning out her spare room. The pub was quiet, so once the meals had been served and eaten Gracie, Clarissa and Cissie had coffee together while Robert Kavanagh and Joe Fisher talked over a couple of pints at the bar.

'The meetings are beginning to seem more like minefields,' Cissie said gloomily and Gracie nodded.

'You're right. Alma has her following, and Moira has hers,' she explained to Clarissa. 'Moira likes to be in control of every part of her life, including her husband and the Rural, and her nose has been put right out of joint. Now she and her friends criticise everything Alma and her committee say and do. It's getting beyond a joke. I don't often get to the meetings, being so busy in the pub, but they're not the pleasure they used to be. I'm thinking of giving up the Rural.'

'Don't do that,' Cissie said. 'We need as many neutral members as possible. I'm sure it'll all settle down eventually.'

'I'm beginning to feel quite glad that I've resisted the attempts to get me to join the WRI,' Clarissa said thought-fully.

'Oh, but it's a wonderful organisation, isn't it, Gracie?'

'Yes it is, and everything was fine before the bickering started. I always thought Alma and Moira liked each other. They're neighbours, aren't they?'

'They are, and they got on well enough before this busi-ness, but unfortunately they're both very competitive. Remember that time you gave the Rural a talk on your travels last April, Clarissa?'

'Not the rock-cake ladies?' Clarissa asked, and when Cissie

7

nodded, went on, 'I do remember, and I don't think poor Alastair Marshall will ever forget them. He only came with me to show the slides, and nobody told us that speakers were always asked to judge competitions afterwards. I did home-made jams and poor Alastair got landed with the baking competition. When the winner was announced more than one lady glared at him.'

'Alastair voted Alma the winner, and Moira Melrose and Ivy McGowan were both deeply offended,' Cissie said. 'I left the hall with Moira and she informed me that Alastair Marshall was a pleasant enough young man, but he certainly didn't know his way around a well-made rock-cake.'

'But surely it was just a little inter-group competition. Why make such a fuss about it?'

'Hear hear!' Robert Kavanagh called over, having caught Clarissa's comments.

'Just you concentrate on your pint and get on with your male gossiping,' his wife told him.

'Women gossip, men talk.'

'Aye, that'll be right,' Cissie said drily, and her husband winked at Clarissa.

'It's a matter of seniority,' Cissie explained, turning her attention back to the matter in hand. 'Moira's in her fifties and she's village born and bred. Alma and George only came here eighteen months ago when he got a job with one of the animal-feed suppliers. She's in her forties, and a really energetic WRI member. When Alma suddenly put herself forward for president Moira never expected her to get voted in but, unfortunately for her, some of the members were in the mood for a change.'

'Specially the younger members,' Gracie added. 'Alma's already come up with some good ideas for future events. Personally, I think we're ready for some new blood.'

'There's nothing wrong with new blood,' Cissie said, 'but when it comes to spilling it I'm not happy. I just hope that Alma and Moira settle their differences before they're much older. If Moira can't accept defeat gracefully the entire Prior's Ford Rural could be the loser.'

'So could the Cuckoo's darts team.' Gracie glanced at the bar, where her husband was polishing glasses while he and Robert put the world to rights. 'George Parr and Dave Melrose are both in the team, and Joe doesn't want to lose either of them. Another coffee?'

'Not for me, I'd best get back to putting the spare room in order. I got a phone call yesterday from someone I met while I was visiting relatives in America last year,' Clarissa said. 'Apparently she's flying over to the UK soon to see friends in England, and she plans to come to Scotland early next year, starting here, with me.'

'That'll be nice for you, seeing your friend again.'

'I hope so, Gracie. The thing is, she was really the friend of friends and I only met her twice. Isn't it silly, the way you say things like, "If you're ever in the UK you must let me know." I suppose we say it because we don't really think the other person's going to take us up on it. But this one has.'

'You must have liked her in order to say it in the first place,' Cissie suggested.

'That's what I keep telling myself. She was vague as to just when she plans to arrive, so I thought I'd better get the room ready now to save a mad dash when she makes contact. Needless to say, I've been using it to store things until I decide where to put them.'

Try as she might, Clarissa couldn't quite place Amy Rose, the woman who had phoned her a few days ago. The name was vaguely familiar and seemed to be linked in her mind to colours, for some reason. Perhaps it was the surname.

The thing to remember, she told herself as she walked the short distance from the Neurotic Cuckoo to her home, Willow Cottage, was that the Americans were wonderful and generous hosts. And so must she be, when Amy Rose arrived.

3

Normally the first thing Moira Melrose did when she got back from a Rural meeting was to make a cup of tea. Tea was always part of the meetings, but Moira, convinced the village-hall water was inferior to the water that ran pure and sweet from her kitchen tap, liked to get the taste of the village-hall tea from her palate.

Today, however, before she had even unpinned the hat she always wore when she left the house, she said, 'Get the loft ladder down, Dave, I want to have a look at the Christmas decorations.'

'Christmas isn't for weeks yet,' her husband protested.

'I want to see if we've got any outside lights.'

'We've never had outside lights.'

'Those Parrs had the outside of their house all decorated last Christmas, and we're going to do even better this year.'

'But you said their place looked common. Like a dog's dinner, you said!'

'Ours'll be tasteful. Nice lights on that tree in the corner of the front garden and things like that.'

'What's Alma done to annoy you now?'

'For one thing, she's breathing, for another she's in our village, and for a third, she's making a right mess of the Rural meetings. They're just not the same. The loft, Dave!'

'I can tell you now we don't have any outside decorations; never have. You need special decorations for outside.'

'Then we'll get them. We'll go into Dumfries on Saturday afternoon and buy some.'

'There's a darts game on in the Cuckoo Saturday afternoon.'

'We'll go first thing in the morning then.'

'Who's goin' to put them up? I'm gettin' too old to climb trees!'

'Our Nancy's husband's good at DIY.' Moira picked up the phone and began to punch in her daughter's number. 'He'll run the show and you can do the fetching and carrying. I'll get them to do their place up as well. We'll all go into Dumfries on Saturday. I'll show that Alma Parr a thing or two!'

To Dave's horror his wife meant what she said about matching and possibly surpassing the Parrs' outdoor Christmas decorations. On the following Saturday morning the entire family – Nancy, her husband Paddy and their three young children in their estate car, and Moira and Dave in their Vauxhall – left the village after an early breakfast, to return just before noon with both cars packed. Nancy and Paddy, who lived only half a dozen doors from the Melroses, had enthusiastically taken to the idea of decorating the exterior of their house as well as the interior.

'Even better,' Moira said. 'We'll have two houses all lit up and they'll only have the one.'

'Oh, I'm not bothered about Alma,' Nancy told her cheerfully. 'She's all right; I just fancy having a nice Christmas garden.'

12

They returned to find George Parr up a ladder, attaching a string of lights to his guttering.

'Look at that – he's started on his lights already. We've made our move just in time,' Moira said as Dave stopped the car.

'Been shopping?' George called down cheerfully as his neighbours each carried an armful of boxes into their house. Moira ignored him, and as soon as she got her husband indoors she issued him his orders. 'Now then, you bring in the rest of the stuff while I get us something to eat. Fast as you can – and don't tell that nosy-parker next door what we've bought.'

George was standing on the front lawn, studying the guttering, when Dave returned to the car.

'Want a hand?' he called over.

'Better not, thanks.' Dave collected another armful and then, glancing swiftly at the windows to make sure his wife was in the kitchen and not watching him, he hurried over to the fence. 'You've got me into a right mess, you have!'

'What've I done?'

'You and your outside decorations. Now Moira wants us to have the same, only better.'

'The more the merrier; it'll brighten the street up. I'll give you a hand putting 'em up if you like.'

'You can't – Moira wants to outdo your missus and I'm not supposed to tell you what we've bought.'

'Why ever not?'

Dave sighed heavily. 'If you must know, it's to do with your Alma being made president of the Rural instead of Moira.'

'Does that matter?'

'It does to my missus,' Dave said gloomily.

'But you and me are in the darts team together – we've got to talk to each other.'

'Of course we will – when Moira's not around. But you know how it is when women get a bee in their bonnet,' Dave

13

said uncomfortably. 'I've got to keep the peace. Don't want to be cold-shouldered in me own house.' And he hurried off.

'Daft article!' Alma said when George told her about the conversation over lunch. 'And poor old Dave, being told who he can and can't be friends with. Talk about small minds! Just because she was born here and she's been president of the Rural twice already she thinks she owns it. I was voted in fair and square and I've got lots of plans for this year. And for the decorations, too.'

'Now don't you start trying to outdo Moira with our decorations, because me and Dave and young Paddy are good mates, and with us being in the darts team it'd cause all sorts of trouble if we fell out.'

'What's Paddy Wishart got to do with it?'

'Apparently Moira's got him and Nancy keen to do up their garden too.'

The smile broadened, and became triumphant rather than amused. 'Well well, so it's two against one. That's not a problem for us, is it? I think we'll pull out all the stops this year, George.'

George eyed her uneasily, past experience reminding him that Alma relished a challenge and hated losing.

'You're not going to make a big thing of this, are you? We like brightening up the area at Christmas, but it's not a competition, love.'

'Don't you worry, pet, it's that Moira Melrose who wants to be cock of the walk, not me. It just so happens we know more about outside decorations than they do. There's more cauliflower cheese keeping hot in the oven. Fancy another helping?' Alma asked and when he nodded, she went off to the kitchen, humming 'Anything You Can Do, I Can Do Better'.

Having arrived in the village a mere eighteen months earlier, the Parrs had only spent one Christmas in Myrtle Crescent.

14

On that occasion their exterior decorations, though they came as a surprise to their neighbours, who had only ever decorated the interior of their houses, had been accepted without much comment. But now bemused neighbours watched in astonishment as the Parrs, the Melroses and the Wisharts began to decorate the walls and front gardens of their council houses.

'It's like influenza,' Steph McDonald said when she arrived home from college to find her parents at the window, watching the work going on across the street. 'Starts with one, then spreads. How many more are going to catch the infection?'

'I'm not,' her father grunted, returning to his armchair.

'Don't you worry, Tom, I'm with you,' Jinty assured him. 'It must have cost them a fortune to buy all that stuff – what a waste of money! And it's not an infection, Steph, it's what's called one-upmanship. It's all part of this silly nonsense going on between Alma and Moira. Just because Alma and George decorate the outside of their house at Christmas Moira's decided that she and Dave have to go one better.'

'The Wisharts are at it too.'

'I'll bet Nancy's under orders from her mother.'

'Poor Dave,' said a voice from the armchair. 'Anyone making a cup of tea?'

'Poor Dave indeed.'

'I wonder,' Steph said thoughtfully, 'what it's going to look like once the houses are all lit up.'

'Like Blackpool Illuminations?'

Steph nodded. 'That's what I think. I'm sorry for the folk who have to live across from all those lights over Christmas.'

'You're ri—' Jinty began to agree before it dawned on her. 'That's us, and next door!'

'So it is. I'll put the kettle on, Dad,' Steph said.

★　　★　　★

15

When all three sets of outdoor Christmas lights were turned on in the same evening everyone poured from their homes to view the brightly lit houses, which had their windows and front doors edged with coloured lights, shimmering golden curtains hanging from the guttering, lights hung in trees and hedges, flashing on and off, and various illuminated Santas, elves, reindeer and snowmen dotted about the gardens. As word went round, people came from all over the village and beyond to see the displays.

'The crescent's been turned into a showplace. I feel like a flamin' circus turn,' Dave Melrose said morosely to George Parr when they met for a pint in the Cuckoo. 'Every time I look out of my front window there's folk gawpin' from the pavement. I've even had to wire up the gate at night to stop kids comin' in. Some of 'em seem to think we're a public park, not a private house.'

'That's because you've overdone it, mate. You should have gone for tasteful instead of throwin' in everythin' but the kitchen sink.'

'I don't think you're one to talk, given the stuff in your garden. That blow-up Santa's an eyesore.'

'Alma happens to be very fond of that Santa,' George said stiffly. 'We've had it for years. And what we put in our garden's our business.'

'The same goes for me and my missus, and you've just told me we've overdone it.'

'That's enough,' Joe Fisher interrupted them from the other side of the bar. 'We all know it's not you two who's at logger-heads, it's your womenfolk and you've already agreed that you're not goin' to get involved in what's goin' on between them. Remember the darts team, lads!'

'Aye, Joe's right.' George drained his glass and set it down. 'Women are touchy and the darts team can't be doin' with

16

any aggro. They'll sort themselves out in their own good time and the best thing for us to do is just stand back an' wait for them to do it. Right, Dave?'

'I'll not say no to that.' Dave drained his own glass.

'Good man. Another?'

Dave hesitated, but only for a second. He had promised Moira he wouldn't be out for long, but to be honest, the Cuckoo was a more peaceful place than home at the moment, with his better half niggling on and on about Alma Parr. And it was soothing to be able to look out of the bar windows into darkness lit only by street lamps rather than the colourful, constantly flashing and moving cavalcade of lights outside his own living-room windows.

'I'll not say no,' he said again, nodding.

Christmas officially began for Prior's Ford on the day that the council workers set up the tree on the little half-moon village green. As darkness fell Clarissa Ramsay looked out of Willow Cottage's main bedroom window at the coloured lights sparkling in the darkness and began to feel the tingle of anticipation that always gripped her at Christmas time.

Keith, her late husband, had considered Christmas to be an overrated excuse to eat too much, drink too much and overindulge children. Clarissa, who, although single for most of her life, had always found like-minded friends to celebrate the festive season with, had endured seven dull Christmases as his second wife, but once widowed and a free agent again she relished the joys of a village Christmas.

In Prior's Ford, members of the church choir went out carol singing in aid of charity, while in the towns and their suburbs youngsters in twos and threes bellowed the first few bars of 'We *wish* you a *merry Christ*muss . . .' and then held their hands out for money. At least one home in every street in the village held parties for neighbours, and those living on their own were never short of invitations to Christmas dinner. This year, Clarissa was cooking for Lynn Stacey, the head teacher of the local primary school, and her neighbours Marcy Copleton and Sam Brennan, who lived together in Rowan Cottage and ran the village store.

Alastair Marshall, the young artist who rented a farm cottage on the fringe of the village and had been the first person to befriend Clarissa after Keith's death would also have been invited to Willow Cottage, but this year he had been summoned to his parents' home in Lanarkshire to meet a new little nephew.

'I'd rather be here with you and the others,' he had said mournfully.

'Nonsense, it'll be lovely to be with your own folk and to see the new baby.'

'I notice you're not hurrying down to England to spend Christmas with Alexandra and Steven.'

'They're my stepchildren, not blood relatives and, in any case, they're both going abroad this year. Alexandra's spending Christmas and New Year in France with friends, and Steven and Christopher are skiing in Austria. I'm looking forward to going to the pantomime and the carol concert on Christmas Eve, then the midnight service, then having a good old traditional Christmas Day dinner in my own home,' Clarissa had said happily.

Hearing voices, she tore her gaze from the tree lights and glanced over at the main road to see a steady stream of people on their way to the first night of the local drama group's pantomime.

Hurrying downstairs, she shrugged on her coat and buttoned it up before going out into the cold night air to join them.

18

4

'The keyboard we're surprising Maggie with isn't a problem,' Andrew Forsyth said, 'but there's no way we can smuggle a live guinea pig and an equally live, noisy kitten into the house without being detected.'

'There must be ways and means,' Jenny said firmly, 'and with a little help from our friends we'll do it. Calum said he wanted a guinea pig and Maggie said a kitten would be nice. If you can survive cancer I can surely come up with a way of surprising them with what they want for Christmas!'

The kitten turned out to be fairly easy, as enquiries round the village revealed that one of the cats at Tarbethill Farm had produced a litter that would be looking for new homes by Christmas. The guinea pig was more of a problem, since it came with a hutch.

Ingrid and Peter MacKenzie and their daughters, Freya and Ella, were spending Christmas in Norway with Ingrid's family. At her suggestion the guinea pig and its hutch were established in the MacKenzie's back garden two days before

Christmas, with Jenny popping over to keep the little animal fed and watered on the pretext of looking after the house.

When Jenny mentioned her dilemma with the guinea pig on a visit to the farm to see the kittens, Jess McNair, the farmer's wife, said at once, 'Our Ewan can probably help you there. He's going to the Cuckoo on Christmas Eve to have supper with the Fishers – he's walking out with their daughter Alison – and I'm sure he'd help your husband to move the hutch. He's in the kitchen, we can ask him now.'

'Alison and I are going to the midnight service after supper, Mrs Forsyth,' Ewan said when his mother explained the situation. 'If you can get Calum and Maggie off to their beds right after the service I'll help Mr Forsyth to move the hutch before I go home.'

'But you probably have to be up early in the morning to milk the cows,' Jenny protested. 'I don't want to keep you from your sleep.'

'I'll survive one late night,' Ewan assured her cheerfully.

Walking home in the early hours of Christmas morning, Ewan felt so full of energy he regretted not being able to rouse the cows and start the milking there and then. The night was cold, with a light frost on the grass and hedges, which was common enough at that time of year, but tonight there seemed to be a tingle of excited expectancy in the air that Ewan hadn't experienced since his childhood, when he had lain awake every Christmas Eve straining his ears in an attempt to hear the jingle of sleigh bells in the starry sky above the farmhouse roof.

His fanciful thoughts might have been influenced by Jenny's almost childish excitement as he and Andrew had quietly settled the hutch into place close to the Forsyths' back door, or they may have had something to do with Alison's young son Jamie's wide-eyed excitement at the prospect of a visit from Santa Claus, but it seemed to Ewan as he started up the farm lane that there was more to the night's magical aura than that.

It had been a difficult year for the McNair family. The farm was failing and Ewan knew his parents were both sick with worry about the future. His older brother, Victor, was engaged to Jeanette, a girl from Kirkcudbright; eager to earn enough money to marry her, Victor had persuaded their father to give him one of their fields which he had planned to turn into a caravan park. When the venture fell through he had sold the field to a builder who was about to develop it into a small housing estate. His decision, taken in secret and not discovered until it was too late for Bert McNair to prevent it, had split the family up. Victor was now living in Kirkcudbright, the nearest town, with his fiancée's family and working for her father, a garage owner. As soon as the housing estate was completed, he and Jeanette planned to marry and move into one of the new houses.

All Ewan had ever wanted was to take over the farm eventually, and since Alison and wee Jamie had come into his life he had found renewed hope and strength. He wanted desperately to marry Alison, but at the moment the farm wasn't bringing in enough money. He was constantly on the lookout for ways to add to their income and fortunately Alison, born and raised in Glasgow, had fallen in love with country life. She had helped him set up the wormery he hoped would eventually bring in some much needed income, and had worked hard alongside him to restore the old, abandoned farm cottage halfway up the lane so it could be used as a holiday let.

The thought of spending the rest of his life without Alison by his side depressed Ewan but, tonight, as he passed the shadowy bulk of the renovated cottage, he was strengthened by the certainty that somehow, from somewhere as yet unknown, he would find the solution to all their problems.

He halted for a moment, looking up at a single star shimmering above his head then, recalling childhood superstition, he closed his eyes and made a wish before continuing on towards the farmhouse where his parents slept.

As he walked he became lost in a dream, imagining what it could be like next Christmas if the fates were kind enough to grant his wish: imagining himself and Alison together in his bedroom in the farmhouse and Jamie in the room next door, waking to find out what Santa had brought him.

A new year was coming, bringing with it new hope.

Everything worked out as Jenny planned. After the ritual present-opening first thing on Christmas morning she handed Calum an envelope, telling him it had been put through the letterbox. Inside was a card with the message: 'See you in the garden'. When he opened the back door to investigate he found the hutch, which Jenny had insisted on wrapping in Christmas paper and tying with ribbon.

The guinea pig, not in the least bothered at being turned temporarily into a Christmas parcel, was greeted with shouts of joy, and promptly christened Frères Jacques.

'That's the song Maggie taught me when she was helping me to learn French. It's his – what d'you call the fancy name that dogs entered in Crufts have?'

'Kennel name,' Jenny offered.

'That's it. Frères Jacques can be his hutch name. I'll call him Jack for short. Want a carrot, Jack?'

Maggie's eyes were like stars when she saw her new keyboard. 'It's – it's fantastic!'

'We'll set it up in your bedroom later. It's got headphones

so you can play it silently and be the only one who can hear the music,' Jenny explained. 'And the man who teaches music every week at the primary school's going to give you lessons, if you want.'

Maggie nodded, and then to Jenny's delighted surprise the girl hugged her and then Andrew. 'Thanks, both of you!'

'You're welcome, love. I just wish we'd known earlier that you had music lessons when you lived with your grandparents.'

'But we know now, and that's all that matters,' Andrew said. 'Anyone fancy some breakfast? I'm starving!'

'It looks as though Maggie's finally accepted us as her family,' he said later as he and Jenny stacked the dishwasher. 'We have a daughter.'

She nodded, beaming.

'Now for the other surprise,' Jenny said when the dishwasher was switched on and the Christmas dinner preparations under way. 'Go and call them, Andrew.'

'In a minute. I've got a gift for you.'

'You've already given me my gift.' She held out her arm to display her new bracelet.

'That was the public one. This is the real one.' He dipped a hand into his pocket and produced a small box. 'I didn't get round to wrapping it.'

'Andrew, it's beautiful!' She stared at the diamond ring. 'It must have cost a fortune – if it's real.'

'Of course it's real. Jenny, will you marry me?'

For a moment Jenny had trouble speaking. When she got her voice back, she asked feebly, 'What did you say?'

Andrew laughed. 'I didn't think it would come as such a surprise after all these years.'

'But – we're fine as we are.'

'I know, but isn't it time to make it official? Even if only for Calum's sake?'

'Being married won't make any difference, darling. You've got me for life, and I'm sure Calum won't worry about us not being officially wed when he finds out. Not in this day and age.'

'Why are you being so obstinate?'

'I – Andrew, when I married Maggie's father I thought it was for ever. I meant it to be for ever but then it turned out to be a terrible mistake, and look what happened. I deserted Maggie, and because of that she and I have both suffered so much.'

'You didn't know what that man was really like until it was too late, but you've lived with me for thirteen years. I'm not going to turn into a bully now, am I? Let me have the ring.' He took her left hand in his and slipped the ring on. 'There – it looks great on you. I'm going to fetch the kids; it's time to go to the farm.'

Alone in the kitchen, hearing Andrew call from the hall, 'Hey, you two, come on down, we've still got one more present to collect,' Jenny stared at the diamonds sparkling beside the plain gold ring Andrew had bought for her when they decided to live together. Everyone had been told they had married quietly, with nobody present except two borrowed witnesses, but in truth Jenny had been unable to sue her husband, Neil, for divorce because she was terrified to let him find out where she was. Her closest friends, Ingrid MacKenzie, Helen Campbell and Marcy Copleton, had learned the truth when her brother-in-law, sent to Prior's Ford when there was talk of the old granite quarry being re-opened, recognised her and told her Neil had died in an accident aboard an oil rig and Maggie was now living with his parents.

Since discovering she was free Andrew had suggested more than once that they should marry, but now – she touched the ring with the tip of a finger – he was clearly eager for a commitment – which made Jenny nervous.

Hearing him come back she swiftly slipped the ring from her finger and returned it to the box, which she put into her skirt pocket.

'They're coming down. I've brought your coat,' he said, and then, as he helped her on with it, 'You've taken the ring off.'

'The children would notice it. Maggie would, for sure.'

'That's not a problem, is it? If you're still reluctant to tell all, we can say it's the engagement ring I couldn't afford to give you years ago.'

'You've taken me by surprise, Andrew. I need time to get used to the idea. Shh, they're coming.' She buttoned the coat with trembling fingers as Maggie and Calum came thundering downstairs.

'Okay, if that's what you want,' Andrew said, his voice flat with disappointment.

5

Jess McNair came out of the farmhouse when she heard the car arrive in the yard. 'Merry Christmas, everyone. Have you had a good day?'

'Brilliant!' Calum told her. 'I've got a guinea pig called Jack and Maggie got a keyboard, but I don't know why we're here.'

'I was hoping you might find room for a cup of tea and some of my Christmas dumpling, but I want you to see something in the barn first. Over here,' said Jess, leading the way.

The farm cat came to meet them as they went into the barn, and Jess bent to stroke her. 'Going to show us your family, Trixie? Here they are.' She went over to a corner where four kittens were curled in a sleepy heap on a snug bed of hay.

'Ohhh!' Maggie and Calum dropped to their knees beside the nest. 'They're beautiful!'

'You can pick them up,' Jess said as the kittens woke, stretching and blinking at their visitors. 'Trixie won't mind. They're all old enough to leave home now and she's beginning to want to be off on her own again. She's the best mouser

27

we've had for a while,' she explained to Jenny and Andrew who, looking at the little cat's lovely face and wide innocent eyes, found it hard to think of her as a hunter. 'Which one do you want?'

'We're getting one of the kittens?' Maggie, cuddling a black kitten to her cheek, asked in disbelief.

'If you remember, when Calum asked for a guinea pig for Christmas, you said you'd like a kitten, but then we discovered you'd had to give up your piano lessons when you came to the village, so we decided to give you the keyboard.' Jenny bent and picked up another kitten. 'We thought we'd get a kitten for the whole family, but ask you, Maggie, since Calum's going to be busy with his guinea pig, to look after the kitten. Okay?'

'Okay,' Maggie said, and her smile seemed to light up the entire barn.

'Did you notice what a lovely smile Maggie has?' Andrew asked his wife as the two of them relaxed in front of the television set after dinner was over. Calum was outside, settling Jack into his hutch for the night while Maggie was on her knees in the kitchen, trailing a ball of wool around to amuse the kitten. She and Calum had finally settled on a marmalade kitten with her mother's innocent little face and wide blue eyes, and Maggie had named her Martha after a stickleback she and her grandfather had once caught in a dam.

'She was actually called the Honourable Lady Martha,' she had explained, flushing slightly, 'and I really loved her. But we'll call this little one plain Martha.'

'The Honourable Lady bit can be her kennel name or whatever cats have,' Calum had suggested, and so it was decided.

'It was great to see her look so happy,' Jenny said now.

'She's going to be a real beauty when she's older. We'll have young men thronging round the door soon.'

'We'll cope. Isn't it wonderful, Andrew? We have a son, a daughter, pets – the lot!'

'All the more reason for us to get married.'

'But everyone thinks we're already married – Ingrid, Helen and Marcy are the only ones who know the truth. How would we explain a wedding to Calum and Maggie?'

'Tell them we're romantic fools who want to go through it all again, with them present. They'd love it,' Andrew said, and then, as Jenny said nothing, he went on, 'You're not having doubts about us, are you?'

'No, of course not. Haven't I just said how wonderful it is to feel like a complete family now? It's just – it might be too soon for Maggie. She needs more time to settle down.'

'I don't think she'd mind, especially if you asked her to be your bridesmaid. Jen, there's a reason for this reluctance, I know it. Tell me.'

'It's daft.'

'I know that already, but I'd still like to hear it.'

'I'm frightened.'

'Of marriage to me?'

'Of marriage. I made a mess of it the last time and we've been so happy just the way we are I don't want to rock the boat.'

'It wouldn't rock any boats, darling. How could it?'

'I don't know, but I don't want to risk losing what we have right now. D'you remember Alice Pemberton in the office where we met?'

'Vaguely, but what's she got to do with it?'

'Alice lived with her partner for three or four years, then they decided to get married, and a year later he left her. He said he couldn't face the thought of being committed to her.'

'But that doesn't apply to us. We've been together for a long time, and we have a son – and a daughter too, now, not to mention the pets. For the sake of that innocent little guinea pig, Jennifer, and that little kitten, we must legitimise our relationship,' Andrew said, but he couldn't even raise the flicker of a smile from her. 'Jen, last year I thought I might die, and when I got lucky and survived, I wanted to celebrate by making you my wife in every way possible. I still want it.'

'Mu-um,' Calum bellowed from the kitchen.

'In the living room, love. Can we leave it for now? I need a bit more time, that's all,' Jenny begged, and Andrew had no option but to nod as Calum burst into the room.

'The committee has decided,' Alma Parr announced at the first January meeting of the local Women's Rural Institute, 'on an exciting new dimension to this year's Daffodil Tea.' The annual event was held at the end of March to raise funds for the Marie Curie Great Daffodil Appeal.

'What d'ye mean, a new dimension?' Ivy McGowan asked truculently from the front row, where she always occupied the same seat. One of the oldest members of the Rural, Ivy hated change.

'Well – we're going to jazz it up a little in a way that'll raise more money.'

Ivy's indignant, 'Do what?' was drowned out by Moira Melrose's, 'And what's wrong with the usual Daffodil Tea? They've always been very popular, haven't they?'

A babble of voices immediately broke out. Those in the area where Moira and her cronies always sat were disapproving, while from elsewhere in the village hall there were more subdued sounds of interest.

'Ladies, please!' Alma banged the gavel on the table before her, but had to use it a few more times before silence fell.

30

'We will of course keep the traditional items such as the bring and buy table, guess the doll's birthday – the doll this year will be dressed by Doris Thatcher – and the cake and preserves table. But the committee has come up with another idea that we're confident will meet with your approval – a fashion show.'

A second excited babble of voices was cut short by a loud and vigorous, 'Nonsense!'

'Excuse me?'

'You heard me. What do we want with a fashion show?' Moira said belligerently. 'A bunch of what d'ye call 'ems – skinny models showing off clothes most of us couldn't get into even if we could afford them, which we can't, or want them, which we definitely don't!'

'Moira's right,' Ivy McGowan boomed. 'We don't need fashion shows, that's not what this group's about. Have you seen those models on the telly? Most of 'em look as if someone's thrown the clothes at 'em and they've only just landed. More bare skin than clothes. Who wants to look at that?'

'You'd be surprised, Ivy,' someone called out to loud laughter.

'Order, please! Sometimes it can be refreshing to ring the changes, ladies.'

'You'll be wanting us to do one of those naked calendars next,' Moira complained, and glared as Alma smoothed her manicured hands over her corseted hips and said amiably, 'Is that a suggestion from the floor?'

'I think it's a lovely idea, Alma,' Doris Thatcher called out. 'The fashion show, I mean. It'd be nice to do somethin' different!'

'Well said!' Alma beamed at Doris who, like Ivy, was in her nineties. Unlike large-boned Ivy, Doris was small and neat with a head of snowy white curls. 'Good for you, Doris, still up for a fashion show at your age.'

A slight frown stitched itself in the papery skin between

Doris's green eyes, as wide and innocent as a child's. 'I might be old, dear,' she said with a slight edge to her normally sweet voice, 'but I'm still all woman.'

'Of course you are,' Alma apologised, once the laughter had died down. 'I just meant that it's lovely to see one of our oldest members so willing to embrace new and fresh ideas.'

'Embracing senility, more like,' Ivy muttered audibly, but Doris, as always, let the comment pass without notice. Her sunny nature made her the more popular of the Rural's two oldest members, and she knew full well this annoyed outspoken Ivy more than any reaction to her sarcasm ever could.

Cissie Kavanagh's hand went up. 'Who'll supply the clothes, and the models?'

'Ah, a sensible question at last. A member of my staff when I was supervisor of a ladieswear department in a well-known Dumfries store' – Alma ignored another audible mutter, this time of 'Not again!' – 'happens to run her own successful dress shop now, and she came up with the idea of bringing some of her wares here for a fashion show. Easter will be approaching by then – the perfect time. As for models, ladies . . .' she spread her arms wide, beaming, 'we ourselves will model the outfits.'

She nodded smugly as there came another sudden babble of voices. As it ebbed, she continued, 'As my former colleague has asked me to point out, she sells her wares to real human beings, not to celebrities – or skinny models, Moira – and she needs real women to show them to their best advantage.' Again she slid her hands over her hour-glass hips.

'You needn't think I'm going to model anything,' snorted Moira, who, in her fifties, was a good twelve years older than Alma, several stones heavier, and never wore corsets.

'But think how exciting it will be to try on the latest fashions. After all, a proper fashion show should demonstrate that the female form can come in all shapes and sizes, and that even the older and least svelte members among us can look attractive with the correct outfits. My former colleague also sells excellent foundation garments.'

Heads swivelled to see what Moira made of that, but she was too busy dealing with her daughter, Nancy, who, in her late thirties, was almost as heavy as her mother.

'It would be fun, Mum,' Nancy was hissing at her. 'Go on, say yes. I want to be a model, Mum!'

'Will you be quiet,' Moira hissed back. She raised her voice. 'I move that we concentrate on having our usual successful Daffodil Tea. Who's with me?'

'Ladies, ladies,' Alma shouted above another outbreak of voices, 'do I have to remind you that all decisions have to be put to the vote? Silence, please!' She banged the gavel down hard on the table and waited, eyeing each face in turn, until even Ivy and Moira subsided. 'Good. Now then, if anyone has anything to say I would be grateful if she would hold her hand up and be recognised in the proper fashion. Yes, Jinty?'

'I'd be willing to do a fashion show,' Jinty McDonald said, 'and I like the idea of us trying on the clothes. It'd be fun. I'd volunteer to be a model.'

'And me,' Doris called out, 'if your friend has any nice clothes for an oldie.'

'Bravo, Doris – I'll make sure there's a lovely outfit for you to wear. Ladies, a round of applause for our first two volunteers,' Alma said, and Doris and Jinty blushed and smiled as they were clapped, while Moira scowled and Ivy muttered, 'Doris Thatcher – a model? That one's a good sixty years past her sell-by date!'

'Can I have a show of hands, please, from those willing to give the fashion show a chance?' Alma watched with satisfaction as hands began to creep up in ones and twos. Even Nancy indicated her approval, almost dislocating her shoulder in her

33

attempt to keep her raised arm behind her mother's back and thus out of her line of sight.

'Agreed by a majority,' Alma said smugly. 'We'll take the names of volunteers during tea. Eleanor, would you be willing to take measurements over the next few meetings for me to pass on to my friend?'

'Of course.' Eleanor Pearce, a trained seamstress, was also wardrobe mistress for the village drama group, run by her husband Kevin.

'Thank you, dear. Any other business before we have our tea?'

'Yes,' Rita Billings's hand shot up. 'When are those Christmas lights outside the houses in Myrtle Crescent going to be switched off and taken in?'

Alma's face went pink. 'I don't think that that has anything to do with the Rural,' she began.

'I know that, but they've been giving me a right headache for the past three weeks, and as three of the people involved are here, I'm grabbing the chance to ask when it's going to stop. I'm tired of trying to sleep in a bedroom that flashes like a fairground until late at night.'

'Decorations should all be down by the evening of the fifth of January, and that's tomorrow,' Alma said.

'That's all right, then. I suppose I can manage one more night. Right,' Rita said, clambering to her feet, 'come on, Jinty, we're on tea duty this meeting.'

6

Frank Billings arrived home from work at half past five on January the sixth to find his wife standing at the living-room window, peering across the road.

'You've not forgotten the Gordons are coming for their dinner tonight? Your clean shirt's laid out on the bed. They haven't started taking in their decorations,' Rita said. 'None of them. I've just had a walk down as far as Nancy Wishart's house. It's past Twelfth Night, too.'

'They'll probably be waitin' until the weekend to start takin' everythin' down,' Frank said easily. 'It took them a whole day to put them up, remember.'

'I hope you're right,' Rita muttered as he went upstairs.

Her sister and brother-in-law, Kath and Maurice Gordon, didn't have far to travel as they lived in Marlot Road, five minutes' walk at the most from Myrtle Crescent. The foursome met every two weeks for dinner, sometimes in the Cuckoo, but mainly in one or other of their homes.

'I know Christmas is over but I thought I'd give it one more outing before it goes into the attic,' Rita said as Kath admired the elaborate holly and frosted pine cone decoration in the middle of the table, which stood in the living room's bay window.

'Quite right.' Kath shrugged out of her coat and handed it to Frank. 'I think it's a shame that Christmas only happens once a year. I hate having to take everything down and put it away again. Ooh, sherry. You're pushing the boat out, aren't you?'

'Left over from New Year, so make the most of it,' her brother-in-law said jovially as he handed a glass to his wife. 'We'll be back to lager next time.'

The meal was finished and they were all lingering at the table with their coffee when the room was suddenly illumin-ated and a battery of coloured lights began to dance outside. Kath, who suffered with her nerves, jumped and then screamed as coffee slopped from her cup and onto her pale cream skirt.

'I knew it!' Rita screeched, jumping up. 'It's those Melroses at it again. And the Parrs,' she added as more lights suddenly appeared.

'Flippin' heck!' Maurice stared out at the night, suddenly taken over by Santas, reindeer, assorted glowing animals and a giant snowman bobbing about in one of the gardens opposite.

'She promised!' Rita almost wept. 'Alma promised the lights wouldn't go on again after Twelfth Night!'

'Never mind her, what about me? Fetch a cloth, quick,' Kath yelped, holding her skirt away from her thighs with the tips of her fingers.

'I'm going, I'm going! Do something about those lights, Frank!' Rita rushed to the kitchen. 'That flashing'll bring on one of Kath's migraines!'

By the time the two men got out of the house someone

was already thumping at the Parrs' door and several other people were emerging from their houses.

It was Alma who opened the door. 'Yes? Can I help you?'

'You can turn those darned lights off for a start. It's like livin' opposite a fairground.'

'I think they're very tasteful.'

'Mebbe at the beginnin', Alma,' Frank cut in, 'but I think we've had enough of them. Rita said you were goin' tae take them down today.'

'We didn't have the time, and when our neighbours put theirs on earlier we decided to do the same, didn't we, George?' Alma turned to her husband, who had appeared behind her, looking uncomfortable.

Before he could reply Moira Melrose's voice blared from the adjoining garden, 'It was you who put your lights on first, not us!'

'Excuse me, I believe you put *yours* on first.'

'I don't give a toss who did what first,' Frank snapped. 'Just put 'em off an' leave 'em off!'

'Hear hear,' a woman called from the roadway.

'Our decorations'll be switched off when they switch theirs off,' Alma said firmly.

'And the same goes for us,' Moira responded, folding her arms tightly beneath her generous bosom.

'Oh, for goodness' sake, you two.' Rita had arrived. 'I'm all for a bit of come and go among neighbours but those lights flashing in at us from right across the road night after night are getting to be too much. Aren't they, Jinty?'

'I wouldn't mind seeing the street get back to normal,' Jinty McDonald agreed. 'Look, why don't you both just switch your lights off – and you too, Nancy,' she added as the Melroses' daughter and son-in-law arrived, 'and agree that it's over for this year. Then we can consider the matter closed. And before

37

any more argument about who switches off first,' she added as Alma opened her mouth to speak, 'it's ten past seven. Christmas ends in Myrtle Crescent at exactly seven fifteen – right?'

'I agree,' George Parr said from his doorstep, and Dave Melrose nipped in swiftly with, 'Me too. Okay, Paddy?'

'I suppose. Ow!' Paddy said as his wife dug her elbow into his ribs.

'Right. Now we can all go home. Tom,' Jinty said as her husband headed for his own gate, 'you wait in the road to see fair play.'

'But it's cold!'

'It's only for four minutes; you won't catch your death. I'll get a cup of tea going.'

'On second thoughts send one of the kids out with my coat. I'll take a walk round to the Cuckoo once the lights go off,' he called after her.

'Hang on,' George Parr said. 'I'll turn the darned lights off and fetch my coat. I wouldn't mind a pint myself.'

'Nor me,' Paddy said, and Dave nodded.

Three minutes later the crescent was restored to its normal peaceful darkness, other than the soothing street lights, and the four men were on their way to the pub.

'Thank heaven that's over,' George said as they hurried along.

'Amen to that,' Dave agreed, little knowing what was still to come.

Sadly, the removal of the Christmas decorations turned out to be the beginning, rather than the end, of the growing animosity between Alma and Moira. Moira refused to have anything to do with the Daffodil Tea fashion show in March and Rural meetings were tense as the members began to group into two camps, one supporting Alma while a smaller clique favoured Moira.

'I'm trying to keep well out of it, but it isn't easy,' Jinty McDonald told Fliss Ralston-Kerr as they gave the gatehouses on either side of the drive leading to Linn Hall an early spring clean. 'Why do people always have to take sides?'

'Human nature, I think. Look at all the wars over the centuries and the way even church congregations can split up.' Fliss sprayed a window and then polished it vigorously. She had always managed to avoid suggestions that she join the Rural, partly because she was shy when it came to mingling with a lot of people and partly because, as the ancient title of laird still lingered in the village, she, like her husband Hector, could never feel comfortable at village functions. Jinty, who lived in the local council house scheme and helped Fliss out whenever needed, was her best friend and the only villager Fliss felt completely relaxed with.

'I forgot to tell you the latest, Mrs F.' Jinty had been quite horrified when Fliss suggested that they should address each other by their first names, but had settled on 'Mrs F' as a compromise. Every time she used it, it gave Fliss pleasure. 'The committee have asked my Steph to model a wedding dress as the highlight of the show. She's chuffed to bits about it and so am I.'

'She'll look wonderful; she's such a pretty girl!'

'Takes after her dad,' said Jinty. 'Merle and Heather are to be bridesmaids and Alma wants Faith to be the flower girl. The bridesmaids'll be all right, but I'm not sure about Faith. If she's having a stubborn day there'll be no controlling her.'

'Oh, I'm sure she'll be fine. Your children are so well brought up, Jinty.'

'But Faith's the difficult one. Sometimes I think that living with her's like eating porridge with ground glass in it.'

'Surely not! D'you know,' Fliss stood back to study the window, 'those gatehouses are in much better condition than the hall itself.'

'That's because they're small and compact. The hall's got so many windows for the weather to damage and so many tiles likely to fall off.'

'You're probably right,' said Fliss, who sometimes scurried up to Linn Hall's top floor on wet days when there was nobody around to revel in the joy of standing in the empty rooms, watching the rain course down the windows and not having to dash around putting vases, ewers and chamber pots down to catch the drips from the ceiling.

The Ralston-Kerrs had lived for years in the big kitchen, using the butler's pantry as Hector's office and their private living room and only going through the baize door and up the wide sweeping staircase to reach their bedrooms on the second floor.

Once a handsome big manor house set in attractive gardens, Linn Hall had gradually but steadily deteriorated due to the Ralston-Kerrs' financial problems. The family – Fliss, Hector and their son, Lewis – had been dependent for years on young back-packers willing to help in the house or on the estate in the summer months in return for their food and accommodation in the gatehouses. Even with their assistance it had been a losing battle until a handsome and unexpected donation a few years earlier had slowly begun to turn the family's fortunes around.

Now the roof and windows were wind- and water-tight and Lewis had made considerable progress towards improving the gardens. Through careful use of their unexpected financial fortune he and his father had managed, with advice from Andrew Forsyth, an architect, to work out a business plan resulting in a bank loan generous enough to enable them to employ a few local people as well as the backpackers.

'Sometimes,' Fliss said, 'I've wondered if we wouldn't be better living down here instead of at the other end of the drive. Nearer to the village.'

'You'd have to move out every summer to let the young folk in. We couldn't expect them to rough it in the big house the way you do. Even young folks would turn up their noses at that.' Jinty always spoke her mind, which was one of the things Fliss most loved about her.

'You're right, and in any case Hector would never come down here to live. He loves the hall too much, bless him – drips, draughts and all.'

'Never mind, we're getting there. Next year you might be able to move into the drawing room instead of using the pantry as a living room, and won't that be something?'

'Mmm.' Fliss looked down doubtfully at her thick jersey, body warmer and jeans. She more or less lived in these clothes and she wasn't sure she had anything, other than the dress and coat kept for events like village fetes, fit for drawing-room wear.

7

'So who's going to be invited to host this year's event?'

'Why not you, Robert? You made a good fist of it last year,' Pete McDermott said amiably. The village progress committee members were crammed into the Kavanaghs' small, cosy living room, organising a Burns Supper for the community.

'Best to let someone else have a shot at it this time. I'd not want to be accused of hogging the limelight.' Robert had been hearing far too much from his wife about the quietly simmering feud between Alma and Moira at Rural meetings and he had no wish to find himself in a similar situation.

'Gilbert McBain asked me just the other day if any decisions had been made,' the Reverend Naomi Hennessey offered in the rich, deep voice that seemed filled with the sunshine that blessed her Jamaican mother's homeland.

'Do we really want Gilbert? He always overdoes things,' Lachie Wilkinson objected. 'Every time I hear the phrase "ham actor" I think of Gilbert in one of the drama club plays.'

'Would you rather do it, Lachie?' Muriel Jacobson enquired gently.

'Good grief, no! I go to a Burns Supper for pleasure as well as for the food and the whisky. I don't want to get involved in any other way, thanks.'

'Same with me,' Muriel agreed, 'so I think we should be grateful for those who offer to do the hard work. Let Gilbert strut his stuff; it doesn't take long.'

'Kevin Pearce has been asking me about the supper too. I got the impression that he would love to be the host this time.' There was a distinct twinkle in Naomi's large dark eyes. Despite being the local Church of Scotland minister she wasn't averse to throwing the occasional spanner in the works, claiming that it kept people on their toes and thus enriched their lives.

'Oh great, two egos clashing and if we pick one the other'll be miffed. So what do we do now?' Pete asked. 'Are you sure you wouldn't like to make it easier for us by agreeing to do it yourself, Robert?'

'And have them both resenting me? Absolutely not. I don't mind helping to organise it, but that's as far as I'm going this year.'

'Let's ask Kevin,' Muriel suggested. 'After all, Gilbert's in every production the drama club puts on, but as their director Kevin has to stay backstage. Let him have his moment in the spotlight.'

'I agree,' Naomi said at once, but the men hesitated.

'D'you think he'll be up to it?' Lachie asked doubtfully.

'I don't see why not. I know he's a rather vain little man,' Muriel ignored the fact that Kevin was much taller than she herself, 'and people tend to look on him as a bit of a joke because he loves to seem important, but I'm sure he'd do well and I think he should have the chance.'

'Muriel's right. I'm giving him my vote,' Robert said decisively. 'I'd go for Kevin as the host, and Gilbert to do the

Address to the Haggis — that needs a Scottish accent and Kevin's English. Kevin could do the Toast to the Lassies, though.'

'So can I note it down as official?' Helen Campbell asked, and when there came a general murmur of consent, she swiftly minuted 'MC — Kevin Pearce plus Toast to Lassies. Haggis — Gilbert McBain.' She had forgotten to record *Desperate Housewives* and was hoping to get home before it started.

'Yes, and then we can get down to deciding who should be invited to take over the other duties,' Robert said. 'I'm going for Lynn Stacey to reply to the Toast to the Lassies and I reckon that Bill Harper'll be willing to do the Immortal Memory again.'

As soon as the meeting closed Helen scooped up her notebook and pen and fled out into the night, anxious to get home in time to find out what the desperate housewives of Wisteria Lane, USA, were up to. One thing she was sure of — it would be much more interesting than recording minutes for Prior's Ford's progress committee. Sometimes she yearned to put a bit more fizz into writing up the minutes — something like Charlie Crandall suddenly rising from his chair to sweep the Reverend Naomi Hennessey into his manly arms and declare his secret passion for her.

Robert was checking his own notes when his wife Cissie arrived home.

'They've gone, then?'

'About ten minutes ago. They all said to thank you for the refreshments. Muriel and Lachie did the washing-up.'

'Good. Put the kettle on, Robert, I'm dying for a cup of tea.'

'Get on with you! You've surely been drinking tea all evening.'

45

'Yes, Eleanor kept everyone supplied through the costume fittings, but tea can't be enjoyed when you're busy trying to keep the peace.'

Robert groaned inwardly as he gathered up his papers. 'We'd a good meeting,' he offered casually. 'Got the list of speakers and entertainers worked out for Burns Night. It's just a case of getting everyone to agree.'

'Moira's blowing hot and cold over this fashion show,' his wife went on, ignoring him. 'First of all she's having nothing to do with it, which is for the best, of course. Then she decides that she'll become involved after all, but we all know that that's only because Nancy insists on being in it. That's the only good thing to come out of this – Nancy's finally found the courage to disagree with her mother instead of always doing as she's told. I think she could be quite an interesting person if she could just break free. So Moira and Alma were both there tonight.'

'Moira's never going to model, is she?'

'Of course not, she's helping with the refreshments, but she turned up anyway and she and Alma were trading snide remarks. I thought they were going to come to blows when Alma started talking about things being years past their sell-by date. She did it subtly, but everyone knew that she was talking about Moira. Everyone, apparently, except Nancy; she took Alma literally and started on about how much she agreed, unfortunately.'

'I'll put the kettle on,' Robert said, making for the door, but before he reached it he was stopped in his tracks by, 'Robert, you're going to have to speak to them.'

'To who?'

'The Parrs and the Melroses – and the Wisharts. From what I'm hearing, things are getting worse in Myrtle Crescent. Apparently last week the Parrs and the Melroses had a real slanging match out in the street because Alma said the Melroses deliberately put their bin out in front of the Parrs' gate the night before the bin collection. I left Eleanor's with Jinty McDonald and Rita Billings, and they said the other residents are beginning to take sides, just like in the Rural. And when I met Gracie on the stairs when I was on my way to the Pearces' bathroom she told me the husbands are rowing as well now, and it's playing havoc with the darts team. Poor Joe's really upset about it.'

'I don't see what I can do,' Robert protested. 'The progress committee doesn't have any authority.'

'Well, if someone doesn't do something soon, Jinty says, things look like getting worse. Neighbours falling out was the last thing I expected in a nice quiet place like Prior's Ford. Haven't you seen to that kettle yet?'

'That,' Clarissa said as she and Alastair Marshall left the village hall, 'was a fantastic evening. Are all Burns Suppers like that?'

'Sometimes they're better. Sometimes the host doesn't plunge the knife into the haggis with such murderous intent that the three people on either side of him flinch back in mortal fear.'

'Gilbert McBain really threw himself into it, didn't he?'

'Into the haggis, or into the Address to the Haggis? He and Cynthia overdid "John Anderson, my Jo John" as well. They were supposed to be a lovely old couple in the twilight of their lives, not two of the witches from Macbeth.'

'Don't be such a killjoy, it was all lovely. Lynn Stacey's reply to Kevin's Toast to the Lassies was superb.'

Frosted grass crackled beneath their feet as they began to cross the village green. Looking up, Clarissa saw the night sky as a huge black velvet dome and the moon as a rotund emperor surrounded by his people, a host of tiny sparkling stars. She dug her hands deep into her coat pockets and took in a breath of cold, sharp air.

'The night tastes like iced champagne,' she said happily.

'Our Rabbie's getting to you – turning you all poetic,' Alastair teased her, and then said in a puzzled tone, 'Are you expecting visitors? There's a car at your gate.'

Peering into the night Clarissa saw a dark mound silhouetted against the glow from a street lamp. 'Not at this time of night. Perhaps someone's broken down.'

As they neared the car they saw by the light of the nearest street lamp that a woman was slumped against the back of the driver's seat, her head at an uncomfortable angle. A floppy sort of beret was tipped at a rakish angle over one closed eye and her mouth was wide open.

'She's asleep.'

'Or ill? She's not . . . ?'

'I can see her breathing. In fact,' Alastair said, leaning forward until his face was almost pressed against the side window, 'she's snoring. Listen.' He made way for Clarissa.

Putting one ear against the icy glass she could just make out faint snoring. 'Is she drunk?' she whispered, her breath misting in the cold air.

'Could be. It can be an almost obligatory state in Scotland on Burns Night.'

'Not for drivers.'

'P'raps she realised that she's not fit to drive and drew in off the main road to sleep it off.'

'We can't leave her out here; it's cold and going to get colder.'

'You're not suggesting we take her into your house, are you? If she's drunk you don't know what she might be like when she wakes.'

'It's at times like this you wish we had a policeman in the

village. I can't leave her here!' Clarissa rubbed the glass and then cupped her hands round her face and peered into the car again. 'Wait a minute – I think it might be Amy Rose.'

'Your expected visitor?'

'Not expected tonight. She said she'd phone me in good time, and I haven't heard a word so far. But I think,' Clarissa said, squirming about to get a better view, 'that it might be. I'm going to waken her.'

'Leave it to me, just in case.' Alastair moved her aside and tapped gently on the window. When there was no reaction from the sleeper, he tapped a little harder.

'I've a feeling that you're being visited by a drunken American, Clarissa.'

'Better drunk than ill. Poor woman, how long has she been sitting out here? Try again, louder.'

This time Alastair rapped loudly on the window and then jumped back, almost knocking Clarissa down, as the woman shot upright in her seat with a screech of alarm. They saw her flailing around, then the window was wound down.

'Get back! I have a gun!' She uttered a dismayed squawk as something thudded to the floor. She dived after it while Alastair and Clarissa stared at each other.

'Don't—' Alastair began, but Clarissa elbowed him aside and opened the car door.

'Amy? Is that Amy Rose?'

'Huh?' The woman shot upright again, the beret finally giving up the struggle and slipping off her head completely. 'Clarissa? Thank God, Clarissa, you've arrived in the nick of time! This highwayman was threatening me.'

'We don't have highwaymen any more,' Alastair informed her coldly.

'You used to have, I've read about them. So what are you – a mugger? Is that what you call them now?'

49

'He's a friend, Amy, and for goodness' sake come into the house before we all freeze to death. Alastair, help her out while I open the door.' Clarissa hurried into the house and switched on the hall and porch lights before turning to see her guest shedding various items over the pavement as Alastair winkled her from the small car.

'My purse is on the floor somewhere, and my coat in back,' Clarissa heard her say when Amy Rose's feet were finally on the pavement. 'I think I lost my gloves on the sidewalk and my bags are in the trunk if you'd be so kind, young man.'

'Are you sure you don't have a gun?'

'Never had one in my life. I find hatpins sufficient. Go get my things.' Amy Rose came fluttering up the path like a large moth; an illusion, Clarissa discovered, created by her clothing – a long skirt floating round her legs at each step, a flared jacket, a scarf looped several times round her throat with the ends hanging to her waist, and a wild mop of hair. As she came into the lit hall she seemed to explode with colour: her hair was almost scarlet, her small face heavily made-up and her clothing in too many colours to count – predominantly greens, blues, yellows and reds.

'Clarissa, honey, it is so good to see you at last! Have I had a ball since I got to Britain!' Red-painted fingernails glittered as her hands accompanied the flow of words. 'It's been the most fantastic time. Why didn't I come over years ago? I must be mad! I meant to be here before this but I was having such a good time in England that I stayed longer than I intended. No matter, I'm in no hurry to get back home. You must have been wondering where I'd got to, though.'

'No, I was just waiting to hear when you were arriving, but – Oh, never mind, come into the living room and get warm.'

'I didn't let you know my plans?' Amy started unwinding

her scarf as she followed her hostess into the room. 'But surely – I thought . . . No, wait a minute – oh, for heaven's sake!' The scarf, a long rainbow of soft wool, was tossed in the direction of a chair but drifted instead to the carpet as Amy began to unbutton her green velvet jacket. 'Did I forget to call you? I could have sworn that I had done but you know how it is when you're havin' a wild time, you keep tellin' yourself, phone, darn you, phone the woman, and then you get so you think you've done it already when you've only been thinkin' about doin' it. What am I like? The visitor from hell, right?' The jacket landed in a haphazard way over the back of a chair. 'I should just turn myself around an' find some hotel somewhere – is there a hotel in this place? – an' come back when you're ready for me.'

'Of course not, Amy!' Clarissa rescued the jacket and hung it over the chair properly. 'You're very welcome, and your room's ready. I just need to put a hot-water bottle in the bed. I've been keeping it aired, and there are towels and so forth.'

'Shall I take your guest's things up to the spare room?' Alastair asked from the doorway.

'Yes please. I've got some home-made soup I can heat up; you must be freezing, Amy.'

'That'd be good. This is a darlin' little home you've got!' Amy said, following her hostess into the kitchen.

'There's enough for three, Alastair,' Clarissa said when Alastair arrived downstairs.

'No thanks, I'll head for home and let you two catch up. Give me your keys and I'll lock your car, Miss – er, Mrs . . .'

'It's the Widow Rose, but my friends all call me Amy. The car doesn't lock too well so just leave it – it'll be fine where it is, I'm sure.'

'It's not a hired car, then?'

'Lord no, I hate drivin' hired automobiles. I bought it when

51

I came over here. I love it – it's eccentric, like me, and we get along just fine together. So where were you tonight, Clarissa? Paintin' the place red, I hope?' Amy raised an eyebrow in Alastair's direction.

'We were at the Burns Supper in the village ha—' Clarissa stopped abruptly as her guest let out a scream.

'Oh no, don't tell me I've missed Rabbie's birthday? It was today? I thought it was next week!'

'January the twenty-fifth.'

'An' it's all over? But it was on my list of got to dos. When does it come round again?'

'Next January the twenty-fifth. It's held to mark his birthday,' Alastair explained.

'Oh darn it! I got myself a book of his poems and everythin'! But there's always next year, I guess. No use gettin' upset over spilled milk.' Amy settled herself at the kitchen table and picked up a spoon as Clarissa ladled soup into a bowl.

'You're sure you don't want some, Alastair?'

'No, I'd best get home.' He turned towards the door. 'I'll see you soon – er – Amy.'

'You can bet on it, Alastair,' she assured him, attacking the steaming soup with relish.

8

February was usually a gloomy month, with its cold weather, long dark nights, short days and all the excitement and fun of Christmas, New Year and Burns Night over, but Clarissa's American guest, fluttering around the village like a multicoloured butterfly, radiating a zest for life that affected everyone she met, changed all that. Her first church-service attendance caused some raised eyebrows when she started clapping to the beat of a particularly cheerful hymn, but when Naomi beamed down at her from the pulpit and clapped along with her almost all the congregation joined in, though some of the older villagers such as Ivy McGowan gripped their hands firmly together and shot disapproving glances in the direction of Amy's bright red head.

'I hope that clapping nonsense isn't goin' to be allowed every Sunday,' Ivy said to the minister on her way out of church.

'I rather liked it, Ivy.' Naomi took the old woman's hands in both of hers.

'So did I,' chirped Doris Thatcher.

'And I have a sneaking feeling our Lord did too, Doris. We all have our different ways of worshipping Him,' Naomi agreed warmly. Doris and Ivy were much the same age, but while Doris's glass was always half full, Ivy's was inevitably half empty.

'But some know better than others what the right way is – and the way to dress for church as well, not like that noisy one. Who is she anyway?' Ivy wanted to know.

'Mrs Ramsay's friend from America,' said Naomi, who with a few others had been invited to Willow Cottage to meet Amy Rose.

'Oh – an American.' Ivy's tone said that explained it. 'This is what happens when outsiders start tae move intae a community,' she added for good measure before stamping off.

'I think,' Naomi said to Clarissa as they walked together to the church gate, 'that your enchanting friend's a little too much for some of our more conventional villagers. If you ask me, though, she's a breath of fresh air. She chases away the winter blues and she certainly enjoys community singing.'

Clarissa glanced over at Amy, talking animatedly to the Fishers from the Neurotic Cuckoo and to Jess and Ewan McNair from Tarbethill Farm, well out of earshot. She smiled at Naomi. 'It's a pity she's tone deaf.'

'Oh, I don't think God objects to that. He probably agrees with me that enthusiasm more than makes up for perfection. And it's much more fun, too.'

On the following day Clarissa arrived home to find the mobile-library van parked outside her gate and Amy and Stella Hesslet, the local librarian, about to have lunch in the kitchen.

'I went to have a look at that cute library on wheels an' discovered that Stella here was plannin' to just sit there and eat sandwiches for her lunch. So I invited her in to have a proper meal. We made enough for three, so sit yourself down.'

'I hope you don't mind, Mrs Ramsay.' Stella was in her mid-forties, a quiet, pleasant woman who lived in the Mill Walk estate.

'Of course not.' Clarissa hung her coat on the hook at the back of the door and pulled out a chair for herself.

'Now Stella, it's Amy and Clarissa. You British are so formal! For gosh sakes, how long have you two known each other?'

'Since I moved here about three and a half years ago.'

'And Stella here's still not callin' you by your first name?'

'It doesn't seem right when Mrs – when Clarissa's a client of the library.'

'Oh, tush, that's got nothin' to do with anythin'.' Amy indicated the pile of books on the kitchen counter. 'Stella gave me a temporary card and I just about cleaned her out of crime novels. Can't get enough of 'em! She likes crosswords too, so I'm goin' to give her some of my own to try.' She slipped Clarissa's oven gloves onto her hands before opening the oven door.

'I'm glad you're here, Stella, because I've got books to return, and I wouldn't mind getting more if you have the time.'

'Of course I do.'

'Food's ready.' Amy set a casserole dish on the kitchen table and steam poured out as she lifted the lid. Stella's eyes widened.

'Goodness, that looks delicious – and what a lot there is. I'm used to a few sandwiches when I'm going round the villages.'

'Not today. You just take your time and enjoy your food, Stella. If you're late back you can just tell them that you'd this mad American to deal with. Not that I was always an American,' Amy rattled on. 'I was born in Nottingham an' I used to be as English as a cup of tea till my parents moved to Chicago when I was ten years old. An' you know what? The minute

55

I stepped off that boat from England I felt as if I'd come home. I guess I must've lived in the US in a past life. I like to think that I was one of the Pilgrim Fathers or, in my case, a Pilgrim Mother.'

Despite her protests Stella managed to clear her plate and have two cups of coffee before she announced that she really had to get back to work.

'That was delicious, and I so enjoyed your company. Thank you both.' She hesitated, then said shyly, 'Would you like to come to my home tomorrow evening for supper? I don't get the chance to entertain much.'

'Sounds grand – we're free, aren't we, Clarissa?'

'Yes, we are. Thank you, Stella, that would be lovely,' Clarissa said, and the librarian flushed with pleasure.

'That's one lonely lady,' Amy said after the mobile library had gone. 'We'll need to see what we can do to brighten up her life.'

When the Rural's guest speaker had to cancel because of influenza Amy stepped in at the last moment and gave a sparkling talk on her life in America and her passion for cross-words, compiling them as well as doing them.

'That's the only thing about having her as a visitor,' Clarissa, who had considered it her duty to accompany Amy to the meeting, admitted to Cissie Kavanagh as the two of them washed up the tea things afterwards. 'I enjoy doing the daily *Times* crossword, but Amy beats me to it every time. It takes me hours to complete it but she races through it like a hot knife through butter.'

'She certainly worked wonders here today – this is the first meeting we've had since Alma was voted in as president without a disagreement over something or another.'

'Oh dear, is there still trouble?'

'I'm afraid so. If the dispute between Alma and Moira isn't settled soon, something's going to give,' Cissie said grimly.

Clarissa and her visitor were also invited to the local primary school, where Amy spent an afternoon telling the children about her American childhood and answering questions such as, 'Do you live next door to any famous film stars?'

'Nope, an' I wouldn't want to,' was her robust reply to that one. 'I like real folks about me, folks like you, not silly pretends. Hi there, what's your question?' She turned to Faith McDonald, who seemed to be trying to touch the ceiling with her waggling fingers.

'Is your hair real?'

'Sure it's real.' Amy grabbed a handful and tugged it. 'See?'

'You mean you were born with it that colour?'

'Oh no, it was just a sort of ordinary colour until I grew up.'

'What happened then?' another child asked. 'Did you get a bad fright?'

'No, I just looked in the mirror one day and I said to myself, "Amy, you're not only little, you're about as exciting to look at as a piece of wallpaper. Nobody ever notices you." If I was the only person at a bus stop the bus driver would drive right past me, and when I went into restaurants the waiters never noticed me. So I decided to do somethin' about it. I started to colour my hair, and I got myself lots of bright clothes. Now nobody misses me and that's the way I like it. Now then, who can guess what I am?'

A hand shot up at once. 'Old?' suggested Faith.

'Good guess, honey, but wrong. I don't ever plan to be old cos bein' old's dull. I'll tell you the answer. I,' Amy announced, 'am a cruciverbalist, and I bet even your teachers don't know what that means.'

The entire class looked at their head teacher, Lynn Stacey, who shook her head. 'I don't.'

'You crucify people?' guessed Lachlan Campbell, and the entire class gasped.

'No, I don't hurt folks, I entertain 'em. I make up crosswords. Anybody here do crosswords?' Amy asked and, when one or two children claimed parents, aunts, uncles and grandparents who liked doing crosswords, said, 'That's great, so you know what a crossword is. Well, I do 'em all the time, and I make 'em up too, for newspapers. I'm a cruciverbalist, that's the proper word for what I do. Write it down and tell your folks tonight. I bet you'll be the only one in the family who knows it,' Amy said, and obligingly spelled the word out several times until even the slowest child had managed to write it down.

The final half hour of her visit passed with the children making up crosswords – pencils gripped tightly, noses almost touching the paper on their desks, tongues protruding between teeth to aid concentration.

'What a wonderful way to get them to learn new words,' Lynn Stacey said later over tea at her house. 'I'm going to start using that system in future; it'll teach them how to use dictionaries, too. You held their attention from start to finish, Amy – were you a teacher?'

'Me? No! I must've been behind the door when they gave the brains out,' Amy said cheerfully. 'Two of my sisters and one of my brothers taught elementary school, and a good half dozen of my nieces and nephews are teachers too. But I never had the learnin'. My mom and dad had ten children and bein' the eldest I had to help Mom with the others as they came along. I always liked children, specially the littlest ones. We lived in farmin' country and Mom helped some of the neighbours when they gave birth. Sometimes I went along with her and that's why I became a midwife. It's really somethin' to bring a new life into the world, you know?'

'More tea?' Lynn asked. She lifted the teapot. 'Do you have any children of your own?'

'Me and Gordon were never blessed, but we'd plenty of nieces and nephews to keep us busy. He was a police officer – an' that suited me, cos crime novels are my favourite fiction. My Gordon was a lovely man. God, I miss him still, though it's been ten years and more. But that's life, I guess,' Amy said. 'Folks come and folks go the world over. Sometimes I think we're only here on loan, or on our way to somewhere else. Could I trouble you for another slice of that terrific fruitcake?'

'I've been thinkin',' Amy said three weeks after her arrival in Prior's Ford, 'of takin' a look at the rest of Scotland while I'm here. I want to see your Highlands and the big cities like Glasgow and Edinburgh.' She pronounced the capital's name with the hard 'g' ending Americans tended to use.

'Would you like me to go with you?'

'No, not at all. I like travellin' by myself and though you've been great, Clarissa, I reckon you could do with some time on your own, same as me. What I wondered was, could I leave most of my stuff here and come back in a while to visit with you again?'

'Yes, of course.'

'It wouldn't get in the way?'

'I'm not expecting any guests, and if my stepson or step-daughter want to come north for a few days I can always store your things in a cupboard. You didn't bring much.'

'I always travel light because of Gordon. I swear that if I packed anythin' larger than a matchbox when we were goin' anywhere he made such a fuss about it. I mind once when we visited his cousin Mavis in Calgary for two weeks her husband, Gerry, couldn't believe how little we brought with us. He said that Mavis needed twice as much luggage as I had just to get downstairs in the mornin's. I'll work out an itinerary,' said Amy, and a week later she was ready to go.

'Let's invite Stella to dinner on my last night,' she suggested. 'I like her, an' she seems to me to be a bit lonely. That nice preacher too, if it's all right with you. She'll draw Stella from her shell.'

'That sounds like a good idea. I haven't had a dinner party for ages. We'll ask Alastair too, shall we?'

'Oh yes,' Amy said, smiling at her hostess. 'We'd never dream of missin' Alastair out, now would we?'

Despite their determination not to fall out as their wives had done, the rubbish-bin episodes proved too much for Dave Melrose and George Parr.

When Moira made a fuss about finding the Parrs' wheelie bin parked outside her front gate on the morning of a bin collection Dave tried without success to get her to say nothing, while George kept quiet about the fact that the night before, Alma had insisted on his having a nice hot bath before bed because he looked tired. She had taken over his usual task of putting the bin out for the early-morning collection.

But when George drove out of his drive on the morning of the following week's collection and found his car bumping over a mass of rubbish spilled from his own bin, his temper finally flared. The bin men, arriving to find him brushing tins and packets from the pavement to the gutter, refused to take it away, pointing out that it was their job to empty bins, not pick up litter.

'It's difficult enough with folk fillin' their bins so full they won't shut, *and* leavin' bags of stuff out as well when it's forbidden, without bein' expected tae sweep the roads as well. We're no' paid for that,' the driver said firmly.

'But you can't just leave it like this!' Alma, wearing her thickest coat over a tracksuit, had brought out a torch to help her husband in his task. 'We pay our council taxes!'

'Aye, ye pay them tae get your bins emptied, pet, but this one's already emptied, isn't it? And it wasnae us that did it.'

'I've a good idea who it was, though!' Alma turned and shone the torch up at the Melroses' bedroom window just in time to see a curtain swing back into place. 'George, get round there and have a word with them.'

George was shovelling rubbish from gutter to bin as fast as he could. 'You do it, I'm busy,' he told his wife breathlessly, 'and I'm going to be late.'

'You're the man of the house, aren't you?'

'Good luck, mate,' the driver said, starting up his engine as his gang moved further up the road.

'Hey, hang on, I'm almost finished here.'

'And I'm on a time schedule. You know the rules – bins have to be on the pavement, ready for collection. If we wait for you we might have to miss out a whole street later. Can't do that,' the driver called as the lorry moved off.

'This is too much! George, what are you doing?'

'Going to work.'

'But there's still stuff to be shovelled into the bin!'

'I've cleared the gateway and now I'm off. You'll need to see to the rest,' he said, slamming the car door.

'George!'

The window was wound down and a piece of cabbage leaf thrown out of the car. 'How many times,' said George Parr irritably to the wife who was used to a yes-dear husband, 'have I told you to make proper use of the compost heap? I'm going because I've got a job to go to. I've done my bit and now it's up to you to do the rest.' Just before he rolled

61

the window up and drove off, he said, 'It's not as if you've got anything else to fill your time.'

'George,' Alma screamed after the departing car. She glanced up to see that lights were on and curtains and blinds twitching in almost every window in the crescent, and yelled, 'Mind your own business!' before storming into the house.

'He's not going to get a nice hot dinner when he gets home tonight,' Moira Melrose said smugly as she dropped the curtain and turned away from the window.

'Was it you that did it?'

'Spilled the stuff from their bin? How could you think that?' She smirked. 'Probably lads bent on mischief.'

'You were out late looking for the cat when all the time he was sleeping by the kitchen boiler.'

'I didn't know that till I came home, did I? He's getting too old to be out all night at this time of year.'

'Moira, let it be.' Dave sat up in bed, what was left of his white hair on end. 'What's done's done and the Christmas lights are all packed away now. There's no sense in going on with this squabble among neighbours.'

'It's more than a squabble and I'm not going to be the first to try to end it. She'll only think she's won.'

'Oh, do what you want, but don't expect me to get involved,' Dave said, disappearing beneath the duvet.

But he changed his mind a week later, when no less than three catalogues extolling the virtues of expensive body-shaping foundation garments arrived in the same post, addressed to Moira. Nobody other than her husband knew how much Moira Melrose, who had once won a beauty contest at a Butlins holiday camp, hated being a victim of the ageing process, especially weight gain. The diets and exercise she had slavishly and secretly followed for years had stopped working efficiently, leaving her with no option but to put on a brave face and pretend she didn't mind being stout and elderly.

The catalogues therefore hit her where it hurt most, and when Dave came home to find her in tears he too declared war on the Parrs. He did it because he loved Moira just as much as he had when he first set eyes on her, a slender girl radiant with happiness as she won the Butlins holiday camp beauty competition. As far as Dave was concerned, anyone who hurt his Moira hurt him.

Which was why he and George Parr almost came to blows in the Neurotic Cuckoo that evening, and why the pub darts team made a right pig's ear of a competition they had until then expected to win hands down.

9

Jess McNair was hanging out the washing in the hope the rain would stay away long enough for the cold February wind to dry her menfolk's heavy workshirts and trousers when she heard a vehicle arrive in the yard. Expecting a feed delivery, she called over her shoulder, 'Won't be a minute,' before being enveloped in the wet folds of the flannel sheet she had been trying to pin to the line. When she finally clawed her way free, grabbed the final peg and secured the sheet, she turned to see her firstborn standing by his car, watching her warily.

'Victor!' Relief swept over her like a sudden warming wave as she went towards him, hands outstretched.

'Mum?' He stayed close to the car, pressed against the driver's door as though ready for a quick getaway, but when she said, 'Oh, Victor, son, it's so good tae see ye!' he gave her the heart-warming smile that had charmed girls ever since his days in primary school – and had charmed Jess since his first tooth-less baby smile, just for her.

'It's good tae see you, too. Is – is Dad about?'

'He and Ewan are in one o' the fields. They'll be back for

their dinner in a wee while. Come on in and I'll put the kettle on. Come on,' she insisted as he hesitated, 'ye've time for a cup o' tea before they get back if that's what ye're worried about.'

Once in the warm kitchen he relaxed, taking off his coat and scarf and sitting down at the table while Jess bustled about, checking the meat cooking in the oven and setting the prepared pots of soup and vegetables on the hob.

'It smells good. I miss yer cookin', Mum.'

'Ye could stay for yer dinner, there's enough tae go round.'

'I doubt if I'd be welcome.'

'Mebbe yer dad'll be pleased tae see ye, son.' Jess longed to give him a hug, but dared not because the McNair family had never been folk to display open affection. She could only show her deep love for her husband and children by feeding them, washing and mending their clothes, dosing them on the rare occasions they were ill and working alongside them in the dairy or even in the fields if needed. And by lying awake at nights worrying about them, as she had often done since Victor had walked out of the kitchen and their lives some five months earlier.

'I doubt that, for nothin's changed.'

'Oh.' Jess's heart sank.

'But I did wonder if Dad and Ewan could dae wi' a hand when the lambin' starts at the end o' next month. I'd be willin' tae help out.'

'Eat up, now.' Jess had poured two mugs of strong tea, added sugar and milk as she always did for her men, and set down a big platter of buttered home-made pancakes on the table. Now she sat opposite her son. 'Wilf's back with us. He says he's tired of bein' retired, and he's as fit and strong as ever he was.' Wilf McIntyre had worked at Tarbethill Farm all his adult life.

66

Victor stuffed an entire pancake into his mouth, as he had done since he was big enough to manage it without choking. Jess had given him countless tellings-off about it, to no avail. She held her tongue and waited until he had chewed and swallowed and was free to speak.

'I'm glad tae hear about Wilf. Is – does my dad ever speak about me?'

'No, but ye know him, he doesnae speak much at all.' She couldn't bear to tell him that Bert had forbidden any mention of their firstborn.

'Thanks for talkin' Alice intae visitin' me when she was up at Christmas.'

'She wanted tae see ye, and tae meet Jeanette. She's vexed about this coldness between you an' yer dad. She tried tae speak tae him about it but he wouldnae. The three bairns are growin' up fast, though. I wish they lived nearer,' Jess said wistfully. Alice and her husband farmed in the Lake District and there were times, especially now, when Jess longed to have her daughter close by.

She watched Victor devour another pancake and wash it down with half a mug of tea. She got up to fetch the teapot from the stove. As she refilled his mug she allowed her free hand to rest lightly on his shoulder.

'Ye're lookin' well. How's Jeanette?'

'She's fine, and so am I. Her mum and dad are good tae me, and I've been put in charge of her dad's second garage.'

'Have ye set a date for the weddin'?'

'We're waitin' until our house is built.'

Jess's heart sank. 'So ye're still goin' ahead with the house buildin'?'

'It's out of my hands, Mum. The land's been sold and the builders'll be moving in soon.'

Jess returned to the stove, leaving her own tea untasted.

Her faint hope of some sort of compromise that would allow her to get her son back was gone.

'How's Ewan gettin' on? Still courtin' that lassie from the pub?'

'Aye, he is.'

'And no further on, I'm guessin'.'

'Ewan takes his time, but he'll get there. An' Alison's a fine girl,' Jess went on, ignoring Victor's sarcastic snort, 'just the sort of wife he needs.'

'She'll be bringin' a ready-made bairn with her as her dowry. Added baggage.'

'I'll have none o' that, Victor!' She swung round from the stove to confront him. 'Jamie's a grand wee laddie an' he and Ewan dote on each other. Jamie needs a father an' he'd not find better than Ewan, so don't you go puttin' him—'

That was when the door opened and Bert McNair stamped in, followed by Ewan and Wilf McIntyre. He stopped on the threshold when he saw the visitor and the other two, about to follow him into the kitchen, were left on the step, peering over his shoulder.

'Hello, Dad – Ewan – Wilf.' Victor's voice was light, but his grip on the mug he had been lifting to his lips was suddenly white-knuckled.

'What's he doin' here?' Bert demanded of his wife.

'Victor's come wi' an offer o' help, Bert. Can ye no' say a welcomin' word tae the man? Bert!' she added sharply as he swung round, preparing to go out. 'Don't you dare turn yer back on yer own son!'

'I've only got the one son and I'm lookin' at him now.' Bert was nose to nose with Ewan, who found himself sandwiched between his father and Wilf, both heavier men than he.

'Come in here, there are things tae be settled.' It wasn't often Jess's voice held such a steely note.

Bert turned again, reluctantly, and stepped further into the kitchen, muttering, 'No' for me, there's no'!'

'I'll just – there's somethin' needin' me in the byre,' Wilf mumbled, and disappeared while Ewan followed his father into the kitchen, nodding a greeting to his brother.

'Sit down, the two o' ye.' Jess seized the heavy teapot and swung back to face the room, seeming to handle it more as a weapon than a supply of comforting warmth. Ewan sat down at once, while his father very slowly pulled out a chair and slid into it inch by inch, not looking at Victor.

'Now,' Jess said when she had filled all the mugs, 'say yer say, Victor.'

'It's just that – I know there's goin' tae be hard work wi' the lambin' startin' come the end o' March and I'm willin' tae help out. That's all.' Victor took a gulp of hot tea.

'Bert?'

'We'll manage.'

'Dad, we could always dae wi' an extra pair o' hands.'

'Hold yer tongue, Ewan, an' just mind that ye don't own this farm yet – I do!' For the first time Bert McNair looked at his eldest son. 'Are ye still of a mind tae put that field under cement an' bricks?'

'I've been told that the work begins next month if the weather goes well.'

'So ye'll no' have the time for farm work, will ye?'

'I've nothin' to do with buildin' the new houses, Dad. I'm here because I know about lambin' and I'm offerin' my help. If the snow comes . . .'

'I'd as soon lose every single lamb tae the snow an' the foxes an' the crows as have you on my land.'

'Bert!'

'Enough, woman!' the farmer thundered, getting to his feet so swiftly and violently that his chair fell with a loud clatter on the stone floor. 'I've come in at your biddin' an' I've sat down at the same table as this Judas at you're biddin', but I'll have no more of it. Ewan, I'm takin' my tea tae the byre an' I'm trustin' you tae get this man off my land. And ye can tell him that if he comes back he'll find himsel' lookin' down the barrel o' my gun!'

He seized the mug and strode out, ignoring Jess's pleading, 'Bert . . .'

As the door swung shut behind him tears flooded down Jess's face and both her sons jumped up to comfort her. It was Victor she turned to, burying her grey head on his shoulder, clutching at him with both hands.

'It's all right, Mum, don't upset yersel'.' He looked over her head at Ewan, who shook his own head helplessly, spreading out his hands. 'Look after her, eh?'

'I'm already lookin' after the two o' them the best I can.'

'I know,' Victor said. 'Give us a minute, eh?'

Caught between his father and his brother, Ewan picked up his tea and went to the inner door, where he loitered in the hallway leading to the farm's front door, which was never used. He drank his tea swiftly then put the mug down on the hall table, empty but for a pretty china ornament that his sister had once given to their mother. Then he went quietly out of the front door. As he rounded the farmhouse Victor's car came towards him.

The brothers looked at each other, but both knew that there was nothing more to be said. Victor drove on down the lane while Ewan went back to work.

10

'I'm goin' to miss you folks, but it's good to know that I'm comin' back here.' Amy Rose beamed round the room at the people who had been invited to Clarissa's dinner party. The meal had gone well and the conversation had flowed effort-lessly from one subject to another all evening. Now, they had moved from the tiny dining room to the living room for coffee.

'Now then,' she produced a notebook and pen, 'I want every one of you to tell me your favourite place in Scotland and I'll try to visit all of them. Alastair, you first.'

'Glasgow,' he said at once. 'You have to see the art school where I studied. It's an art noveau building designed by Charles Rennie Mackintosh and well worth seeing. He designed other buildings in Glasgow too – the House for an Art Lover in Bellahouston Park is one of them and again, it's worth a visit.'

'And the school in Scotland Street,' Stella Hesslet chimed in. At first she had been too shy to say much, but as the meal progressed she had gradually emerged from her shell as Amy had hoped. 'It's a school museum now, but it still has that smell of chalk and wet coats that schools had in my young days.'

'Sounds good.' Amy scribbled busily. 'Where's your favourite place, Stella?'

'The Isle of Arran. My parents used to take me there on holiday when I was young. My father came from a big family and we all met up there for two weeks – aunts and uncles and cousins.' Stella smiled at the others. 'It was my favourite time of every year.'

'D'you still see your cousins?'

'No. They're scattered all over the world. I'm the only one who stayed put.'

'You should visit with them.'

'Och, I don't know about that. I've never been one for travelling around. I've a friend from childhood who lives in Whitby and I spend my annual holiday with her every year, but that's all.'

'Any cousins in America or Canada?'

'Quite a few.'

'Tell you what,' Amy suggested, 'you should visit with me next year and we'll look in on your cousins together.'

'Go to America? I couldn't!'

'Yes, you could. Clarissa managed it, so why can't you?'

'Amy's right.' Clarissa smiled at the librarian. 'I was scared when I set off, but it turned out to be the best thing I've ever done.'

'We'll keep in touch when I go home,' Amy promised. 'Now then, let's have some more places for me to visit.'

'Did you mean it when you invited Stella to visit you in America?' Clarissa asked when the guests had gone, the kitchen was set to rights and she and Amy were drinking hot chocolate in front of the fire before going to bed.

72

'Of course I did. I love havin' folks to stay and I'd have fun takin' her around an' meetin' with her family. She needs a bit of joy in her life, and I aim to see she gets it.'

'You're a very generous person, Amy. I'm glad you decided to come over to see me.'

'Not as glad as I am. I'm havin' a ball, and I'm not generous, I just love bein' around folks. My Gordon was the same. Our house was always busy with comin's and goin's. Half the time we didn't know who most of the folks were. A burglar could've come in an' taken valuables from right under our noses and then had a cup of coffee before leavin' and we wouldn't have known it.'

'That's what I missed when I was married, being around "folks". Keith didn't care to mix with people. I scarcely knew anyone in Prior's Ford until after I was widowed, and now I've got so many friends here.'

'Uh huh. Young Alastair's a real nice boy, isn't he?'

'He was my first friend. I don't know what I would have done without him.'

'He's real fond of you. Real fond.' There was something about Amy's voice that made Clarissa look up at her.

'What are you saying?'

'I'm sayin' that he really cares for you, just like you really care for him.'

'Amy, he's thirty-seven and I'm in my fifties.'

'So what's age got to do with anythin'?'

'It's got everything to do with it.'

'You think?' Amy stood up and collected both mugs. 'I'll rinse them out and we can wash them properly tomorrow. You go up an' use the bathroom first; I've got some last-minute packin' to do. G'night.'

'I thought I was late, but apparently not,' Helen Campbell said when she found Jenny on her own in the Neurotic Cuckoo.

73

'Where's Ingrid? I thought you two were going to have lunch here and I was arriving for the coffee.'

'She's waiting for a phone call from her mother. She'll be here as soon as she can. Marcy too, if the shop isn't too busy. So I just went ahead and ate here on my own rather than at home. Thanks, Gracie,' Jenny said as the landlady came to clear away her lunch plate. 'There doesn't seem to be much point in waiting for the others, so I'll have a black coffee, please.'

'White for me.'

'Won't be a moment, loves.' Gracie Fisher returned to the bar.

'I can't wait for the day when I'll be able to meet you for lunch here now and again.' Helen's voice was envious. 'Two years before Lachlan goes to the Academy and another two years before Irene joins him. Then I'll be a free woman during the day.'

'Don't be too quick to wish the time away. I still miss Calum coming home in the middle of the day.'

'That's probably because he's your only chick. I'm looking forward to getting down to some serious work on my novel and I'll need most of the day for that. At the moment the mornings are taken up with shopping and housework and then my two youngest arrive home for lunch, and when they go back to school I've usually got to finish off the house-work. And when I do get time at the computer there's the agony aunt page to do.'

Helen wrote a weekly news report on Prior's Ford activities for the *Dumfries News* and was also the newspaper's agony aunt, Lucinda Keen, a secret known only to Jenny, Ingrid and Marcy, her closest friends. 'And between March and November there's the garden to look after, of course,' she added.

'Poor Helen, you're like the cobbler's children who never get new shoes.'

Helen nodded mournfully. Although Duncan Campbell was the one and only gardener employed at Linn Hall now, his wife had to look after their council house garden. As far as Duncan was concerned gardening was paid work and he had no intention of making it his spare-time hobby as well.

'You describe me perfectly. But at least I've been finding half hours here and there to read over what I've written so far of the novel and to start noting down ideas. Having had to leave it aside once I was offered work with the *News* seems to have given me a fresh outlook.'

'Good. Thanks, Gracie,' Jenny said as the landlady brought their coffees. When they were alone again she went on, 'Before Ingrid arrives, have you noticed anything different about her since she came back from Norway in January?'

'Not particularly, but I don't see as much of her as you do.'

'She seems to be very absent-minded, and for another thing, the Gift Horse should be opening in April for the tourist season but when I mentioned that it was time to start filling the shelves she didn't appear to be very interested in it.'

'D'you think she's ill?'

'Doesn't seem to be. I've been making things for the shop, but I can't contact suppliers or make decisions because it's Ingrid's shop, not mine.'

Jenny and Ingrid were keen on crafts and both made items for the Gift Horse, though most of the stock was bought in. 'Alastair was asking me the other day how many paintings we want from him and I couldn't say.'

'I hope there's nothing wrong between Ingrid and Peter.'

'I doubt that; they dote on each other and the girls seem to be fine. Ella was playing football with my boys the other day and she was her usual cheery wee self.'

'And Freya was at our house yesterday. She and Maggie

75

have become good friends now and I'm really pleased about that. Freya's such a sensible girl; just like her mother.'

'Maggie's really settled in now, hasn't she?'

Jenny nodded. 'She still gets a bit stroppy at times but that's probably down to her age. It's great to feel that she's part of the family at last.'

'I'm so pleased for you, Jen,' Helen told her friend warmly. 'You had a horrible time last year between Maggie being difficult and Andrew being ill, but it's all behind you at last.'

'We've been very lucky. Andrew's going to see the oncologist for his first check-up on the twentieth of this month, so I'm feeling a bit jittery.'

'He'll be fine.'

'Yes, of course he will.'

'I've just remembered – Alma Parr came round this morning to ask me to type out the programme for the Rural's Daffodil Tea, and I saw Ingrid's put in an advert for the Gift Horse.'

Jenny brightened at once. 'That means we're definitely going to open, so I'd better get cracking with those little dolls I was going to dress. The last lot sold well.'

'There you are then, all sorted.'

'There's something I wanted to tell you.' Jenny glanced round the almost deserted lounge bar, then lowered her voice. 'Andrew wants me to marry him.'

'Oh, but that's lovely – isn't it?'

'I'm not sure.'

'Why? You plan to stay together for ever, don't you?'

'Of course we do, and now that he's recovered from cancer and Maggie's stopped being the stepdaughter from hell I've never been happier.'

'So?'

'So why change things?'

'Perhaps Andrew just wants to feel more secure.'

'Marriage won't make us any more secure than we are now. I've *been* married, remember, and it was terrible. I was locked in a nightmare, Helen.'

'But it could never be like that with Andrew!'

Jenny nodded slowly, then said, 'I think deep down I've become scared of the sort of commitment that comes with marriage. Neil made it so clear once we were man and wife that he owned me and there was nothing I could do about it, except run away – then when I plucked up the courage to do that I lived in fear of being found until I discovered he'd died and I'd been free of him for years. I suppose a part of me's afraid that marrying again might lock me back into that nightmare. It's got nothing to do with Andrew, it's this apprehension inside my own head. I know it's daft, but supposing I can't get rid of the fear, Helen? I might ruin things for the two of us.'

'Does Andrew know what you've just told me?'

'I've tried to explain and he's tried to understand, but of course he keeps saying that he's not Neil, which is true.' Jenny's fingers twisted the gold band round and round on the third finger of her left hand. 'I know he's disappointed and I feel terrible about it.'

'He must feel as if you don't trust him.'

'I suppose. Perhaps I'll find a way to get over this stupid fear,' Jenny was saying as Ingrid and Marcy arrived together.

'Everything all right, Ingrid?' Jenny asked. 'Did your mother phone?'

'Yes to both questions. My father hasn't been very well, so I just wanted to find out the latest news. He's doing well. A latte for me, please,' Ingrid told Gracie.

11

'Why do I always get sent to these domestics?' Constable White complained.

'Will you stop whining?'

'I do not whine!'

'Oh, come on, Neil,' Constable Frost said, 'everyone at the station knows you can whine for Scotland. I just wish I'd been quick enough to realise it before you got me up the aisle.'

'I didn't exactly have to drag you up it. You were keen enough at the time, as I remember. Desperate for a big white wedding, you were.'

She'd looked fantastic, walking up the aisle towards him on her father's arm, Neil White recalled, with her blonde hair gleaming beneath her lace veil and the off-the-shoulder wedding dress moulding her perfect body. He'd thought himself the most fortunate man in the world that day. How wrong he'd been!

'Time you stopped living in the past,' she told him. 'Move on, Neil. And move out – when are you going to apply for that transfer?'

'I like Dumfries and Galloway. I was born here.'

'So was I.'

'Anyway, ladies first.'

'Last in, first out.' Before he could find a smart retort, she went on, 'I'm not the one who should move. I've been in the force longer than you and I'm getting tired of us having to pretend to be nice to each other at work, Neil. Tired of being paired up with you, too. I need to be free to concentrate on studying for my promotion. I could get on faster if you'd do the right thing and move to Glasgow or Edinburgh. Timbuctoo would be even better. First left then first left again. A nice wee estate,' she said as the car turned into Myrtle Crescent. 'It looks peaceful enough – not that that means anything nowadays. There they are – number sixteen and—'

'Number eighteen next to it.'

'Right where we'd expect to find it – well spotted!'

'D'you have to be so sarky?'

'It's one of the few pleasures I have in life.' Gloria flipped open her notebook. 'We'll start with number sixteen since Mr and Mrs Parr were the first to put in a complaint, then we'll see the other complainants – Mr and Mrs Melrose at number eighteen.'

'Wouldn't it be better if I interviewed the Melroses while you're dealing with the Parrs?'

'No it wouldn't because then we'd have to waste time comparing notes,' Gloria said in her most withering voice. 'Better for us to work as a team – if that's possible. With any luck we'll sort the four of them out within half an hour. Neighbours who can't get on together get up my nose. They're a waste of time in my opinion.'

Curtains twitched as the police car drew to a halt outside the Parrs' house. Gloria got out first, clamping her hat firmly on her blonde head. 'Let's get it over with,' she snapped, and by the time Neil had emerged, hat in hand, she was halfway up number sixteen's garden path. 'Leave things to me,' she told him when he caught up with her at the door, 'this needs a firm hand.' She stabbed at the doorbell with a firm finger.

'Bad cop, good cop. Obviously you'll be the bad one.'

'Shut up!' Gloria hissed at him as the door opened.

'At last,' Alma Parr greeted them.

'Mrs Parr? Constable Frost,' Gloria introduced herself coldly, and, as though suddenly discovering that an unexpected and unwanted constable seemed to be trailing in her wake like a bit of toilet paper stuck to her shoe, went on, 'and this is Constable White. May we come in?'

'I'm certainly not going to discuss my private business in full view of all the neighbours,' Alma retorted, opening the door wider as her husband appeared in the hall behind her. 'Inside, quick.'

In the name of the wee man, Neil thought as he followed his estranged wife into the house, two strong women in the one building! He shot a sympathetic look at George Parr, who had stepped back to let them into the immaculate living room.

Once in, Alma Parr wheeled round to confront the two of them. 'So . . .' she began truculently. Neil took off his hat and she had her first clear look at him. 'Oh! Would you like to sit down?' Suddenly she was simpering. 'A cup of tea? Coffee?'

Gloria's hackles were immediately raised. At one time she had enjoyed the way Neil's dark good looks could turn other women, even women like Mrs Parr, into giggling teenagers, but now it was just downright irritating.

'No thank you, I don't believe this is going to take long. I understand you're having problems with your next-door neighbours?'

Alma's attention was suddenly brought back to the reason

81

why the police officers were in her house. 'Problems? That's putting it mildly, isn't it, George? It's a vendetta, that's what it is, and you've got to put a stop to it. I want the four of them behind bars!'

'Four?'

'It's not just the Melroses next door harassing us, it's the Wisharts further along the crescent – their daughter and her husband.' Alma stopped as someone launched a thunderous attack on the front door. 'And it doesn't take a mind-reader to tell us who *that* is. Go and tell her to get lost, George.'

'Neil, if that's the neighbours, bring them in,' Gloria said as George Parr hurried to do his wife's bidding.

'I will not have those people in my house!'

'At the moment, Mrs Parr, this is the scene of a crime investigation.' Gloria fixed the other woman with a glare known to have caused hardened criminals to break down and cry for their mothers. Alma flinched noticeably before rallying and glaring back. 'So we need to interview everyone involved. Here and now suits me.'

'Now just a min—' Alma began as Moira Melrose charged in, having pushed past George and almost knocked Neil down when he tried to speak to her. She was followed by her husband.

'*I* was the one who phoned for the police,' she said furiously to Gloria.

'Actually, I think you'll find that *I* phoned first.'

'And if you're them you should be at my door, not hers,' Moira went on, ignoring Alma.

Even on her feet, Gloria was smaller than Moira but her air of steely efficiency seemed to give her added height. 'We are the police and I take it you're Mrs Moira Melrose?'

'I want to see your credentials.'

'Certainly.' Gloria whipped out her warrant card and swept

82

it past Moira's face at speed. 'Sit down please, Mrs Melrose and – Mr Melrose?' As Dave gave an embarrassed nod and huddled down on the sofa she resumed her own seat on a straight-backed chair.

Three strong women in the same room, Neil thought, and began to feel slightly panicky. Gloria had fallen for him because he was over six feet tall, good-looking and a keen sportsman. He had fallen for her because she was small, beautiful and, he had foolishly thought, feminine. It wasn't until the wedding ring was on her lovely finger that he realised men are only the stronger sex in the physical sense. Women like Gloria didn't need physical strength to emasculate the strongest man.

Now he was trapped with two more like her. He wished he could open the window to let in some fresh air.

'To save valuable time,' she was saying crisply, 'Constable White will read out the list of complaints received.'

Neil opened his notebook. 'Bins blocking gateway and bin contents spilled across gateway, unsolicited mail of a personal nature—'

'Corset catalogues,' said Moira Melrose, 'and brochures and phone calls from estate agents saying we want to sell our house – it's a council house, we couldn't sell it even if we wanted to, which we don't!'

'Unauthorised advertisements in the local paper—'

'Saying our car was for sale,' Alma interrupted him. 'We were inundated with phone calls. George loves that car and there's no way he'd sell it, as you well know, Dave Melrose!'

'Are you insinuating that my husband would stoop so low as to spread lies about your man?' asked Moira.

'Who else? Either him or you or your precious daughter – the one who's been encouraging her children to ride their bikes up and down past our house singing rude songs and staring in our windows!'

'For goodness' sake, children are children.'

'Some of them are spoiled little monsters!'

'How dare you criticise my grandchildren! And while we're talking about phone calls, young man, you can include being pestered by folk claiming that we want to be fitted with burglar alarms.'

'And someone put an advert in the paper to say I was selling second-hand furniture. One woman got quite stroppy when I refused to let her in to have a look at my three-piece suite,' Alma complained.

'That's not as bad as a funeral director wanting to fix a time to come and discuss my funeral,' Moira screeched. 'And what about the girlie magazines that arrive in the post day after day? Go next door and fetch them, George. I want to show them to the constables.'

'Do I have to?'

'No you don't, Mr Melrose. And while you're both pausing for breath, can I just say that the four of you are well on the way to being charged with wasting police time. There are people out there,' said Gloria, pointing to the window, 'committing serious crimes and my colleague and I would prefer to be dealing with them than with a situation like this.'

Glancing out, Neil could see a knot of women and a few men gathered in the middle of the road, gawping at the police car and the Parrs' house. None of them looked capable of or interested in committing serious crimes, other than having a good nosy.

'Shall we continue with the list?'

God, what a woman, Neil thought. It was when she was exerting her command over people, as now, that he knew that estranged or not he was still madly in love with her. Couldn't live with her, couldn't live without her and her wide blue eyes that a man could easily drown in. She was the most passionate, most exasperating, most difficult . . .

He noticed the wide blue eyes were impaling him on a pin like the latest addition to a butterfly collection rather than drowning him, while her voice, sharp and cold as an icicle, repeated impatiently, 'Shall we *continue*?'

He scurried back to his notes. 'Starting bonfire deliberately while Mrs Melrose had washing out; dousing the Parrs' cat with a hose.'

'The washing was out before the bonfire was lit,' Moira muttered. 'Dave was only trying to save my whites by putting the fire out.'

'George didn't see the washing, and our poor cat was traumatised. Terrified!' The two women were trying to maintain the former level of anger, but they were definitely beginning to crumble. Gloria managed to do it every time, Neil thought. What a woman!

'Honest, I didn't see the cat,' Dave Melrose offered. 'Like Moira said, I was just trying to put the fire out.'

'It was so terrified it wouldn't come from behind the sofa for a whole day, poor little kitty. Totally traumatised, it was!'

'This, I take it, is the animal in question?' Gloria indicated the cat, which had climbed onto Dave's lap and fallen asleep. 'It seems to have made a full recovery.' She briskly got to her feet. 'My colleague and I are returning to the police station, where we would like to report that you have resolved whatever problem started this storm in a teacup and no further action will be necessary. By further action,' she went on, fixing her gaze on each of them in turn, 'I mean that nobody will be arrested, charged, or forced to undergo a court appearance that would stand against them for the rest of their lives. Are we agreed? Good,' she finished as they all nodded meekly. 'Mr and Mrs Melrose, you will leave with us.'

'See you at the darts practice tonight?' George said to Dave as they went into the hall.

'Sure.'

As the door opened the crowd outside scattered. Gloria chivvied the Melroses down the path before her and then swept the crescent with gimlet eyes before getting into the car.

The Myrtle Crescent feud was over.

'You sorted that in double quick time,' Neil said as he reversed the car into the Parrs' driveway so he could head back the way they had come.

'Easy-peasy. Now you know how to deal with domestics in future.'

'I'd like to remind you that I've been on the force for over two years now. I am not a rookie any longer, and I could have managed that little domestic upset perfectly well on my own.'

She said nothing, though her silence bellowed, 'No you couldn't because you're only a man!' into his ear so loudly that it hurt.

Where had it all gone wrong? Neil wondered as they left Prior's Ford behind. She had been fantastic during their courtship and the first six months of their marriage. Sweet, funny, loving, cuddly. What had he done to turn her into the shrew she had suddenly become? Or was it all her fault? Could it be because of her ambition to climb the promotion ladder? He'd never have stood in her way, so he couldn't see how that had ruined things between them.

Perhaps he should do as she asked; move on, apply for a transfer to another district, start a new life with someone else. He'd never had any trouble attracting women – quite the opposite: he'd been able to take his pick since he'd become skipper of the football team in his first year at secondary school. He could get married again, this time to someone who wanted a peaceful, loving, happy family life with kids. He should think seriously about that.

Then he slid a sideways glance at Gloria's perfect profile and knew he couldn't do any of these things. That was why he refused to apply for a transfer – he didn't want to be where she wasn't.

Couldn't live with her, couldn't live without her.

No way.

Life could be a right bitch at times.

12

Ginny Whitelaw arrived at Linn Hall in her camper van in early March in the middle of a snowstorm, to be warmly welcomed by the family when she walked into the kitchen, shedding snowflakes from her short, spiky black hair and her heavy anorak.

The Ralston-Kerrs were all sitting at the long wooden table, the remains of their lunch pushed aside to make way for a sheaf of papers.

'Ginny, how lovely to see you! Tea?' Fliss jumped up and headed for the big old stove.

'I'd love a big mug of hot chocolate, if you have any. That was a hair-raising journey. The camper van was skidding all over the place for the last few miles. Hello, Mr Ralston-Kerr. Lewis, how are the gardens?'

'Doing very well. We're having a look at the new business plan and you're just in time to help me decide what part of the estate should get priority.'

Ginny's heart leapt at the words, but she managed to hide her delight behind a carefully casual nod. Two years earlier her mother, actress Meredith Whitelaw, had come to Prior's Ford to sulk or, as she herself put it, 'to rest, darling,' after being axed from a lead role in a popular television soap. Ginny was her reluctant companion, but her own life suddenly brightened when she met Lewis Ralston-Kerr and discovered that he was struggling to renovate his family's rundown estate.

Ginny, who had been working in a garden centre, immediately volunteered her services and within months she had restored the overgrown and neglected kitchen garden to its former glory. She had returned the following summer and now Lewis, who was eager to open the gardens to the public, had come to look on her as a partner in the enterprise. He was totally unaware that it wasn't just Ginny's love of the estate that made her want to be there.

Now she dumped her own bulky folder on the table before slinging her anorak over the back of a chair and sitting down. 'Remember that day last summer when we climbed the hill at the back of the house and discovered that the water used to feed the lake and the pond in the rose garden had been dammed up with rubbish? I did an evening course on horticultural archaeology over the winter and it turned out to be very useful. If it's all right with you, I'd like to concentrate this year on getting the water flowing down from the top of the hill again, but first we'd have to get the lake dredged and relaid – clay or sand, possibly sand. And have a good look at the pond, too. Now that the kitchen garden's up and running it should be fairly easy to maintain. Young Jimmy McDonald could see to it. You'll be getting backpackers in again?'

'As always, and we're going to have enough in the kitty this year to pay for local help as well, even if it's only evenings and weekends. There are quite a few folk in the village keen to help us. We'll add your water project to the business plan; it'll help to show the bank that we mean business.'

'We'll need to hire a small JCB to clean out the lake and open up the channels that carried the water from the hill to the lake and pond. Thanks, Mrs Ralston-Kerr.' Ginny picked up the mug that had been set before her and dipped her face into the rising steam, inhaling. 'Mmm, lovely!'

'Who'll run the JCB?'

'I will, I've been working with one over the winter.'

'How's your mother, dear?' Fliss wanted to know. Meredith Whitelaw had caused quite a stir in the village and great upheaval in the local dramatic club before leaving to pick up her acting career again.

'Oh, she's having the time of her life, filming for her new television series in Spain.'

'That's good, I can't wait to see it. We bought a television set during the winter,' Fliss said happily. 'It's in the butler's pantry, so we won't have to go down to the pub to see her now.'

'The series is due to start in the autumn. I'll keep you informed,' Ginny promised before returning to garden talk. 'I want to climb the hill at the back of the house again to find out just how badly the water's dammed. A garden like this needs water features.'

'Are you sure we can afford to spend time and money on the lake while there are so many other things to be done?'

'It's been niggling at me all winter, Lewis. I want to have a proper look at the situation as soon as possible, but that doesn't mean I won't be doing other things. I was thinking,' Ginny told the family, her blue eyes sparkling with excitement, 'about the entire estate. It's small compared to some but we can use that to attract visitors. Linn Hall estate doesn't need to be grand – leave that to others. We should be friendly and colourful and make use of every piece of ground there is.

'I know you want to open to the public all summer this year, Lewis, and there's nothing wrong with people seeing it as a work in progress. We can put up notices telling them what plans we have for certain areas – perhaps you could get Alastair Marshall to do sketches for them to look at. That might persuade them to return year after year, just to see the place develop. We'll need to photograph every step of the way.' She paused before suggesting, 'I thought it might be an idea to ask Cam Gordon to do that for you since he's already taken some excellent photographs of the place.'

Lewis and Cam had been firm friends since their first day at primary school and had looked forward to attending the same university. Sadly, Cam's hopes were dashed by his father's insistence that earning was more important than learning: bitter at having to begin his apprenticeship as a builder while Lewis became a university student, Cam had ended the friendship.

Three years earlier, Lewis had fallen in love with Molly Ewing, a backpacker who had spent the summer working at Linn Hall. They were now engaged, and had a daughter, Rowena Chloe, and the rift between the former boyhood friends had been reopened when Lewis discovered that Cam and Molly had once met while holidaying abroad. A teasing remark from Cam, hinting that he and Molly had been more than just friends, had led to a fist fight between them in the Neurotic Cuckoo.

Now, Lewis said reluctantly, 'I'll think about it.' The building firm Cam worked for had been repairing Linn Hall's leaking roof the year before, and during the process he had taken photographs of the hall and its grounds. Cam was a talented photographer and when Lewis, at Ginny's urging, reluctantly agreed to sell them as postcards in the shop set up in the old stables they had proved to be popular.

'There's another thing – every plant on the estate needs to be identified, named and labelled. Records were probably kept when the gardens were first landscaped. Do you happen to know if they're still in existence?' Ginny looked hopefully at her listeners.

'I think they might be among a lot of papers and files upstairs, on the third floor or in one of the second floor rooms,' Hector said.

'Let's hope if there are any records they're on the second floor,' Fliss said, 'because until last year the roof leaked like a sieve and they might have been ruined. Alexandra Ramsay may have come across them when she did all that cataloguing for us about eighteen months ago. I know where her lists are.'

'Then I'll start with them. And old photographs might help as well.'

'You're taking on a lot of work, Ginny.'

'I'm hoping Lynn Stacey will help during the school's summer holidays.' Ginny and Lynn had become friends after Lynn had taken the primary-school children to see the kitchen garden. 'And I don't mind hard work,' Ginny added, 'not when it means getting your grounds back to the way they were. I love this place!'

The blizzard had sent Bert and Ewan McNair and their farm-hand, Wilf McIntyre, to the furthest fields to round up the pregnant ewes, now within three weeks of giving birth, and bring them down to the 'in-bye' land close to the farmhouse, where they could be watched. If the heavy snow persisted, animals sheltering by walls and hedges could easily be buried, which meant, in the worst weather, locating them by prod-ding a stick through the snow. But they were fortunate, for after the first heavy fall that blinded the men and hampered their struggle to get to the animals, the blizzard began to ease and they were able to round up the sheep and bring them closer to home without too much trouble.

Most of the ewes were now safely settled in the field nearest the farmhouse. A barn had already been prepared for the few considered at risk of complications. Bert McNair took no chances with his beasts and since calling in the vet cost more money than he could afford, a sturdy box in the kitchen was stocked with syringes, antibiotics, vitamins and minerals. A larger box by the fire awaited lambs whose mothers might be unable or unwilling to look after them.

The task of settling the sheep in their new home and moving those at greatest risk into the barn took most of the day. Ewan had been looking forward to seeing Alison Greenlees that evening, but as happened so often now that the lambing and calving seasons were near it was not to be. His mother had promised to let Alison know he would be working even later than usual, so when he went straight from the field to the milking shed and found her helping Jess to wash the cows' udders his heart gave a sudden lurch and sheer joy at the sight of her warmed his chilled limbs.

She smiled at him. 'I knew when I saw the snow piling up that you'd be out in the fields and I couldn't leave your mother to start the milking on her own, could I? Lucky I've helped often enough now to be of use. My parents are looking after Jamie.'

The milking over, she was easily persuaded to sit down in the warm kitchen with them to eat the meal Jess had prepared earlier and kept hot. They were all ravenous and scarcely a word was spoken until the last plate was empty and the last mug drained. By then Alison was almost falling asleep.

'Come on, lass, I'll walk ye home.' Wilf pushed back his chair and got to his feet.

'I'll drive you both home.'

'No need, Ewan, you're exhausted. You need to get to your

bed.' There were dark shadows beneath Alison's brown eyes and her face was white with fatigue. 'Wilf and I can manage fine.'

'I'm takin' you both home,' Ewan insisted doggedly.

It was still snowing when they left and the Land Rover bounced over frozen ruts as they went down the farm lane, and had to be handled carefully once on the road. Wilf insisted on being dropped at the end of the road leading to the council estate and within minutes the Land Rover had halted outside the Neurotic Cuckoo.

Ewan switched the engine off. 'You didn't need to come to the farm in that snowstorm. You should have stayed with Jamie and your parents.'

'I wanted to help your mother. I've learned enough about farming to guess that you and your dad and Wilf would be looking after the beasts and she'd p'raps have to start the milking on her own. Lucky I've been learning about farming since I started seeing you,' Alison said. 'I love it, and I want to learn more.'

'It was good of you and I know my mother appreciated it. We all di—' He was stopped by an enormous yawn.

'You're worn out – I'm going to let you get home to your bed.' Alison started to open the passenger door, protesting, as Ewan opened his door, 'I can manage fine.'

He was out before her and hurrying round the bonnet to help her out, holding her arm to make sure she didn't slip. He led her to the side of the pub to the door leading to the family quarters.

'I wish we'd been able to spend more time together tonight, but this is a busy time for us, and the snow just made it worse.'

It was dark at that side of the building and when she leaned back against the door and looked up at him her face was little more than a pale oval.

95

'I know, and I suppose I should admit that I didn't go to the farm just for your mother's sake; it was to spend some time with you as well.' She reached up to put a mittened hand on either side of his face, drawing him towards her. 'I love spending time with you, Ewan McNair. If it wasn't for Jamie and having to help in the pub, I'd talk your father into giving me a job so we could see each other all day and every day.'

The snowflakes on her lips melted as they kissed and kissed again. Then with a sigh of regret, she pushed him away.

'Go home and get some sleep. See you soon,' she said, and was gone.

On the way into the village Ewan had driven carefully, partly because he knew that Wilf would comment if he didn't, but mainly because Alison was precious cargo. But now she was safely at home he increased the Land Rover's speed, not in the least bothered about the way it slithered over the empty, snow-packed road. He and Victor had learned to drive round the farm at an early age, and they were both totally at home behind a steering wheel. Revitalised by the memory of Alison in his arms and the taste of her mouth beneath his, he whooped 'Yahoo!' every time the Land Rover fish-tailed.

In the third week in March Andrew Forsyth had the first check-up since his operation to remove a malignant tumour. When he came back to report that he was absolutely fine, Jenny hugged him hard.

'I've been so worried!'

'No need to be.'

'I can't help it. After the shock of you falling ill last year I don't think I'll ever feel completely safe again. We take so many things for granted in this life and it's only when something bad comes along we realise the need to live for the moment.' She hugged him again.

'That's what I've been trying to tell you. That's why I bought you that engagement ring.' He took her left hand in his. 'The ring that's still in its box. Have you had any more thoughts on that?'

Rather than meet his gaze Jenny looked down at the gold band on the third finger of her left hand; the plain ring he had given her when they decided to live together as man and wife. 'I've been so busy lately. You know I was worried about Ingrid being vague about the Gift Horse, but now she's started taking an interest in it again we're working really hard to get it ready for opening next month.'

'So still no decision.'

She finally found the courage to look up at him. 'Andrew, I don't know what to say. I'm happy as I am and I don't want to do anything that might change things.'

'I don't see how it could change anything.'

'So why . . .'

'Because I love you and I want us to be united in every way. Nothing could change the way I feel about you. Are you saying that being married to me would stifle you and make you want to break free?'

'Of course not! It's just – Oh, I don't know *what* it is! Would it make you happier if I wore it and told everyone it's an eternity ring?'

'It's an engagement ring, Jen. Eternity rings are different.'

'We could tell people it's the engagement ring we couldn't afford when we got married.'

For the first time irritation was in his eyes and in his voice. 'An engagement ring is a commitment to marry. A pledge. Once I can get you to wear that ring we'll start planning our wedding. No more pretending, no more made-up stories.'

'But what about all the people who think we're already married? Think of what they might say.'

'I don't care what they say. This will be for us, but it has to be out in the open. Look, Jen,' he began, then had to stop as Maggie and Calum arrived home from school, both anxious to hear how Andrew's check-up had gone.

13

Although Amy Rose's visit had been quite brief Clarissa missed the American's colourful figure and equally colourful character. She enjoyed living on her own but Amy was such a vibrant person that for weeks after her departure Clarissa felt as though a light had gone out in the house.

But now that spring was on its way she looked forward to getting out into her garden again, and to exploring more of Dumfries and Galloway in her little car, as she had done the previous summer. There was something about the place, with its rich farmland, lovely little villages, bustling towns and rivers, lochs and coastal areas that filled her with peace and tranquillity. The move from England had been her late husband's idea; she had been dismayed at the time because she was being uprooted from familiar places and good friends, but now she was grateful to him.

There were occasions such as when she was contentedly loosening up the earth in the flower beds or stopping the car in a lay-by to drink in a particularly striking view when she recalled Amy's comments about the friendship between herself and Alastair Marshall. She wondered just what the American was getting at when she had said on the evening before she left: '. . . he really cares for you, just like you really care for him . . . what's age got to do with anythin'?'

Then she would push the thought away and remind herself that she and Alastair were firm friends, and differences in age certainly weren't a barrier to friendship.

Work had begun in earnest on the small housing estate planned for the field Victor McNair had persuaded his father to sign over to him. At his first sight of the somewhat stunted trees being cut down and bulldozers uprooting bushes and hauling rocks out of the ground, Bert seemed to Jess to age overnight. He began to stay on farmland, only leaving it for the occasional evening drink at the Neurotic Cuckoo when the workmen had gone and the machines stood silently in the midst of the destruction they had wreaked that day.

'I'm worried sick about him,' Jess confided to Naomi Hennessey over a cup of tea in the manse. 'The heart's gone out of the man.'

'Do you want me to speak to him?'

'No offence meant, pet, but my Bert was never one for religion as ye'll have noticed for yersel' since he's never at a Sunday service. I doubt if he'd listen tae ye, and he'd be angry if he knew that I was here now, but I needed tae speak tae someone. The lambin' season starts soon and even with Wilf back it's goin' tae be hard. I'm worried about Bert's health; he's not gettin' any younger, an' like I said, it's as if the heart's gone from him.' Jess shook her head. 'That wee field was no use for plantin' or grazin', and I've tried tae get him tae see that there's no sense in frettin' for it now, but Bert's loved the land all his life and it's destroyin' him tae see even a wee patch o' it disappearin'. The real hurt is knowin' that it's our own

100

son who should love the land as much as we do who sold it for the building.' Tears glistened in her tired blue eyes and Naomi reached out to put a warm hand on the older woman's arm.

'I can understand how he feels – and you and Ewan too. It's sad to see land disappearing beneath concrete no matter how poor it might be. I know a lot of the folk in the village feel the same about that field as Bert does. I'm praying for you and Bert, but I wish I could find some other way to help as well.'

'Just knowin' you're here an' that you understand how we feel helps me, pet.'

'Victor only got that one field, didn't he? That's one blessing at least,' Naomi said when Jess nodded. 'At least you won't lose any more McNair land. But there's nothing any of us can do about what's happening now. It's a pity the houses will be right opposite the farm lane, where you'll see them every day. We can only hope Bert comes to terms with that.'

'I think he's too old and too stubborn. There's Victor too, my own son that I cannae see any more because Bert's refused tae have him near us. I miss him,' Jess said, and this time the tears flowed freely. She covered her face with trembling hands and Naomi rose and went round the table to hold her visitor close until the weeping slowed and stopped.

'I'll make a fresh pot of tea.' She pushed forward the box of paper tissues she always kept handy.

'I've already taken up too much of yer time.'

'Jess, you could never take up too much of my time,' said the minister.

For the first time since she had come to Prior's Ford to live with the Forsyths, Maggie Cameron woke on the morning of her birthday looking forward to the event:

101

She stretched luxuriously, pushing her feet down to the coolness at the bottom of the bed, and smiled up at the ceiling. She had come to the village filled with resentment against everyone in the whole world – her mother for dying when Maggie was too young to remember her; Jenny, her step-mother, for leaving her and her father when Maggie was a toddler; her father for having died in an accident on the oil rig where he worked; her beloved grandparents for not being able to keep her in their safe, loving home when her grand-father's health had broken down.

She had been bundled off to live with the Forsyths, feeling just like a hurriedly wrapped parcel with 'Not Wanted' stamped on it, and had stormed into their peaceful home determined to punish Jenny for destroying her chance of growing up in a proper mum-and-dad family. She had resented Andrew for replacing her dad as Jenny's husband, and saw Calum as a smug little boy enjoying the safe life she herself, passed from one person to another, had been denied.

She had been the daughter from hell, the Demon Seed, and at first she had revelled in it, being spiteful to Calum when nobody was there to overhear, and watching with contempt his parents struggle to make her happy. But Naomi Hennessey was right when she said that disliking people and trying to make their lives difficult was not only tiring, but downright boring. It had been almost a relief when Andrew fell ill and had to spend time getting treatment in an Edinburgh hospital. Jenny had gone with him and Maggie and Calum had moved temporarily into the manse. It had been Maggie's chance to change, and with Naomi's help she had more or less managed it.

She bounced out of bed, grabbed her dressing gown, and hurried to get into the bathroom before Calum.

★　　★　　★

102

'You would think,' Maggie said during breakfast, 'that being sixteen should mean not having to spend the day at school.'

'Dream on,' Andrew said mildly, while Calum asked, 'Can I stay off too?'

'Nobody is staying off school or work,' Jenny told him.

'But sixteen – I'm old enough to get married!'

'And if your new husband let you stay off school he'd be doing you no favours. You're going.'

'That's mean!'

'I have a diploma in meanness,' Andrew told her. 'I'm very good at it.'

'I'm planning your favourite dinner,' Jenny said from the cooker, 'and you can open your presents this evening before we eat. In the meantime, have a look at your cards. There'll be more once the post arrives.'

She and Andrew smiled at each other as Maggie began to open the cards. A year ago the girl would have demanded a day off from school and flounced back to her room, slamming the door, when it was refused.

There were more cards and some small gifts when Maggie met up with her classmates, and she returned home in a good mood to unwrap the family presents, including gifts from her grandparents and her aunt and uncle that had arrived a few days earlier and been hidden by Jenny. There were presents, too, from friends in the village, including a lovely diary from Naomi and Ethan with a card that read, 'What goes on between a person and her very private diary is legal, so let it all hang out!'

'And now to start on the dinner,' Jenny announced when the living room was littered with wrapping paper.

'Dinner's going to be later this evening because I've got a promise to keep,' Andrew told her. 'Calum, gather up all the paper – Maggie, you've got five minutes to make yourself beautiful. You and I are going out.'

'Out where?'

'Last year I promised to buy you a gin-and-tonic at the Cuckoo when you reached sixteen. Be ready in five minutes.'

'Andrew, she's only just sixteen,' Jenny protested while Maggie was upstairs. 'Too young to drink in a pub.'

'It's okay, I had a word with Joe Fisher on my way home. Although the official age's eighteen, a sixteen-year-old can drink alcohol in a Scottish public house providing it's bought by a responsible adult and the landlord gives permission. Technically, it's only possible if the party are having a meal, but Joe's agreed that just this once, he'll go along with me. And if she still wants a gin-and-tonic, he's going to make it very weak. Trust me,' Andrew finished as they heard Maggie run down the stairs.

'I'll get the drinks. Gin-and-tonic all right?' Andrew asked when he and Maggie went into the Neurotic Cuckoo.

'Actually, I think I'd prefer an apple juice, if you don't mind.'

'It's up to you. Take that table in the corner.'

'Can I have a packet of ready-salted crisps?'

'Won't they spoil your dinner?'

'It's my birthday!'

'Then you shall have them. We're in the clear, Joe,' Andrew said when he went to the bar. 'The young lady would prefer apple juice after all.'

'Very sensible choice.'

'And I'll have a half pint of beer. Quite sure about the gin-and-tonic?' Andrew asked as he put the crisps and the apple juice down in front of Maggie.

'To be absolutely honest, I've had G and T before. Ryan used to buy tins of it.' It wasn't entirely the truth – Ryan, her boyfriend no more, tended to steal what he wanted rather than pay for it. It was one of the reasons she had stopped seeing him.

'Did you like it?'

'I'd rather have a soft drink.'

'Talking of this boyfriend of yours . . .'

'Ex-boyfriend.'

'Jenny was disappointed when you stopped going out with him. She seemed quite taken with him when they met at the Scarecrow Festival.'

'It turned out that he wasn't what he seemed to be.'

'Ah,' he said, and to her relief he changed the subject.

'You didn't open your crisps,' he pointed out as they got up to go.

'I'll give them to Calum for after dinner.'

It was cold outside and almost dark. Andrew slipped her hand through the crook of his arm as they crossed the green. 'I like having a grown-up daughter.'

'Mmmm.' She wasn't yet ready to say that it was nice to be someone's daughter again.

Though it was.

14

Because Hector Ralston-Kerr was a painfully shy man who preferred to hide away in the pantry – used by the family as their living room – when people other than his wife, son and Jinty McDonald were around, Ginny was surprised to find him willing to help in her search for the history of the Linn Hall gardens.

While she and anyone else she could coax into working with her started on the task of clearing the dry, choked lake, Hector spent hours collecting together photograph albums and accounts books going back over a hundred years. In the evenings, when Ginny had finished outdoor work for the day, the two of them sat at the kitchen table, often with Lewis, going through the books in search of clues, Ginny armed with an exercise book and a large sketchbook in which she had done her best to draw layouts of different parts of the grounds. The idea was to gradually fill in each area with the plants it had once held and, if possible, cross-reference them to entries in the accounts books of plant purchases.

Fliss left them to it. She was to be found every evening in the pantry with a large mug of coffee, enjoying the television set they had recently been able to afford. Now, when Jinty referred to a programme she had watched on the previous evening, Fliss knew what she was talking about and was able to launch into a discussion about it.

Once he got started on the photographs Hector began to reminisce over childhood holidays spent at Linn Hall with his grandparents. 'We lived in Edinburgh, but my parents brought me here every summer, and I walked with my grandfather around the estate every morning. In those days there were several gardeners, but by the time my father inherited the money was beginning to run out. I was in my mid-teens when my grandfather died and I came to live in Linn Hall with my parents.'

The photographs were all sepia, but Hector still recalled exactly what the grounds had looked like in his younger days, and as his voice flowed on and Ginny scribbled busily, the photographs seemed to her to burst into colour. Very gradually, the estate as it had once looked began to reveal itself to her mind's eye.

She and Lewis agreed that a lot of the original plants and shrubs were probably still in situ, though overgrown, clogged by weeds and hidden by larger plants that had been left to grow out of control.

'But if they're there, they can be located eventually and with any luck we'll be able to save them. It's not too late,' Ginny enthused one evening, running a work-roughened hand through her spiky black hair.

'A nice young woman, that,' Hector said to his son when she had gone. 'Useful.'

'Useful?'

'Like your mother.' Hector mused in silence for a moment,

108

then said, with a sidelong glance at Lewis, 'That's what this place needs – women who are *useful*.'

On the day the costumes arrived for the Rural Daffodil Tea fashion show the lesser village hall had been turned into a large dressing room. Alma Parr and Ashley Hodges, the woman supplying the clothes, handed out outfits from the stands at one end of the room and women of all shapes, ages and sizes were stripping to their underwear. Those who had volunteered for kitchen duty helped the models to dress while a few, such as Ivy McGowan and Moira Melrose, had only come to criticise, though their voices were lost in the general babble of excitement.

'I've often wondered what it must feel like to be Kate Moss or Naomi Campbell, and now I know. It feels terrific!' Jinty announced when she had donned a patterned mid-calf-length skirt and silky black cowl-necked sweater.

'Jinty McDonald, I never knew you had such elegant ankles!' Alma exclaimed.

'That's cos I'm always wearing trousers. This . . .' Jinty spun round so that the cotton voile skirt swung out, 'feels much better than trousers.'

'You should get Tom to buy it for you.'

'Give over, Alma, when would I ever get the chance to wear something like this? But it'll be fun to wear it tomorrow. Oh, look, there are the wedding outfits!' She scurried off to join her excited daughters.

Nancy Wishart was posing in front of a mirror in a silky jade-green dressing gown with exotic red and pink flowers scattered round the neckline, sleeves and hem. 'Isn't it lovely, Mum? And look at this . . .' her plump fingers fumbled with the buttons, finally releasing them to reveal a matching nightdress with thin shoulder straps, 'it's beautiful!'

109

'Now when would you ever wear that sort of thing?' her mother snorted. 'Fripperies like that are for the idle rich. When you've got kids throwing up all over you and housework to do and meals to cook you can't afford to dress like a strumpet.' The excited smile faded and her daughter's face fell. 'You need decent easy-wash flannel pyjamas and a warm woollen dressing gown.'

Ashley Hodges bustled up to tweak Nancy around, patting and smoothing the garments into place. 'They suit you, dear. You look lovely,' she said warmly, and the smile returned.

'It feels wonderful.' Nancy ran her hands down her body, relishing the soft silky feel of the material. 'I wish we could keep them!'

'You can buy any of the clothes on show at a special discount for Rural members,' Ashley told her.

'I knew there'd be profit in this idea for someone!' Moira muttered, and Ashley turned to smile at her.

'Of course – I'm a businesswoman. And I did say, at a discount,' she pointed out sweetly. Moira's face went brick-red. 'Half the proceeds from sales will be donated to Marie Curie Cancer Care.'

'I bet your Paddy would love to see you in that,' Naomi, who had come along to help and to join in the fun, said to Nancy. 'P'raps you should ask for the outfit as an early birthday present – for both of you.'

'Sometimes I wonder if she's really cut out to be a minister,' Moira said when Naomi had gone off to talk to Doris Thatcher, who had donned a beautifully fitting blue and cream tailored woollen suit.

'Doris, that fits you perfectly, dear!'

The old woman's face was pink with excitement and her eyes sparkled, giving an insight into the young girl she had once been. 'I feel like royalty,' she admitted with a giggle. 'This

110

is the sort of thing the ladies wore when they visited Linn Hall years ago. I was a domestic there,' she explained to Ashley, 'in the days when the Ralston-Kerrs had enough money to pay for proper staff. Oh, it was a lovely big house in them days!' She stroked the jacket gently. 'I never in all my wildest dreams thought I'd ever get to wear something like this.'

'You look as though you were born to it, believe me.' Ashley stood back, head to one side. 'You've got very good posture for your – for an older lady. You look just like the Queen Mother in that outfit.'

'Given that the Queen Mother died all of five years ago,' Ivy McGowan commented to Moira Melrose, 'I could agree with that.' Then she gave a hefty sniff and flounced off as Naomi glared at her.

'How much is it?' Doris asked timidly. As Ashley murmured into her ear, her eyes widened. 'Is that all?'

'There's a discount for the Rural members.'

'Oh – well, I think I might just manage that. I've got some savings put by and not much to spend it on now.'

'Why not, Doris, you deserve a special treat,' said Naomi.

The old woman's shoulders went back, her chin lifted, and she gave the minister a radiant smile. 'You're right,' she said. 'I've worked all my life and at my age, I do deserve a treat!'

In the corner set aside for the show's finale, the bridal group, Jinty had dissolved into tears at the sight of Steph in a high-necked wedding dress, the fitted bodice and three-quarter-length sleeves scattered with crystals and the skirt full, with a short train. Her red hair had been anchored on top of her head by a circlet of small white roses and the veil was waist-length.

'Oh, pet, you look so beautiful!'

'There's no need to cry, Mum, it's only pretend.'

'What about us?' Merle and Heather clamoured. 'What

111

about the bridesmaids?' While Faith kept repeating, 'Where's my flower basket? You said I could have a flower basket with sweeties at the bottom for after!'

'You're all lovely,' Jinty said, her voice choked. The bridesmaids and flower girl were all dressed in green silk and Merle and Heather carried small copies of Steph's bouquet of white roses and green fern. 'You're the most beautiful wedding party I've ever seen!'

'Come with me, dear.' Ashley bore down on her. 'Let's get that face dried and then I'll redo your make-up. Girls, you look lovely. Go and sit over there until the rehearsal starts.'

'Where have you put my flower basket?'

'I'm so sorry, poppet, I forgot to bring it. But you'll get it tomorrow,' Ashley promised as she led Jinty away. Faith, who hated being called baby names, stuck her tongue out at the woman's retreating back and was immediately whisked off to a corner by her sisters.

The first rehearsal took a while because so many problems had to be ironed out, but the second was almost a success, other than the final moments when the flower girl marched in before the bride with arms swinging, for all the world like a sergeant major.

'Hold your flower basket nicely, Faith,' Jinty called, cupping her own hands demurely at her waist. 'And remember to *scatter*.' She mimed tossing petals.

'I can't hold a basket,' Faith yelled back, 'when I haven't *got* a basket, can I? And I can't scatter *nothing*!'

'It'll be fine tomorrow,' Ashley said hurriedly. 'Well done, everyone. Back to the dressing room and take the costumes off carefully so they can be hung up. Then we can all go home.'

To Ivy McGowan's and Moira Melrose's chagrin the fashion show turned out to be a great success. Every table in the village hall, decorated that morning with vases of daffodils, was taken and Alma fretted in case there weren't enough sandwiches, cakes and biscuits to go round.

'It'll be fine,' Jinty assured her, 'I've done this often enough to judge a crowd's consumption to the last slice of Swiss roll and we don't want too many leftovers, do we?'

'I can just feel Moira willing it to be a failure, and old Mrs McGowan too. They'll never let me live it down if something goes wrong!' It wasn't at all like Alma to doubt her own abilities, but she had woken that morning in sudden panic, wondering if she was expecting too much of the local Rural.

'Never mind them, they've always been right Jonahs. Concentrate on thinking about how much we'll raise for charity if it works, and how pleased me and the others are to have the chance to wear such lovely clothes for the afternoon.'

It had been decided that once the guests had settled themselves at the tables and been welcomed, the fashion show would take place with the models walking in turn down the space left in the centre of the room, then grouping together so that when the bridal party joined them they could all receive a final round of applause before being led back up the centre by the bride and bridesmaids. Because there were so many tables, and not many Rural members, the models, other than the wedding party, would then whisk into the lesser hall to don large aprons so they could help serve refreshments. Once that was done they would remove the aprons and move among the tables to let their audience have a closer look at the garments.

To Jinty's relief Ashley remembered the flower basket, tied with a big yellow bow and with multi-coloured artificial petals for the flower girl to scatter. Jinty whisked it away and tucked some miniature Easter eggs, Faith's reward for behaving herself, beneath the petals.

113

Cam Gordon had agreed to record the occasion for posterity, snapping each model as she walked down the centre of the room towards him. Once word had spread that the costumes could be purchased from Ashley's dress shop in Kirkcudbright, many of the women brought their husbands along in the hope of a pleasant birthday surprise in the future.

It all went beautifully, other than a slight hitch when the pretty little flower girl, hurling fistfuls of petals energetically to left and right, accidentally threw an Easter egg, which landed on one of the tables. Steph, walking behind her little sister, managed to grab her hand in time to prevent her from going to retrieve the sweet.

'Walk beside me!' she hissed as Faith tried to pull away.

'That's mine and I'll be back for it,' Faith told the people at the table as she was marched on. Steph smiled apologetically at Cam, who was so taken by the sight of her in her wedding finery that he had forgotten to photograph her. He jumped as though stuck by a pin, and began hurriedly to concentrate on the job he was supposed to be doing.

Once the bridal party took their places the models received a final round of applause – and some enthusiastic wolf-whistles – before leaving for the lesser hall, where large aprons were awaiting everyone other than Steph, her sisters and Doris Thatcher.

'You've been fantastic, love, but I don't want you to do too much,' Alma told her. 'So you just sit yourself down here and someone will bring you a nice cup of tea and something to eat. Have a rest, then come in when you're ready to speak to your friends.'

'Can I keep my outfit on?'

'Course you can, we'll tuck an apron over it to keep it nice.'

Once the old lady was settled with a beanbag tray on her

lap and an assortment of sandwiches and cakes on a small table by her side, the others donned their aprons and rushed to help the kitchen staff.

Jinty was right – there was still food left over when the guests finally left, but very little, and Cam soon disposed of that. He had brought his laptop and the women crowded round to look at the slideshow of photographs.

'Where's Doris? She has to see this.' Ashley suddenly remembered her.

'I'll fetch her,' Jinty volunteered. She hurried into the lesser hall, where Doris was still comfortably ensconced in her chair, fast asleep and smiling as though enjoying a lovely dream.

It was only when Jinty touched her soft, wrinkled cheek that she realised how deep and how final the sleep was.

15

Ivy McGowan and Doris Thatcher, the two oldest residents in Prior's Ford until Doris left Ivy as sole holder of the title on the day of the Daffodil Tea, had fallen out many years earlier.

Needless to say, the grudge was over a man. Until Norman Cockburn arrived in the village Ivy and Doris had been close friends from childhood: they had played with each other as toddlers, gone through their school years together and were in domestic service at Linn Hall, home of the Ralston-Kerrs, when Norman joined the team of gardeners who tended the estate. That was the day Ivy and Doris fell out of friendship and into love.

A cheerful young man who liked female company, Norman enjoyed their attentions. Ivy had a quick, sometimes sharp tongue, but she was also very pretty, while Doris was quite plain but with a sweet and biddable nature. They vied openly for his company and longed secretly for his proposal, each considering that snatching the prize away from her rival would be sweet indeed. But Norman had some living to do before settling down, and when war was declared in 1939 he was one of the first to enlist, leaving his sweethearts with a passionate goodbye kiss to each, but no promises.

A year later he was married. It had been a shotgun wedding to the sister of a fellow soldier who had taken Norman to his home when they were both on leave. The only war wound Norman received came from that shotgun . . . he survived the war and in 1945 returned to Prior's Ford with his wife and their five-year-old son.

By then Ivy was married to a farmhand and Doris to a joiner. Some thought their mutual disappointment at losing Norman might have drawn them close again, but if anything they grew further apart. Ivy became bitter about the fact that Doris's husband could afford to buy a nice little cottage by the river, close to where the council housing estate was built after the war, while Ivy and her man lived in a small and fairly uncomfortable tied farm cottage.

Norman became head gardener at Linn Hall and over the next eighteen years, during which time he and his wife produced another six children and the Ralston-Kerrs' fortunes began to shrink, he became the only gardener.

Meanwhile Ivy and Doris carried their feud to the Women's Rural Institute, where the other members grew tired of their determination to outdo each other in every competition, and to the Horticultural Society, where every year they clashed in the best flower arrangement, the tallest sunflower, and the best fruit and vegetable entries. Oddly enough, they both got on quite well with Norman's wife.

Widowed, and marching with clenched fists and set lips into old age, they both set their sights on becoming the village's oldest inhabitant. Ivy, the elder by three months and ten days, won the battle in 2007, on the day of the Daffodil Tea.

Ivy was also the sole survivor of the love triangle, since

Norman and his wife had both died in the late 1990s. Most of their offspring had moved abroad and only one daughter, Jinty, still lived in Prior's Ford. Following in her mother's footsteps she, too, had married a charmer, Tom McDonald.

Doris's only child, a daughter, lived in New Zealand and was in poor health, so was unable to be present at her mother's funeral, which was attended by the entire village and many people from the surrounding area. Ivy set herself up as chief mourner, pointing out that she had known Doris for longer than anyone else in the church.

'And fought with her for most of that time,' someone murmured as Ivy hobbled down the aisle to take her seat in a front pew. 'How can she be poor Doris's arch enemy *and* chief mourner?'

'If you want to challenge her, go ahead,' her friend whispered back. 'I'd not want to take her on. She's got a tongue like a cheese knife, that one. Pity it was Doris who went first, she was such a pleasant old lady. She'd do anything for anyone – not like Ivy at all.'

'When we moved into the village Doris was the first person to call on us. Brought us a lovely home-made cake.'

'I can believe it. She was a bit of a gossip, but there was no harm to her, or malice – unlike some I could mention. Poor Doris just found everyone interesting, even the dull ones.'

When Naomi Hennessey spoke of Doris's sweet nature Ivy gave a sniff that echoed round the church. Naomi smiled down at her.

'It's fitting that as we mourn the passing of a loved member of our community we have with us someone who knew Doris throughout her life.' Her rich voice touched everyone present like a blessing. 'Our thoughts today are with Ivy as well as Doris, for this must be a sad day for her . . . the end of an era.'

119

Ivy's head jerked up and she glared at the minister. Naomi replied with a loving smile that shamed the old woman into turning the planned sniff into a gusty sigh. But as she led the mourners from the church she was hard put to it to hide the satisfied smirk pulling at the corners of her mouth. It had been a long-fought battle, but from now until the day of her own death she was safely and undoubtedly the village matriarch.

Doris's daughter arranged for her mother's furniture to be disposed of at an auction held in the village hall. Again Ivy was in the forefront, running a critical eye over each lot and making disparaging remarks, though not so critical that she didn't put in a successful bid for one or two pieces.

'Sentimental reasons,' she told those brave enough to wonder, which only made them wonder something else – how did Ivy know what sentiment was?

Finally everything was sold and the proceeds sent to Doris's daughter. A 'For Sale' notice went up in the front garden of the little cottage by the river. The inhabitants of Prior's Ford settled back into their usual routines, unaware of what was to result from the death of their second oldest inhabitant.

The person who bought Doris's wardrobe was very content with it. It was old, but roomy and well preserved and it looked good in its new home. The new owner put hangers in the wardrobe section and began to check the drawers. A deep drawer running the length of the wardrobe promised to be useful. Kneeling down, the successful bidder reached into the back to assess the space available then frowned as the back of their hand caught on something sticking down from above. Fingers probed and fumbled, then pulled, and there was a gasp of surprise as a muffled click was heard and the shelf or whatever it was dropped down, releasing something that had been hidden there for years.

And, unfortunately for several local people, was hidden no longer.

Jess McNair had missed out on the Daffodil Tea because by that time Tarbethill Farm's lambing season had just started, and the three McNairs and Wilf were kept busy day and night.

For once things went their way. Only two lambs were born dead and only two ewes, both in their first lambing season, rejected their young. Three mewling motherless babies occupied the big box in the kitchen, and Alison and young Jamie were more than happy to come to the farm every day to help feed them.

'That lassie's a natural,' Jess told her son. 'Ye'd never think that she's city bred. I think she'd jump at the idea of livin' here an' becomin' a farmer's wife – you could do a lot worse, son.'

'The thing is, Mum, she could do a lot better. How can I ask her tae spend the rest of her life workin' as hard as you have for as long as I can remember?'

'D'ye no' understand women at all?' Jess wanted to know. 'Have ye never heard o' love? I chose tae be a farmer's wife because I wanted tae be with yer father and I love the land. Alison's chosen you for the same reasons. When are ye goin' tae open yer eyes an' see that?'

'The farm was larger and bringin' in more money when you married my dad. Farmin''s different now. If Victor had only stayed here an' worked alongside me I might have been able tae offer Alison a decent future. But now, the way things are' – Ewan threw out his hands in despair – 'I don't know what's goin' tae happen; I just know that I'm torn between her and Tarbethill, Mum, an' I've got tae give the farm a

121

chance. I can't walk away from it the way Victor has, no' even for Alison an' Jamie. I'd rather leave her free tae find a better life wi' someone else than have tae watch her scrimpin' an' worryin' day in an' day out, the way you do.'

Jess wanted to shake him, while at the same time her heart ached for him. He was torn between the land, his parents and the woman he loved. It would have been much easier for him if he could have followed his brother's example and left her and Bert and the farm to whatever fate awaited them. But she knew he couldn't do that.

She could only hope that somehow things would work out for all of them, although it seemed impossible.

'It's nothin' more than a disgrace if you ask me,' Doug Borland was saying when Robert Kavanagh went into the Neurotic Cuckoo. 'Local cottages for local folks, I say!'

'Ye're right there. The usual, Robert?' Joe Fisher reached for a pint glass when Robert nodded.

'I'm just sayin', Robert, that it's a disgrace. Can the progress committee no' do somethin' about it?' Doug wanted to know.

'Depends on what it is.'

'I'm talkin' about old Doris Thatcher's cottage. Now that my lad's gettin' wed to Tricia Harper that cottage'd do them nicely, but when Derek made enquiries he found out the estate agent's askin' far more than him and Tricia can afford. I mean, look at the place,' Doug appealed to the row of men standing by the bar, 'two up an' two down, with a nice bit o' garden for veg and some flowers, but it's not got what you'd call mod cons, has it?'

'Seems to me,' a voice agreed, 'that it's ideal for a young couple startin' out in life together an' willin' tae do some improvements tae it.'

'Exactly what I say. Doris an' her husband can't have paid

more than a couple of hundred for it, if that. Now the estate agent's lookin' for thousands more than it's worth.'

'He'll never get it. The price'll come down,' another man assured Doug.

'I'd no' be so sure,' someone else said. 'The cottage belongs tae Doris's daughter now, doesn't it?'

'Brenda. I mind her when she lived here,' a grey-bearded man chimed in. 'Went to work in a bank, which wasnae a surprise, given that all she thought about was money. Used tae charge the lads tuppence a kiss in the playground, she did. Then she got married and went out to New Zealand and never once came back tae visit her old ma. If she's still the same Brenda Thatcher that I mind she'll want as much as she can get for that cottage, and she's probably got the time tae wait till the right buyer comes along. I'm talkin' about folk with more money than the likes o' us, Doug. Holiday cottages.'

There was a general rumble of disapproval. 'We're surely not goin' tae have any o' that in Prior's Ford,' Doug boomed. 'Who wants cottages lyin' empty most of the year, then the folk who bought them swannin' round in the summer as if they own the place? It'll take the heart out of the village!'

'Holiday homes are all the rage among those with money tae burn,' Cam Gordon said, 'an' this is a bonny part of the world. If you ask me, that cottage'll be snapped up by some stranger in no time.'

'And we won't have any say in the matter,' Robert Kavanagh pointed out. There were many incomers in Prior's Ford, including Doug, Robert and Joe, the landlord, but they were all permanent residents and they had become part of the village. Doug was the local butcher, Joe and his wife Gracie ran the village pub, Robert was chairman of the progress committee while his wife was a member of the Women's Rural and sang in the church choir. The thought of cottages lying empty during most of the year and incomers who only appeared briefly and did nothing to further the village's interests appalled him.

'When are Derek and Tricia gettin' wed, Doug?' Joe asked.

'When they can find somewhere tae live. Neither of them want tae leave Prior's Ford; Derek's a good butcher, and he'll be takin' over the shop in a few years, and with Patsy's mother bein' in poor health she wants tae live near her.' Patsy's father, Bill, ran a small garage at the end of Riverside Lane and he and his wife lived in a bungalow beside the garage. 'We've no' got room for them, and neither have the Harpers. In any case, they want a place of their own. They've put their names down for a council house, but God knows when they'll get one. Might be Darby and Joan afore they get tae totter up the aisle, poor souls.'

Doug drained his glass and thumped it down on the counter. 'Put another in there, Joe, I need it!'

'Hi, Ginny!'

'Oh – fish!' Ginny Whitelaw muttered. She had worked hard since arriving back at Linn Hall, and had managed to drain the small neglected lake of its stagnant scummy water. Today, with enthusiastic assistance from Jimmy McDonald and his younger brother Norrie, she was scooping muck, stones and rubbish from the lake bed – until Lewis arrived. Normally, Ginny would have welcomed his appearance, but not today since his red-haired fiancée, Molly Ewing, was with him, her hand in his.

'How's it going, Ginny?'

'Very well. The boys have been a great help.'

'Oh, golly, what a stink!' Molly wrinkled her pretty nose.

'You get used to it after a while.' Ginny, shovelling lumps of watery mud into a bucket, paused to rub the back of one hand over her face, dirtying it even more.

'What are you supposed to be doing, apart from playing at making mud pies?' Molly wanted to know.

'Ginny and I discovered last year that the water that's

supposed to feed the lake and the pond in the rose garden's dried up because the burn at the top of the hill's dammed,' Lewis explained. 'That means the water still left in the lake's stagnant and the lake's choked with rubbish and weeds. We have to clear the dam and let fresh water through, but first the lake has to be cleaned out and relined. Ginny's taken this over as her new project now the kitchen garden's up and running.'

'Is it worth it? I mean, the kitchen garden's useful because it provides food, but this?'

'It's going to be a great focal point for visitors once the gardens are open to the public on an annual basis. Keep going, lads,' Ginny yelled at the McDonald boys, who had stopped work to goggle at Molly. 'This area's going to look lovely when the lake's filled and stocked and the area round about replanted.'

'And how long will that take?'

'With any luck we might have it up and running by the end of next summer.'

'Next summer? When's this place finally going to get finished, Lewis?'

'It's been falling into disrepair for years, and it'll take years to put it right.'

'Mmm. What are you going to do with that?' Molly waved a hand at the growing piles of mud on the banks.

'Get rid of the stones unless we can find a use for them. The mud and dead vegetation can probably be recycled as compost.'

'Well, whatever turns you on, I suppose. C'mon, Lewis, let's go and find your dad and Weena. See you later, Ginny. Bye, boys,' Molly called as she turned away, pulling Lewis behind her.

Ginny heaved a silent sigh. She had been enjoying the day

up until then, sloshing about in the mud with a huge sense of satisfaction. Each time she looked up from her labours she had visualised the lake fed with fresh, sweet water, its surface covered with mats of pink, red and white water lilies open to the sunshine. Well laid-out paths edged with flowering shrubs and shady trees would lead visitors towards the lake and the landscaped garden surrounding it.

But right now she saw what Molly had seen – a huge hole in the ground edged by great piles of smelly muck, tangled neglected bushes and weeds.

Looking down at herself she saw something else that slender, pretty, gloriously red-headed Molly had seen: a sturdily built Ginny covered with muck. No wonder Lewis was crazy about Molly! And now that she and Lewis's baby daughter had returned to Linn Hall he would be too busy cooing over Rowena Chloe and fawning over Molly to concentrate on turning the estate back into the place of beauty it had once been.

Without thinking she ran her free hand through her short black hair, only realising what she had done when a blob of mud landed on her nose.

'Oh, fish!' she said again.

'D'you really think it's worth it?' Molly was saying to Lewis as they left the lake.

'Worth restoring the estate? Of course.'

'But it's taking so long!'

'As I said, darling, the place has been suffering from years of neglect. We can't turn it around in twelve months. I want it to be something wonderful for Rowena Chloe to inherit – and any other children we have. Once the restoration's finished we'll be able to afford to get married.'

'And who's going to look after the place?'

'We are, of course. You and me. That's what you want, isn't

it?' he asked as she kicked moodily at an abandoned brick on the overgrown path.

'What I want is for us to be together properly, having fun – travelling around with Weena. But you seem to be quite happy just staying here, working away and getting older with every year that passes.'

'We'll manage to fit in some travelling as well, once the place is earning enough to pay for responsible staff.'

'I was just thinking the other day,' Molly said thoughtfully, 'about that money your parents got the other year. Two hundred thousand pounds, wasn't it?'

'That's right.'

'Think what we could do with that sort of money!'

'It's all gone now, but because it got us started on the hall and the grounds we've managed to raise a bank loan to keep us going, and Dad and I are working on a new business plan. It takes time, but we'll get there, step by step.'

'Mmmm.' Molly reached up and pulled a twig from a tree, then began stripping the leaves off and tossing them away.

'Don't, love. Trees are living things.'

'No they're not,' Molly said sharply. 'They're just trees!' Then, as they arrived in the rose garden, 'Hello, Cam!'

'Hi, Molly – Lewis.'

Lewis groaned inwardly, much as Ginny had done earlier when she saw Molly. He had agreed reluctantly to Ginny's suggestion that Cameron Gordon should be asked to photograph each stage of the renovations and now Cam had free run of the place. Fliss and Hector, who had always liked Cam, saw it as a return to the old days, when he and Lewis were inseparable school friends.

Lewis could only just cope with Cam being around Linn Hall and its gardens in his spare time, but seeing Cam and Molly together wasn't easy.

'We're looking for my father,' he said now. 'Have you seen him?'

'He was here ten minutes ago – I got a great picture of Rowena Chloe. Want to see it?' Molly scampered over to him at once to look at the picture. Their two heads, hers fiery in the afternoon sun, his dark, were close together.

'Oh, Cam, it's so sweet! Can I get a print?'

'Of course.'

'Come and see this, Lewis.'

Reluctantly, he joined them. Now Molly was cuddled between him and Cam. Photography had always been Cam's passion and he owned a top of the range camera. The picture of Rowena Chloe perched on the former pond's low stone wall in her striped jersey and blue overalls, her head a mass of red curls and all her attention fixed on the golden buttercup clenched in one little fist was, Lewis had to admit, perfect.

'A good one, Cam,' he acknowledged. 'Dad mention where they were going next? I want to see him about something.'

'Helen? It is, isn't it? Oh, my goodness, Helen McKillop! I can't believe it!'

Helen, having a quick morning coffee in the Neurotic Cuckoo with Marcy, stared up at the woman standing by their table. 'Yes, I'm – I was Helen McKillop. Sorry, I can't recall . . .'

'I've changed, but you haven't. Remember Carrie Wilson?'

Helen's eyes widened. 'Carrie? It can't be!'

'I told you I'd changed.'

'I haven't seen you since we were eleven years old. What are you doing back in Prior's Ford?'

'We've been in the area on business and I told Bernie that I simply had to revisit my old haunts. I'm Carrie Alston now. Bernie,' she called over to a grey-haired man buying drinks at the bar from Joe Fisher, 'come and meet my former schoolmate Helen. I don't seem to remember you.' Carrie turned to Marcy.

'Marcy Copleton. I'm an incomer. My partner and I run the village store,' Marcy was explaining when Carrie's husband arrived, a drink in each hand.

'We'll sit here, Bernie. You don't mind, do you?' Carrie asked when the introductions were over. 'Actually, I've got something to tell you, Helen.'

'Hold on, darling, it's still early days.' Bernie set his glass on the table. 'Can I get you ladies a drink?'

'We've just had a coffee and I've to get back to work soon,' Marcy said, while Helen shook her head.

'Marcy runs the village store, darling.'

'That's useful to know.' Bernie settled his girth into the fourth chair. 'Carrie's been wondering if she'd meet any of her old friends on this flying visit, and bingo, Helen, here you are.'

'So what do you do, Helen?' Carrie asked eagerly. 'Are you a career girl?'

'Not unless you call looking after a husband and four children a career.'

'My kids are in boarding school, which is a blessing because Carrie and I have our hands full with our cabinet-making business.' Bernie slipped two fingers into his top pocket and pulled out a couple of business cards. 'There you are – exclusive furniture hand-made to order. No two pieces alike.'

'Actually, Helen's being modest,' Marcy said. 'She writes a weekly column for the local paper and she's working on a novel.'

'But that's wonderful! You were good at English when we were in school together, weren't you? I wasn't much good at anything – too busy enjoying myself.'

'Organising the games in the playground, more like. My wife's a born organiser and a great saleswoman. She can charm

130

money out of our clients' pockets with no trouble at all,' Bernie said proudly.

Carrie's cap of burnished auburn hair, worn in a long bob, swung silkily as she turned to smile at her husband. Her hazel eyes were thick-lashed, her features neat and her make-up perfect. Bernie's brown eyes were heavy-lidded and his grey, neatly trimmed moustache and curly hair showed that he was quite a bit older than Carrie. They were both expensively dressed, Carrie in a dark green flared skirt with matching jacket over a soft cream-coloured polo-neck sweater, her husband in grey trousers and a tweed jacket over a deep blue polo-neck.

'In fact, she's just charmed thousands out of my pocket,' Bernie went on. Carrie's laugh was like a chime of musical bells.

'You'll love it by the time I've made improvements, I promise you.'

'As long as *you* love it I'm happy.' He reached across the table to take her hand.

'Can I tell Helen and Marcy – please?' She fluttered her eyelashes at him.

'Oh, go on then. Women can't keep news to themselves, can they?'

'We've been impulse buying!'

'Something else she's good at. Damned good – nothing's ever turned out to be a turkey. I keep trying to persuade her to take up gambling and break the bank at Monte Carlo.'

'Oh, you! The thing is,' Carrie said excitedly, 'our business is in Berwick on Tweed, where we live, but we've been in Dumfries for the past few days, seeing a new contact. Last night I persuaded Bernie to drive over here so I could wander round the village, and we found the sweetest little cottage for sale down by the river. D'you know it?'

131

Marcy and Helen glanced at each other. 'That would be the cottage Doris Thatcher used to live in,' Marcy said.

'That's right. It was dark, of course, and too late to see inside, but I immediately had one of my special feelings about it. Didn't I, darling?'

He nodded, smiling at her. 'The sort of feeling that always costs me money. Wouldn't rest until I agreed to phone the estate agents and arrange a viewing today.'

'We've just been shown round, and it's perfect,' Carrie said excitedly.

'We should be driving back home at the moment but here we are, back in Prior's Ford.'

'Helen, I'm coming home to my roots! Isn't it exciting?'

'You're really going to buy that little cottage?' Helen asked in disbelief.

'We've more or less done it. Carrie nagged me into offering the asking price there and then.'

'But what about your business in Berwick on Tweed?' Marcy wanted to know.

'Oh, we're not going to live here all the time, though we'll probably end up opening a second branch of the business in Dumfries and Galloway now that we're going to be in the area frequently. We'll use this place as a lovely little bolthole where we can relax whenever we find the time.'

'It's far too small for us, of course, especially if the girls are there as well,' Bernie added. 'We'll have to extend it, but the garden's large enough for that, and it'll more than double the value of the house if we ever decide to sell. A sound business investment – thanks to my clever little wife!'

He and Carrie showered each other with loving smiles while Marcy asked, 'You have daughters?'

'Maureen and Rhona are actually my stepdaughters,' Carrie told her. 'Twins, fifteen years old and such sweet girls.'

132

'They're at a really good boarding school just now. Only the best for all my women,' Bernie patted his wife's hand. 'As I was saying, we'll have to do a lot of work on the cottage to make it comfortable, but we're getting it for a very reasonable price. Cheers!'

He and Carrie clinked glasses, beaming at each other.

17

'Oh dear,' Marcy said when the four of them had left the Neurotic Cuckoo, the Astons in a sleek dark blue Jaguar, Carrie's manicured hand waving an elegant farewell from the passenger window, and Marcy and Helen walking across the green together. 'So Doris's home's to become a holiday cottage. There's been a lot of talk about the danger of that happening, and now it has. I'm not sure how local people are going to take to the news. Your friend's quite stunning, Helen; she doesn't look like someone from Prior's Ford at all. Did you see her engagement ring? Elizabeth Taylor would envy it!'

'I'm in shock. Carrie talked today about concentrating more on enjoyment than learning at school and her husband reckons she's a natural organiser, but the Carrie I remember was a timid mouse. On our very first day at primary school I found her weeping in the girls' toilets at playtime because she'd wet her knickers. She hadn't had the courage to ask permission to go to the toilet, poor wee thing. She was a skinny, carroty-mopped child in those days.'

'Hard to imagine now.'

'Very. She was in such a state and so afraid of getting a row that I swapped knickers with her and then told the teacher I'd wet myself.'

'Now that,' Marcy said, 'I can believe because you're always the first to offer help when it's needed.'

'Miss McEwan gave me the dry pair of knickers kept for emergencies and at home time we swapped back again. Ever since then Carrie relied on me to look after her and I did, until her family moved out of the village when she was eleven.' Helen finished the story as they arrived at the store, where Marcy took control of the till and Helen picked up a wire basket and began the rounds of the shelves.

When she arrived home she dumped her laden carrier bag on the kitchen table and fished Carrie's card from her pocket. Gold letters on a pale cream background gave the address and phone number in Berwick on Tweed of a company producing exclusive hand-made furniture, naming Bernard Alston as managing director and Carrie Alston as sales director.

When she agreed to take on the job of being agony aunt for the *Dumfries News* Helen had panicked at the sight of her first batch of letters, all asking for her advice, until she recalled how as a little girl she had managed to solve every problem Carrie brought to her. And all at once, by pretending that each letter she opened came from Carrie, she had found the confidence to help the writers.

It was just as well, she thought as she finally began to unpack the shopping, that she had become used to being an agony aunt and no longer needed to summon the memory of skinny, timid Carrie, for that Carrie was already fading from her memory, replaced by the gorgeous, glamorous, confident woman of the world Helen had just encountered.

'And what have I done with my life?' she asked the fridge

136

freezer. Already well past its sell-by date, it could only manage a mournful wheeze in reply.

'Very wise,' Helen agreed. The last thing she wanted was for a clapped-out piece of kitchen furniture to tell her she hadn't done much. She was still living in a council house in Prior's Ford, struggling to raise four children on the small wage her gardener husband earned. And still dreaming of becoming a successful novelist.

'I've got to get on with that novel!' she said aloud. And this time the fridge freezer kept its opinions to itself.

'I've got that Maeve Binchy you asked for, Mrs Ramsay.' Stella Hesslet reached below the counter in the mobile-library van and produced the book.

'Oh, lovely – and it's Clarissa, remember?'

'Sorry – Clarissa.' The librarian's neat little face went pink with pleasure. 'I got a letter yesterday from Amy Rose. She's in Fort William.'

'The last letter I got from her was written in Plockton. She certainly gets about. I'm returning this lot and taking that lot out.'

'She sends me her latest crossword in each letter and I have to let her know how long it took to solve,' Stella said as she stamped the books. 'She's very good at compiling them. Keeps me busy in the evenings, I can tell you.'

On her way out of the van Clarissa met Alastair on his way in.

'I haven't seen much of you recently,' he said.

'I've been putting the garden to rights and enjoying the countryside.'

'You know where I am if you need help with the garden.'

'Oh, it's just a matter of keeping the weeds down now. Jimmy McDonald's giving most of his time to Linn Hall this year, but he dug the beds and borders last month and all I need do is make sure they're kept tidy.'

'Fancy a drink in the Cuckoo when I've finished here,' he indicated the library van with a jerk of the head, 'or a coffee in the Gift Horse?'

'I've got a stack of ironing waiting for me, and some phone calls to make as well. Another time?'

He looked down at her for a long minute, a slight frown creasing his brows, then said, 'Sure – see you,' and hurried up the van steps.

Why, Clarissa asked herself as she opened Willow Cottage's gate and went up the path, had she not accepted his invitation? Normally she would have set aside the ironing and the phone calls – both fictional excuses in any case – to enjoy a chat with Alastair, but not now. Not, she realised as she let herself into the house and put her books down on the hall table, since Amy had spoken of the friendship between Clarissa and Alastair the night before she left to see more of Scotland.

Her words ran through Clarissa's head as she went to put the kettle on. *'Alastair's a real nice boy . . . he really cares for you, just like you really care for him . . . so what's age got to do with anythin'?'*

'Shut *up*, Amy!' Clarissa said aloud.

'So what's age got to do with anythin'?' Amy persisted.

It had everything to do with it. And in any case, whatever she was hinting at wasn't true. Clarissa felt her face going hot at the very thought. She liked Alastair very much – he was a friend, her best friend. He was the son she had never had. What exactly was Amy getting at? Was she, Clarissa, taking Alastair for granted, becoming possessive in some way? If so, was there any possibility that Alastair might notice it as well? After all he had done for her she couldn't bear to think of hurting or embarrassing him in any way.

138

She switched the kettle off before it was near boiling and went out to the car in the hope that a long drive into the countryside might help clear her mind of such disturbing thoughts.

All day and every day Ginny worked on the lake and in the evenings she sat in her little camper van close to the Linn Hall kitchen door, poring over the books and photographs that Hector and Fliss had found in drawers and cupboards, trying to get a clear idea of the way the gardens used to look in their heyday, and seeking, in the beautifully handwritten accounts books and diaries, information about the purchase of plants.

Until Molly and her daughter arrived Lewis had worked with her in the evenings, the two of them drinking mugs of hot chocolate and eating biscuits with one hand while they scribbled with the other. But all that had changed.

Ginny had no objection to Rowena Chloe, an enchanting miniature of her mother with her red hair and wide smile. She was two months from her second birthday now, trotting round the kitchen and the gardens, making friends with everyone she saw, even Duncan Campbell, Linn Hall's one and only gardener. Duncan was a dour man who tended to leave the raising of his own four children to his wife, Helen, but even he melted slightly when Rowena Chloe headed towards him calling, 'Ducken!'

The year before, when the baby's idea of petting him was along the lines of pulling at his long shaggy coat, Muffin, the Heinz-variety dog the Ralston-Kerrs had inherited when his elderly owner died, had been wary of Rowena Chloe. But now she could walk and was big enough to enjoy a bit of rough and tumble, the dog had become her greatest friend and went everywhere with her. 'Like Nanny the dog in Peter

139

Pan,' Fliss said. 'We can always rest assured that if she goes where she shouldn't or gets herself into a mess, Muffin will let us know about it.'

Not that Rowena Chloe was ever on her own. She and Molly lived with Molly's parents and sister in Inverness, so Lewis made the most of her infrequent visits. During the day he took his little daughter round the grounds with him, and she was often to be seen travelling atop his shoulders clutching fistfuls of his dark brown hair or with her blue-jeaned bottom stuck up in the air as she dug busily at a patch of earth with the plastic trowel and fork he had bought for her.

Sometimes Molly was with them but, unlike her daughter, she became easily bored with gardening and preferred to sit in the kitchen, especially now that the first few backpackers who had arrived to help in the garden were in for their meals.

'And getting a bit too friendly with the lads, if you ask me,' Jinty McDonald, who helped Fliss in the kitchen, said to her daughter Steph. 'She's a natural flirt, that one. That's how she managed to nab Lewis.'

In the evenings after Rowena Chloe had gone to bed Molly demanded Lewis's attention. At first she joined him in the camper van, driving Ginny mad by the way she flipped through photographs, getting the carefully organised piles mixed up and going on about the old-fashioned hairstyles, clothes and hats worn by the ladies pictured during house parties.

Lewis couldn't take the distraction either. For a few evenings he put up with his fiancée's prattle for about half an hour before taking her off to the Cuckoo for the rest of the evening, then he gave up and Ginny was left to work on her own.

'Which is a relief,' she admitted to Lynn Stacey when they met at the pub. Desperate to get some time on her own, she had gone there for a hasty lunch and ended up sharing a table with Lynn. 'It's difficult to concentrate on things when

140

someone's talking about fashion all the time. To tell the truth, I don't even notice the people, all I'm looking at are the plants in the background.'

'Could I help at all? Not with the photographs, because I can't tell one tree from another and I'd probably be more interested in the people too. But I know when not to prattle, and you said there were accounts books and diaries as well. Could I concentrate on them and leave the pictures to you?'

'To be honest, I was about to ask for your help, but are you sure?'

'Absolutely. It would be good for my brain to think about something other than school business. I have supper round about seven-thirty every evening, if you'd like to join me tomorrow. Would you be allowed to bring the photographs and books with you? My place would give you lots of room to spread all the photographs out.'

'I think the Ralston-Kerrs would agree to that. They know they can trust me,' Ginny said eagerly. It would be good to have a change of scene, and a break from watching Lewis simpering over Molly.

Not that Lewis ever simpered, she corrected herself as she walked back to Linn Hall. That was unfair. But he did seem to think he was lucky to be engaged to her, while it was Ginny's opinion that he deserved much more than an empty-headed flirt.

Somehow, she couldn't see Molly settling down to be the lady of Linn Hall once she realised what hard work it was. Nor could she see Lewis ever being happy away from the place.

141

18

Ten days after Helen and Marcy had met Carrie Alston and her husband at the pub a scarlet open-top sports car with cream leather upholstery drove past Prior's Ford Primary School. Lynn Stacey, busy getting her small pupils to form a double line before marching indoors to start the day, suddenly lost their attention.

'What on earth is going on?' she asked the staff member assisting her as the children broke ranks and dashed to the railings. And then, seeing the car, 'Who can that be?'

The driver, a woman with her hair protected from the elements by a pretty scarf, tooted her horn and waved to the children, now pressed against the railings. The male driver of a Range Rover following close behind also banged his horn and waved. The children cheered, jumping up and down, and waved back vigorously.

The car and its escort were both signalling a turn down Slaemuir Road, in the direction of the river. 'I think that woman must be the person who has bought Doris Thatcher's cottage – the one down by the river with the pretty garden.

They're saying in the village that it's been snapped up by rich folk to use as a holiday home. Shall I round them up?' The young teacher nodded towards the children.

'They'll come back to their lines in a minute,' said Lynn. 'No harm done.'

As far as most of the residents of Prior's Ford were concerned a lot of harm was being done to their village. Until now every house had been occupied all year round and the prospect of holiday homes was abhorrent to most people.

'We don't want houses lyin' empty most of the year, then when the owners come in the summer they don't know us and we don't get the time to know them,' said Bill Harper, the local garage owner. 'And I'm willin' to bet,' he added, turning from the bar to face the table where Sam and Marcy were sitting, 'they'll charge about the place in one of those big four by fours and do all their shoppin' in Kirkcudbright or even Dumfries.'

'That's a thought,' Sam agreed. 'But I don't see what we can do about it.'

'We managed to put a stop to the quarry bein' opened, didn't we?' Doug Borland put in.

'That was because they discovered peregrine falcons nest in the quarry every year, Doug.'

'So this is what the country's comin' to, is it, Robert?' Doug slammed down his pint glass and folded his beefy arms. 'It's a sorry day when *birds* have to be protected while youngsters who've lived here all their lives and want to find a nice wee home so's they can get married are priced out of the place without so much as a by-your-leave.'

'Doug's right, it's a disgrace and a miscarriage of justice,' Bill agreed. 'God knows when his Derek and my Tricia'll be able to set a wedding date now. It'll take years for them to

144

work their way up the council housing list, an' that wee cottage would've been just right for them. Almost next door to my house, too. My missus was desperate to know that Tricia wouldn't be far away. And I'll bet you the new people will want conservatories and all that sort of nonsense. The place'll be over-run by workmen and the noise'll be terrible.'

'All so's it can be lived in for a few weeks every summer,' someone said sadly. 'Poor old Doris must be turnin' in her grave at the thought of what's goin' to happen to her nice home.'

'Then a few years down the line they'll get bored with it and sell it on for more than any of us could afford to pay – you just wait and see. Robert, is there nothin' the progress committee can do?' Doug asked. 'Our Derek loves this village and he's all set to take over the butcher's shop when I retire. As Bill says, that wee cottage would have been just right for him and Tricia.'

'I know how you feel, and I feel the same way – I think we all do,' Robert said, and was met by a rumble of agreement, 'but Doris's daughter owns the place and she's entitled to get as much money as she can from it.'

'If falcons saved the old quarry, we could always try to persuade a colony of bats to set up home in Doris's attic,' Cam Gordon suggested with a grin. Molly Ewing, who was sitting at Cam's table with Lewis and some of the backpackers from Linn Hall, gave a shriek of laughter. 'Bats are protected too, aren't they?' Cam went on, winking at Molly. 'I'm not talkin' about the old human variety that's in bed by nine every night; I mean the ones that come out after dark for some fun. What you might call the clubbing bats.'

Molly gave another peal of laughter while Bill Harper snapped, 'What about the ones in your belfry, Cam?'

'Lewis, could your dad write to the council or our MP on the village's behalf?'

'I doubt if anyone'd pay attention to a letter, Doug. My father's got no more clout than anyone else here. I have to agree with Robert – we're helpless.'

'Sometimes,' Doug said bitterly, 'I don't know why we should have to pay taxes, since falcons and bats seem to have more rights than we do!'

Again, there was a rumble of agreement.

The transition from winter to late spring kept the McNair family working from morning to night. No sooner had the lambing season ended than the calves began to arrive, then came the task of checking the previous year's lambs and calves – the best of the lambs to become the following year's new mothers and the calves, just under a year old, to be sold on.

Every year it seemed there were fewer young ewes to produce lambs in a year's time, and fewer calves to sell. The farm's livestock was gradually dwindling because feed had become so expensive.

'It's a vicious circle,' Ewan said in despair as he and his parents sat at the kitchen table working on the farm books. 'We need the money from the sale of the young rams and calves, but we're not producing enough of them to keep the others going for the rest of the year.'

'So what d'ye suggest we do about it?' his father growled back. 'Sell the lot an' hand our land over tae that no-good brother o' yours so's he can cover it wi' houses for rich folk?'

'Of course not, but sooner or later we're going to have to decide between the sheep or the dairy herd, since the cost for both herds is greater than the money we make from them.'

'We've always had sheep an' cattle at Tarbethill and while I'm in charge we'll keep both,' Bert snapped. He pushed the papers away and rose from the table. 'I'm away out tae see the calves settled for the night.'

'I'll come with ye, Dad.'

'Stay where ye are, I can manage.'

'I'll have a cup of tea ready when you come back,' Jess said. When the door had closed behind her husband's back, she went on, 'Let him be, son. He needs tae be on his own for a wee while. I know ye're doin' ye're best tae find ways tae keep Tarbethill goin' but Bert cannae face lettin' the stock go. It'd make him feel like a failure.'

'That's the last thing he is, Mum. It's the system that's failin' farmers, no' the other way round. Too much kow-towin' tae the EU. Can they no' understand that what suits one country doesnae suit another?' Ewan burst out impatiently. 'Can folk who think they're fit tae govern a country really be so stupid?'

'Money an' power don't add up tae brains, or even common sense.' His mother put her palms flat on the table, using them to lever herself up. 'And there's no sense in frettin' about the folk that make the laws,' she said over her shoulder as she poured hot water from the kettle on the range into the big teapot, 'better tae concentrate on what we can do tae keep things goin' here.'

'I suppose so. The cottage could be ready for June – I think I'll ask Alison to write an advert to put into the *News* an' some of the other papers. It would help if we could rent it out over the summer.'

'There you are, then.' Jess turned to smile at him. 'That's what I mean. Good for you, Ewan!'

'Jenny, I have news.' Ingrid MacKenzie, who had just ushered the customers she had been dealing with from the Gift Horse, closed the door and locked it before turning the notice to 'Closed'.

'It must be something important to make you shut up shop.' Jenny felt butterflies stir and stretch their wings in the pit of her stomach. For months she had been concerned about Ingrid's unusual lack of interest in the shop and in village life in general. She had wanted time and again to come right out and ask her friend what was wrong, but now she was about to find out she was uneasy.

'It is. We're moving to Norway.'

'What? All of you? For how long?'

'I don't know. A year at least.' Ingrid started reorganising a stand of greetings cards she and Jenny had made. 'My parents run a small hotel in my home town, and my father's health has not been good for some time.'

'That's why you went back home for the Easter holidays as well as at Christmas?'

'Yes. It's his mind, Jenny. We thought at first there was a brain tumour or something of that sort, but he's had all the tests and it seems to be early senility.' Ingrid's voice shook slightly as she gave up her pretence of being busy and turned to face Jenny.

'I'm so sorry!' Normally Ingrid was so capable and sure of herself that Jenny would never have thought of hugging her, but now she did so without thinking, and felt her friend's slender body melt into the embrace.

'So am I. He's no longer able to take any responsibility for the hotel and my mother can't manage it on her own as well as caring for him. She needs me, Jenny, and I must put my parents first.'

'Of course you must. When are you leaving?'

'We've been talking about it for months now. You've probably been aware that I've had something on my mind, but I had to work things out before I could tell anyone. Peter's going to take a sabbatical and we leave in mid-July.'

'Oh.' The Gift Horse opened every year in April and closed in October. Although Ingrid owned the shop, she and Jenny

148

ran it more or less as a partnership. 'So what's going to happen to this place?'

'That's what I have to talk to you about. I would like you to keep it going if you can, but the decision has to be yours. My main priority in Norway will be to help to look after my father, of course, but Peter and I will also have to take over the hotel. My parents love the place and it would upset both of them to let it go. My mother feels, too, that it would worry my father because at the moment he still goes in every day and the staff keep watch to make sure he doesn't do anything to cause problems. If his normal routine was stopped it would only add to his confusion. But the business is suffering because he's always been the general manager while my mother supervises the housekeeping duties. We may eventually be able to appoint a reliable manager and return to the village but at the moment' – Ingrid spread her hands out in a helpless gesture – 'I can't say anything for certain. If you feel the Gift Horse would be too much for you to run on your own, then you must, of course, say so, and we'll close it until such time as I know where my future lies. The decision is yours, Jenny, and you must take time to think about it. If you do take it on, then you will be free to take full control.'

By the end of May the village was filled with colour. Clematis and wisteria scattered their blossoms over fences and walls and even on the roofs of some sheds and garages. Rhododendrons and azaleas were massed with colour, lilacs perfumed the air and golden laburnum blossoms were thick on the trees. Gardeners were hard at work, especially at Linn Hall, where the restored kitchen garden seemed to be trying to make up for the years it had lain neglected and unproductive.

The motor mower that the Ralston-Kerrs had finally been able to afford arrived, and for once Duncan Campbell had a smile on his face as he made short work of tending grass that had been carefully nourished over the past eighteen months. When he had finished, and the cut grass was raked up, he insisted on Fliss and Hector coming to have a look at the result.

'They're just as they looked when I was a boy,' Hector marvelled as he stood on the flagged terrace and surveyed the three smooth green levels, linked by gentle slopes.

'I only knew them as patchy ground. Oh, Hector,' Fliss's eyes filled with tears, 'isn't it lovely to see them looking so good? I wish your parents were here.'

Molly handed her daughter to Lewis. 'Hold her for a minute,' she said and ran across the top level then threw herself down on the ground and rolled out of sight. 'Wheee!' She appeared on the second level, jumping about like a child, arms in the air and with loose grass clinging to her clothing, then ran to roll down the next slope.

'Me, me!' Rowena Chloe struggled in her father's arms.

'Come on then.'

'Lewis, you'll make her sick!'

'She'll be all right, Mum.' He went more than halfway down the first slope before putting the little girl down. She rolled to the bottom almost at once, squeaking her delight, and scrambled to her feet as her mother came racing back, laughing and brushing grass from her clothes.

'Nice to see young people playing in the grounds again,' Hector said happily.

19

'Would it matter if the Gift Horse closed down for one summer?' Andrew asked.

'I suppose not, but on the other hand, it's all stocked and there are the suppliers to think of. Some of the items were made by people in the area – Alastair's paintings, for instance – and it means they'd lose money. And I feel,' Jenny said, 'that I should keep the place going in the hope that Ingrid will be able to come back to the village. But what if they have to stay in Norway?'

'We'd keep having conversations like this one.'

'Sorry, it's not fair to expect you to help me make my mind up.'

'Why not? I'm your husband,' he said, but couldn't help adding, 'At least, everyone here thinks I'm your husband.'

'Of course you are! We're legal under Scottish law, aren't we?'

'So why not make us legal under every law?'

'Andrew, I've got enough on my mind right now!'

'I don't see why a gift shop should be more important than

us making a full commitment to each other.' Andrew's tone was mild but every word seemed to have a sharp edge to it.

For a moment he and Jenny glared at each other before saying together, 'I'm sorry . . .' and starting to laugh.

'Truce?' Andrew asked.

'Truce,' she agreed.

'Let's get back to the Gift Horse then, since you're clearly still not ready to talk about us. You want to keep it going.'

'I don't know.'

'I wasn't asking a question, I was stating a fact. You hate the thought of seeing it closed during the summer, don't you?'

'Well, I – yes I do. Ingrid and I worked so hard to get it up and running, and since the peregrine falcons were found to be nesting in the old quarry we've become quite a little tourist village.'

'Okay, so that's one thing settled – you're going to tell Ingrid you'll hold the fort for her.'

'I don't know about next year, though. If she . . .'

'Let's take it one step at a time, love. The next question is, how are you going to manage the place on your own?'

'I had thought of asking if Alastair would put in some hours there, as and when he can.'

'Why don't you ask Maggie to work for you at weekends?'

'Maggie? Do you think she'd want to?'

'It wouldn't hurt to ask. I've a feeling she'd like to be useful and if I'm wrong I'm sure she'll not be shy about turning you down. You'd have to pay her, though. If the shop doesn't make enough to justify that, I'll cover her salary.'

'You've grown really fond of Maggie, haven't you?'

'I'll admit that when you first announced your bullying ex-husband's teenage daughter was going to become part of our family I had my reservations, and I'm sure you agreed with me for quite a while.'

152

'She was the stepdaughter from hell, wasn't she?'

'Indeed she was,' Andrew agreed heartily, 'but once she learned to trust us things changed. I am fond of her and I think you did the right thing. In fact,' he went on as the front door opened and shut, 'why don't you ask her right now?'

'Ask who what?' Maggie wanted to know as she came into the living room. The marmalade cat followed her, mewing for attention. 'Hello, lovely Martha!'

Martha, who seemed to have known from the start that she was more Maggie's than anyone else's, bounded into the girl's arms.

'Gorgeous kitty,' Maggie crooned. 'Ask who what?'

'Maggie, the MacKenzies are going back to Norway for a year.'

'I know, Freya told me. I'll miss her.' At first rebellious Maggie and laid-back Freya MacKenzie had been like chalk and cheese, but as Maggie gradually began to settle into being part of the Prior's Ford community the two girls had become firm friends. 'Her mum said I can visit them, though – that'd be cool.'

'It certainly will, and Freya can come here as well. I wanted to talk to you about the Gift Horse, Maggie. I've decided to try to keep it going while Ingrid's away and I wondered – would you be willing to help me at the weekends?'

'Would I get paid?'

'I told you she'd want money,' Andrew butted in. 'Don't we give you enough pocket money?'

'Pocket money's different. The labourer is worth her hire,' Maggie informed him.

'Andrew, stop teasing her. Of course you'll be paid. I'm sure we could come to an agreement that would suit us both.'

'Great! I'm going to get in some practice on the keyboard,' Maggie said, and wandered off upstairs with Martha draped round her neck like a golden boa.

153

'She never ceases to surprise me,' Jenny marvelled.

'That's what teenage kids are created for: keeping parents on their toes,' Andrew told her.

It seemed to the driver of the post van that Prior's Ford was a very popular village. Deliveries took him longer than usual and meant that he spent the rest of the day trying to catch up with himself, finally going home in a bit of a temper. Once there, he snapped at his children, growled at the dog, and annoyed his wife by criticising her cooking.

He wasn't the only one to have a bad start to the day.

★　　★　　★

To Moira Melrose

You are the most selfish woman in Prior's Ford. Just because you didn't get to be president of the WRI this time, you're trying to wreck it for everyone else. If you had any decency in you, you would resign before you're found out and barred.

Moira read the letter for the second time, and then once more, her face swelling with rage. This was too much! This time she was going to take the matter all the way to court and that snooty blonde policewoman wasn't going to get her to change her mind.

She picked up the phone and dialled the first four digits of the police-station number then banged the receiver back onto its rest. Before bringing the police into it, she was going to tell that Alma Parr exactly what she had coming to her! She charged out of the house, down the path, through her gate and had to do a swift and somewhat awkward U-turn as it was only separated from the Parrs' gate by a gatepost. Up her neighbour's path she went like a charging hippo and on reaching the door she banged the polished knocker hard against its brass plate.

Five minutes earlier Alma Parr had arrived back home from the village store to find the post on the doormat. She had taken off her coat and hung it up, filled the kettle and switched it on, then riffled through the mail delivery, setting obvious bills aside for George's attention and tossing the junk mail straight into the kitchen bin. That left only one envelope, handwritten and addressed to her.

Fetching the pretty letter-opener she had bought a few months earlier because she could no longer stand the messy way George ripped envelopes open with his thumb, often sending tiny shreds of paper floating to her immaculate carpet, she withdrew a single sheet of handwritten paper.

Alma Parr
There is no place in Prior's Ford for ambitious cheats. You were so keen to take over the WRI you went out of your way to bribe decent honest women to vote for you. It is only a matter of time before you are found out and thrown out. This is a decent village and there is no place in it for the likes of you.

She gasped, one hand flying to her bosom in an attempt to calm her heart, which was beating like a jungle drum. Then, as a ferocious attack was launched on her front door, she jumped and squealed. The world was going mad!

'Right, lady,' Moira said as soon as the door was opened, 'you've done it now. You've gone too far. I was willing to forget, even if I could never forgive, but this is the last straw. I'm going straight back home to phone the police and I'm going to press charges, and this time there'll be no changing my mind. This time I mean it!'

'What are you talking about?'

'About this!' Moira shoved a letter almost into her neighbour's face and Alma backed off, waving it away.

155

'How dare you come onto my property with your threats about the police after what you've done to me? I'm the one who's going to phone them right here and now and I'm going to tell them that this time— Oh,' she said as she recognised the sheet of paper Moira appeared to be trying to force-feed her, 'where did you get that?'

'Don't try to pretend you don't recognise it!'

'I'm not. Come in, quick,' Alma said as she suddenly noticed a woman passing along the crescent had paused to watch the two of them. She caught Moira's arm and dragged her into the hall.

'Get your hands off me! That's assault and battery!'

'I won't have the neighbours seeing you bellowing on my doorstep,' Alma snapped, shutting the door. 'In here.' She led the way to the kitchen then held out her hand for the letter. 'Give me that.'

Moira passed it over, saying, 'Don't try to pretend you haven't seen it before.'

Alma scanned the few lines hurriedly. 'Where did you get it?'

'Just now in the post – as you well know.'

'That's how I got this.' Alma picked up the sheet of notepaper she had dropped on the floor when Moira began trying to batter her door down. 'Here, read it.'

Moira did as she was told, then put the letter on the kitchen table. 'What's going on?'

'Someone's writing to the two of us. Someone who knows us. Poison-pen letters, they're called. Look' – Alma put Moira's letter on the table beside hers – 'it's the same handwriting.'

'How do I know you didn't write one to yourself so you could pretend they came from someone else?'

'Oh, for goodness' sake!' Alma rummaged in a drawer and produced an exercise book. 'Here's a recipe I copied down.

156

That's my writing. And *that*,' she said emphatically, pointing to the two letters, '*isn't* my writing.'

'Poison pen? You mean one of the neighbours sent these letters?'

'Or a member of the Rural. D'you recognise the writing? I don't.'

Moira studied both pages closely. 'Nor me. But why would anyone do such a thing?'

'Out of sheer badness. What are we going to do?'

'I think we should keep the police out of it. I don't know about you, but I don't fancy havin' to speak to that bossy woman PC.'

'Nor me,' Alma agreed. 'I wouldn't mind speaking to the man again, but they'd be sure to send her as well and he didn't get a word in last time, poor lad. She's got him well under her thumb, that one.'

'Mebbe we could find some way to get the rest of the Rural to write something down so we could compare this writing with theirs.'

'That's an idea.' Alma's eye fell on her recipe book. 'Get everyone to write their favourite recipe.'

'Perfect!'

They both glanced down at the letters, lying side by side on the table. Alma studied the page Moira had brought to her door and knew, with a sense of inner triumph, that she was right – the letter writer, whoever it was, had realised that Moira was indeed trying to wreck the Rural rather than let Alma take her rightfully won place as the new president.

Moira, reading the page Alma had received, noticed smugly that she wasn't the only one to be convinced that Alma had stooped to bribery to get the votes she had needed to defeat Moira. But they both realised they couldn't use the other's letter as proof without being forced to reveal the accusations levelled in their own letter. And neither of them wanted to go another round with Police Constable Gloria Frost.

'I don't even want my Dave to see what that – that person's said about me.'

'I think you're right, we shouldn't let anyone else see them. I could murder a cup of tea,' Alma said. 'Fancy one?'

Moira hesitated, but only for a second. 'I suppose I could do with it after the shock of gettin' that horrible letter.'

'I've got some nice biscuits.'

'Okay.' Moira agreed, and the two women, united by a mutual problem, prepared to let bygones be bygones as they drank the cup of peace and broke biscuit together.

20

The phone in the manse rang just as Naomi was stacking the breakfast dishes.

'Ethan, can you get that for me?' she yelled, and then, as there was no reply, she realised that for once he must have left in good time for the school bus.

'Oh – bother!' She was having problems with Sunday's sermon and was hoping, as had happened before, that washing up might just trigger off an idea. Why washing dishes helped to create a sermon she had no idea, but it was true that God did work in mysterious ways.

However, an early phone call almost certainly meant someone had a problem and that didn't bode well for the sermon. Sighing, she made sure the dishes weren't going to teeter and crash into the sink, then hurried to the hall.

The six identical little terraced houses on Main Street had once been almshouses for impoverished elderly villagers with no family to care for them. Although they had long since been modernised and renamed Jasmine Cottages the villagers

159

still referred to them as the almshouses, a term of endearment accepted by the inhabitants. Because they shared an open-plan back yard with flower beds, drying greens and a flagged area outside each back door, they knew each other well and were inclined to look out for one another and especially for Ivy, the village's oldest inhabitant.

When Naomi arrived at the old woman's house the door was opened by Dolly Cowan, one of Ivy's close neighbours.

'Thank goodness you're here, Naomi.' Even the blonde curls that usually danced perkily around Dolly's still pretty face looked upset. 'Poor Ivy's in a right state!'

'Where is she? Are you sure she doesn't need a doctor?'

'I don't need a doctor,' Ivy's voice boomed from beyond the cluster of women in her small living room. 'I need a priest!'

'And I'm the nearest to a priest Prior's Ford has,' Naomi said from the doorway and Muriel Jacobson, Cissie Kavanagh and Hannah Gibbs, other Jasmine Cottages residents, parted to let her through to the old woman's high-backed fireside chair. 'Now then, Ivy, what's upset you?'

'Not what's, it's who's upset me – and the answer's Doris Thatcher, that's who. I want her excised or whatever you call it! I want you to do that spell that sends her to where she should be instead of *lingerin"* – Ivy said the word in sepulchral tones, and Dolly shivered – 'in this world upsettin' innocent old bodies who've done nothin' wrong except for livin' longer than her, and that's not a crime, is it?' Ivy appealed to her audience. 'That's God's wish, that is, and it's not my fault He chose me over her.'

For a moment Naomi thought the woman's ravings indicated a stroke, but there was no tell-tale droop on one side of her face, and her voice was as loud and clear as ever.

'Here, Naomi, you sit by her and I'll fetch you a cup of

160

tea and a scone.' Cissie indicated the small nursing chair nearby. 'Then Ivy can tell you what's happened.'

'If I sit on that, my love, you'll have to call in the army to get me to my feet again.' Naomi fetched one of the chairs pushed in beneath Ivy's small table, turned it round and lowered herself gently on to it. 'Now then, start again, Ivy. It's too early in the morning for my brain to take everything in at once.'

'Where is it? Where's me letter?'

'Here it is.' Muriel held out a sheet of notepaper to the old woman, who grabbed it and passed it over to Naomi.

'You read that an' tell me what you think about it! And I'll have another cup of tea while you're at it, Cissie. Am I to die o' thirst and hunger in me hour o' need?'

The letter was written in a neat hand and was unsigned.

Just because you go to church every Sunday, Ivy McGowan, and sing the hymns louder than anyone else doesn't mean that you're a better person. Or are you trying to make up for all the sinning you did when you were younger?

What would folk say if they knew you stole men from another woman and had to get married quick to hide your shame?

'Oh dear.'

'An' well you might say that. Came in the mornin' post an' gave me a right turn, it did. Me heart's still thuddin'. It's a blessed wonder that it didn't stop altogether with the shock. Though that's prob'bly what she was hopin' for.'

'You know who sent it?'

'Course I do! It was Doris Thatcher, I told you that when you came in.'

'Ivy, Doris is dead. I officiated at her funeral, and you were there. Don't you remember?'

161

'Am I ever likely to forget? She might be dead, but she's not finished with this village yet. That's why I want you to do that exercisin' or whatever it is that makes dead souls stop botherin' decent livin' folk. Good,' Ivy said as Cissie set a mug of tea on the occasional table by her side. 'Did you put in plenty of milk an' three sugars?'

'I did. Here you are, Naomi.'

'Thanks. Ivy, for one thing I'm not the sort of minister who exorcises spirits, and for another I very much doubt that poor Doris is haunting you or anyone else.'

'An' who else would know what's written in that letter? Doris an' me used to be good friends; we knew everythin' about each other an' no livin' person knows about what she wrote there.'

'Are you saying you did the things you're accused of in the letter?' Hannah asked the question nobody else was willing to voice.

Outrage made Ivy puff up like an irate turkey. 'Of course not! It's all lies! Mebbe I wasn't a saint in my younger days – nor was Doris, come to that. But I wasn't a sinner neither. Mebbe me an' John had to get married sooner than we'd planned cos of our Cathy bein' on the way, but at least I wasn't like those loose women who flaunt their bairns and their lack of a weddin' ring nowadays. We had self-respect, we had. We got married, even if it were later rather than sooner.'

'Is this Doris's handwriting?'

'Could be. I don't recall seein' any writin' of hers before.'

'There you are, then.' Naomi took a sip from her mug and almost choked. 'I think you got them mixed up, Cissie.'

'Sorry.' Cissie snatched the other mug from beneath Ivy's reaching fingers and replaced it with the one Naomi handed her. 'There you are.'

'I said I don't recall seeing her writin', but I doubt if you've

162

ever seen it either, Naomi. So how d'you know it *isn't* her that wrote it?'

'That's true, but I can't believe Doris is writing to you from beyond the grave. Did you say it came in the morning post?' Ivy's white head bobbed up and down emphatically. 'I can't believe spirits would need to use the postal services to contact the living.'

'That's what I thought,' Hannah volunteered. 'More likely to use mediums than stamps.'

'Where's the envelope?'

'Here you are. It's the same handwriting,' Muriel said. 'It's a poison-pen letter, isn't it? Should we contact the police?'

'Best not if we can help it,' Cissie advised. 'They were here not that long ago because of that carry-on between Alma Parr and Moira Melrose. I don't fancy the idea of calling them back to the village so soon.'

Naomi nodded. 'I agree. This is probably a one-off prank – someone's idea of a joke. I think it's best ignored.'

'Well, I'm keepin' it just in case,' Ivy said. 'Evidence, that's what it is.'

Naomi was on her way back to the manse when her name was called and she turned to see Dolly Cowan running after her.

'I didn't want to say to any of the others,' she said breathlessly when she caught up with the minister, 'but Harold and I got a letter just like Ivy's this morning. Unsigned and the same handwriting, as far as I could see.' She looked around before drawing an envelope from her pocket. 'You might as well read it.'

Naomi took the single sheet of writing paper from the envelope and scanned the few lines written in the same hand as Ivy's letter.

What made you choose to come to Prior's Ford? Everyone who lives here knows each other's business but nobody knows about you. What have you got to hide? We don't like secrets here. Be warned that someone will find out sooner or later and then you'll be unmasked.

'This is just silly. Why on earth would anyone worry about your past?'

'I know. We only kept it quiet when we came here because before then, every time people found out Harold had been a circus clown they kept wanting him to do turns at children's parties and he got fed up with it, so—'

'Dolly,' Naomi finally managed to interrupt the gabbled words, 'you don't need to explain anything to me. I'm quite sure you and Harold aren't guilty of any – did you say he had been a circus clown?'

'A very successful one before he had a fall from a tightrope and had to retire,' Dolly said proudly.

'Good gracious. I mean – clearly whoever wrote this letter doesn't know your secret, so I wouldn't worry about it if I were you.'

'That's what Harold said. He thinks it's just a silly prank.'

'Not a very nice one, but he could be right. Try to forget about it, Dolly, and be assured I won't say a word about this to anyone.'

'Thank you,' Dolly breathed, and scurried back to the almshouses.

'Good gracious,' Naomi said again as she made for the manse. She had always thought of Harold Cowan, with his long, rather expressionless face, as a clerk in an office, or perhaps a shopkeeper. The thought of him as a clown, especially one who could walk a tightrope, was difficult to grasp.

As she went up the manse path, fumbling in her pocket for

164

her door key, a sudden vision came into her mind of Harold edging his way along the washing line at the rear of the almshouses, balancing with the aid of an open umbrella.

Despite the seriousness of the poison-pen situation, she giggled.

Clarissa had woken early to a beautiful morning and settled down to some serious gardening as soon as she had breakfasted. It was almost one o'clock when she returned to the house. She made herself some lunch and was on her way upstairs to make her bed when she found the post on the doormat. It consisted of two unwanted catalogues, a bill she had been expecting, a letter from her stepson, Steven, and another letter addressed in an unknown hand. She put Steven's letter, the bill and the catalogues on the hall table and opened the remaining envelope. It held a single page and there was no opening, and no signature, just a few lines.

It's not proper, a woman of your age carrying on with a man young enough to be your son. That sort of behaviour belongs in the gossip magazines, not in a respectable village like ours. Where's your self-respect?

Clarissa's heart seemed to pause for several seconds then just as she began to wonder if it had stopped for good it crashed back into action, beating out a fast, erratic rhythm. Her head felt light and floaty and her breath fluttered in the region of her throat, seemingly unsure as to whether it was on its way into or out of her lungs. She sank on to the bottom step of the staircase, her free hand gripping the banisters while she concentrated on breathing in and out, in and out, slowly and regularly.

Once she had regained control she read the letter again,

feeling colour rush into a face that had been drained of it only seconds earlier. It was cruel, malicious, wrong! She must – but she didn't know what she must do. Take it to the police? The very thought of anyone reading such an accusation, possibly asking questions, wondering if the things it insinuated were true, was unbearable.

She would destroy it, she decided, then changed her mind and put it back into its envelope, which she then stuffed into the pocket of her cardigan. Destroying it wouldn't undo the damage it had already done to her, wouldn't take away the vile taste it had brought to her mouth. What if there were more letters, or – the very thought made her feel sick – what if the writer decided to send letters accusing her of chasing after Alastair to other people in the village? Perhaps she should keep it in case she needed evidence.

She jumped and gave an alarmed whimper when the door-bell rang. Her first reaction was to pretend she was out, then realising that if the caller peered through the letterbox she would be clearly seen, she got to her feet. Opening the door, she found Alastair on the doorstep, grim-faced. A guilty flush warmed her neck and cheeks.

'So you got one too,' he said.

'I got one what?'

'Letter. Anonymous, unpleasant, mentioning me. One like this.' He held out an envelope. 'Don't try to deny it, Clarissa, I could tell by the look on your face when you saw me. Can I come in?'

She stepped back reluctantly to allow him entry, casting a swift look at the road outside and along Main Street beyond in case anyone noticed him being admitted.

He had gone straight to the kitchen, as he usually did when entering her cottage, and when she followed he turned and handed her the single sheet from his envelope. 'Read it.'

166

'I'd rather not.'

'You need to, Clarissa, and I need to read the letter you got. Please. This – this person, whoever it is, has targeted both of us and we have to work together to sort it out.'

He was right. She withdrew the letter from her cardigan pocket and handed it over.

His letter had been written in the same hand as hers.

It's disgusting to see a lad like you lusting after a woman old enough to be your mother. The whole village is talking about you. There are plenty of nice single lassies around, why don't you see sense and pick one of them?

'This is horrible – and ridiculous! Why would anyone write such stupid letters?'

'God knows.' He peered at her envelope. 'Your post mark is a bit clearer than mine. It looks as though they could have been posted locally.'

'We should probably show these letters to the police – but I'd rather not.'

'Nor me. I wonder if anyone else has had letters. Not about us,' Alastair added hurriedly as Clarissa put a shaking hand to her mouth, 'I mean, about themselves.'

'Who's likely to tell if they do?'

He nodded, then said, 'Are you all right?'

'Not really.'

'Sit down and I'll make some coffee. Have you got any brandy? We could both do with a drink.' As he spoke he made for the cupboard where the coffee and sugar were kept, then halted as Clarissa said, 'No!'

'No coffee or no brandy?'

'I think you should just go, Alastair. Go now – and don't come back. I think it would be best for us not to speak to

167

each other unless it's in public,' she hurried on as he stared at her.

'But we're not guilty of the accusations in the letters.'

'I know that and so do you, but others might not agree.' She indicated the two letters on the kitchen table. 'At least one person in this village believes we are.'

'Even if that were true, it wouldn't be anyone else's business.'

'It's for the best, Alastair. It's what I want us to do.'

'Are you saying that we should let this malicious person spoil a good friendship?'

'I think whoever it is already has,' Clarissa said sadly.

21

'Here, Mum.'

Jess backed away from the envelope Victor held out to her, shaking her head. 'Put it away, son, I don't want it.'

'It's no' a case of wantin', it's a case of needin' it. I'm gettin' good money from Mr Askew — what's wrong wi' givin' some of my wages over tae my mother? It's what me an' Ewan have always done.'

'Yer father wouldnae like it.'

'That's why I'm no' offerin' it tae him. Just because I've chosen tae work in a garage instead of on the farm doesnae mean that I've disowned my fam'ly. Oh, I know,' he went on as Jess continued to shake her head, 'that my fam'ly've disowned me — my dad has, I mean,' he added hurriedly as hurt filled his mother's eyes, 'but I still care for ye. For all of ye.'

'It's no' just you turnin' your back on farmin' as well you know. It's what's goin' on in that field. That's what's torn Bert apart.'

'I know.' The hand holding out the envelope full of notes fell back against Victor's side and his shoulders slumped. 'An'

I'm sorry that it's split the fam'ly like this, but I love Jeanette, Mum, an' I had tae sell the land tae safeguard our future.'

'Ye should be puttin' yer wages aside for the future too, instead of givin' some tae me.'

'The money I got from the sale of the field's banked so ye don't have tae worry about that. Just let me help ye when I can, Mum. Dad doesn't need tae know a thing about it. Please!' Victor held the envelope out again and this time Jess took it. There was no denying that she could do with it.

Bert and Ewan had taken some of last year's calves to the market and Wilf was working on one of the furthest fields, out of sight of the farmhouse. Sometimes, when she knew it was safe, Jess phoned Victor and if he could get away he hurried over to the farm. She felt like a traitor to Bert, but seeing her son helped to ease the ache that had nagged at her heart since the night he moved out of Tarbethill to live with his fiancée's family.

'So,' she said now, putting mugs of tea and a plate of freshly buttered scones on the table, 'how's Jeanette?'

'As bonny as ever. We're thinkin' of settin' a date for next year. Our new house'll be ready by then. It was good tae see Alice at Easter and tae know that she doesnae bear me any ill will.'

'She spent most of her week here workin' alongside Bert and Ewan.'

'She told me that an' I felt bad about lettin' you all down, but you know I tried tae get Dad tae let me help. Alice is worried about ye,' Victor said through a mouthful of scone, 'same as me. She says you an' Dad both look so tired.'

'That's because we are, all the time,' Jess said tartly, then regretted snapping at him as she saw his face cloud. 'I'm no' blamin' you, Victor, there was no sense in stayin' on here if yer heart wasnae in it. It's just that farmin's got so difficult. But what else can we do but try tae keep goin'?'

'There's other farmers who'd be willin' tae buy the land off ye. You an' Dad could live on the money an' Ewan can always find work on another farm. Then he could afford tae marry Alison. I suppose he still wants tae?'

'Oh, aye, and she's the right one for him, but there's little chance of a marriage.'

'There could be, if Dad could be talked intae seein' sense.'

'If you're trying tae say that I should get him tae sell off Tarbethill land, Victor, ye can forget it. It'd be kinder tae push that bread knife intae the man's heart an' you know it. I nearly forgot – a letter came for you the other day.' Jess fetched it from behind the clock on the mantelpiece.

Victor studied the envelope before running a thumb beneath the flap and pulling out a single sheet of paper. His face shaped itself into a puzzled scowl as he read the few handwritten lines.

'It's no' bad news, is it?'

'It's no' anythin'.' Victor read it again, then handed it to Jess. 'I can't make head nor tail o' it.'

Jess had to put on her reading glasses before she could make out the spidery script. There was no opening and no signature, just three or four lines that she, like her son, read with mounting astonishment.

You should be ashamed of yourself, letting your parents down the way you have. If you have any decency you will return to Tarbethill Farm and help them and your brother instead of losing your head over the wrong sort of girl. You will pay the price in the end if you don't.

'What does it mean?'

'I told ye – nothin'.'

'But – someone must have written it and posted it.'

'Aye, someone who doesnae know where I'm livin' now. Have ye been talkin' about me tae folk in the village?'

'As if I would dae a thing like that! How could ye think it? An' even if I wanted tae, which I don't, when would I find the time? I've scarcely been off the farm since ye – all year,' Jess said hotly. 'In any case, everyone knows. Ye cannae keep a thing secret for long in a wee place like Prior's Ford.'

'Aye, of course. I shouldnae have accused ye, Mum, I know ye'd never gossip about anyone, let alone yer fam'ly. It's from some old fool wi' wandered wits an' nothin' better tae dae.' Victor took the letter from his mother's hand.

'But why would anyone want to attack you like this?'

'God knows, but if ye happen tae find out, let me know an' I'll sort her out – or him.' He screwed the page up and tossed it at the range. 'I'd best go. I'll see ye again, soon.'

When he had gone Jess cleared the evidence of his visit away, washing and drying the two mugs and clearing up the crumbs he had sprayed over the table. She had never been able to teach her firstborn not to talk with his mouth full but she was quite sure that Jeanette, a prim young woman, would succeed where she had failed. Marriage to Jeanette would turn her Victor from a farm lad to a townie in no time.

Throwing the crumbs into the fire, she saw that the crumpled letter had hit the bars of the range and bounced off instead of being gobbled up by the glowing coals. She picked it up and smoothed it out, reading the few lines again.

There was an air of malice about them that made her give a sudden shiver, as though someone or something had walked over her grave. For a moment she contemplated burning the single page as Victor had intended, then she smoothed it out on the table, folded it again, and slipped it back into its envelope.

The post mark over the second-class stamp was smudged and she couldn't make anything out.

She pushed the envelope into the bottom of the drawer where she kept the clean kitchen towels and went out to see to the calves.

'Good Lord,' Hector Ralston-Kerr said mildly, passing his letter across the table to his wife, 'what d'you think of that, Fliss?'

She scanned it, then remarked, 'Your great-grandfather seems to have had an interesting life, dear. According to this you're related to half the village.'

'Looks that way, doesn't it? Mind you, I seem to recall my father telling me once that no woman was safe when the old man was around, be they guests or servants, so whoever wrote this could be right.'

'I wonder who it was? It's not got a signature, Hector. I think it's what's called a poison-pen letter. I read about them once in a crime novel by – Agatha Christie, or perhaps Dorothy L. Sayers. I got it from the mobile library years ago. A good book, as I recall.'

'Let me have another look.' Her husband took the letter back and read it again. 'Mmm. Well, all I can say is, I wish one of those relatives I seem to have in the village had inherited this place instead of me.'

'It had to be you, dear, because as far as we know, you were born on what's called the right side of the blanket.'

'Pity in a way. We could have had a much more peaceful life if I'd been born on the other side, Fliss.'

'Yes dear, we certainly could.'

'Oh well, never mind, all water under the bridge now, eh?' Hector said, and crumpled up the letter before going back to his newspaper. They both forgot to mention it to Lewis and he didn't mention the letter he had received that morning, but not because he had forgotten about it.

He had got up early and was pruning back some bushes near to the big front gates when the post van arrived. Seeing him, the driver banged his horn and waited until Lewis walked to the van before handing a bundle of post through the open window.

'Saved me a couple of minutes, you bein' here,' he said before driving off.

Lewis thumbed through the letters and plastic-covered junk mail and was surprised to find a handwritten letter addressed to him. He shoved everything else into one of the two big pockets in his body warmer and opened it.

The letter was brief and unsigned.

A fool and his money are soon parted. You should ask that flighty girlfriend of yours for proof that you're the wee one's true father. Most of the village think otherwise. There's talk going round and it's time you either made it all legal or called an end to it.

The accusation hit him like a punch in the mouth. He gasped with the shock of it, feeling colour surge into his face. 'Most of the village think otherwise.' So he and Molly and wee Rowena Chloe were the subject of village tattle? His first reaction was to go down to the Cuckoo that very evening to face the lot of them and demand an explanation. And if anyone dared to repeat the letter's accusations or seemed to agree with them, he would damned well drag them outside and teach them a lesson. He stormed up to the house and tossed the rest of the post on the kitchen table, then left again while his mother was in the middle of asking him something.

174

As he went round the side of the building he met Jinty on her way to help Fliss.

'Morning, Lewis,' she said cheerfully, then, as he glared at her, 'Oh dear, you got out of bed on the wrong side, didn't you?'

'No!' he snapped as he hurried past her, suddenly eager to put as much distance between himself and the house as he could. Molly had taken Rowena Chloe to the village and he was glad of that because he needed to clear his head before seeing them again. They meant the whole world to him, and being with them had, until then, made him happy. But whoever had written the letter in his pocket had spoiled everything for him and he didn't know what to do.

'Helen? It's Carrie. I'm coming to Prior's Ford tomorrow to do some measuring at the cottage. We're going to move in some furniture from the warehouse to make it liveable until the extension's been built. Let's meet up for lunch in that nice little pub, just the two of us, for a catch-up.'

'Oh.' The phone call took Helen by surprise and as she hadn't time to think of a swift excuse she had no option but to say, 'Yes, that would be nice – but it'll have to be after one because my children come home from primary school for lunch.'

'Quarter past one do you? Good, see you then, must dash.'

The following day was Wednesday, and Helen usually devoted Wednesdays to being Lucinda Keen, agony aunt for the local newspaper. Everyone knew that Helen wrote Prior's Ford's news column for the paper, but Lucinda's real identity was a secret. Every Thursday afternoon Bob Green, the reporter who had persuaded her to take on both jobs, collected the village news and handed over the letters that had come in for Lucinda.

Now, although there was a great stack of ironing awaiting her in the living room, a task only made bearable because it gave her the chance while working to watch previously recorded television programmes in peace, she was going to have to put on her Lucinda hat, so to speak, and hurry upstairs to her computer to start on the letters.

Naomi sat in Robert and Cissie Kavanagh's cosy little living room enjoying home-made fruitcake and a mug of strong coffee.

'I need advice, Robert, and as chairman of the progress committee, you seemed the obvious choice. I take it that Cissie has told you about the anonymous letter that poor Ivy got a few weeks ago?'

'And he's been sworn to secrecy along with everyone else in the almshouses,' Cissie put in.

'Of course. Several other people have approached me since then with similar letters, addressed in what looks like the same writing, and all unsigned. They came to me in confidence so I'm not going to name names or discuss contents, but all the accusations were along the same lines as Ivy's – fairly mild and concerning past misdemeanours, none of them serious.'

'So we do have a poison-pen writer in our midst? Are any of the letters threatening?' Robert wanted to know when the minister nodded.

'None that I've seen or heard of, although the people they were aimed at tended to worry in case the contents had been passed to others in the village. But as far as I know that hasn't happened. I haven't heard of any new letters over the past week. The epidemic or whatever it could be called may be over. I just wanted to know what you think we should do about it.'

Robert passed a plate of home-made shortbread to her. 'If

it's over I'd say let sleeping dogs lie – unless anyone wants to bring the police in.'

'Nobody does. What worried most, if not all of them, was the fear that others might hear about their alleged sins and believe them.'

'Ivy's still convinced her letter came from poor Doris Thatcher,' Cissie said. 'But then, Ivy blamed everything on Doris when she was alive.'

'I doubt if the police would believe her theory in any case.' Her husband chuckled. 'Sounds as though it's been some stupid prank that's over and done with now, Naomi.'

'I hope so, but I'm wondering if it might be an idea to mention them very carefully during the Sunday service, letting anyone who might have received one and been fretting about it know that they can come to me for reassurance, and perhaps letting the perpetrator know that his or her actions have caused unnecessary anxiety and it has to stop – if it hasn't already stopped.'

'I suppose you could, but only if you were very careful about it.'

'Perhaps we could work it out together?' Naomi suggested. 'Cissie, I shouldn't, but yes, I will have another slice of that gorgeous fruitcake.'

'And take some home to share with Ethan,' Cissie said placidly. 'There's far too much for us to manage.'

22

Carrie was already in the Neurotic Cuckoo when Helen arrived on the following day. The large glass of red wine before her was half empty and Helen's excuses for being late were cut short with, 'Never mind, you're here now. What d'you want to drink? This is all on me.'

'Fresh orange, please.'

'Oh, come on, live a little! This wine's quite good. Landlord,' Carrie waved at Joe Fisher, 'can we have a bottle of this wine?'

'A bottle? I'm not used to drinking in the middle of the day.'

'Time you started to get used to it. We're going to have such fun when I'm staying here, Helen. Such a lot of catching up to do! Let's decide what we're going to eat first. So,' Carrie went on when Joe had taken their orders, 'what have you been doing with your life since primary school?' She filled Carrie's wine glass and then drained her own and refilled it.

'Not a lot. Went from primary to Kirkcudbright Academy, left at sixteen, worked in an office, married Duncan when I was nineteen, had four children and that's about it.'

'Didn't you say you were a novelist?'

'It's my ambition, but so far I've only sold one short story. Looking after the family takes up most of my time. A few years ago when there was the possibility of the old quarry reopening a protest committee was set up and now it's become the village's progress committee. I'm the secretary and from that I got the chance to do a regular weekly column in the *Dumfries News* covering village activities, so that's cut into my spare time. And there you are – what you see is what you get with me,' Helen finished. She took a gulp of wine and had to grab a napkin as the drink went down the wrong way.

'Steady there, lassie.' Joe, who had just arrived with their soup, set the bowls down hurriedly in order to thump her on the back. 'Want a glass of water?'

'Yes, please!' she gasped, mortified. Carrie must think that she was a real country bumpkin.

'I did a course in a secretarial college after I left school, then like you I opted for an office job,' Carrie said when order had been restored and they had both picked up their soup spoons. 'I'm so glad my dad's new job took him and Mum and me to Berwick on Tweed just as I was finishing primary school here, because otherwise I might never have ended up working for Bernie. I started as his secretary and then it turned out that I had a flair for encouraging people to buy the furniture he makes. So I was promoted to head of sales, married the boss and now . . .' she picked up her drink, and finished with, 'I'm living happily ever after,' before emptying the glass.

'Sounds like a fairytale come true.'

'If it is, it's Cinderella, complete with ugly sisters. Only in my case the sisters are the stepdaughters from hell.'

'Last time we met you said they're sweet girls.'

Carrie grimaced. 'That's because Bernie was there. He spoils them rotten and thinks they're a couple of angels. Fortunately they go to boarding school and for most of the holidays they live with their mother, who of course encourages them to make my life as miserable as possible when Bernie has them. To me, they're the ugly sisters and to them I'm the wicked stepmother, but in front of Bernie we all get on well together. I'm aware I sound like a gold-digger, marrying the boss, but to be honest, Helen, I've adored him since the first moment I set eyes on him. He's the only man in the world for me and I really do want to make him happy. If that means putting up with his daughters then I'll do it, though sometimes it can be very exhausting.' She poured some more wine.

Helen waited until Joe cleared the soup bowls away and set the next course down before saying, 'So he and their mother are divorced?'

'Indeed they are, and it's cost him a lot in alimony, I can tell you. But I certainly wasn't going to be his bit on the side, and I made it very plain to him that it was marriage or nothing with me. Drink up, I can't finish this bottle on my own,' Carrie said, topping up her half-empty glass. 'We're really strong together, me and Bernie. He'd do anything for me and I'd do anything for him. So – tell me all about your husband.'

'Duncan? He was in the year above us at primary. He's the head gardener – well, the only gardener, actually – at Linn Hall and he's kept pretty busy because there's a lot of restoration going on up there. The Ralston-Kerrs are hoping to be able to start opening the gardens to the public every year from now on.'

'And are you happily married?'

'Oh yes,' Helen said at once. As Carrie picked up the wine bottle she tried to put a hand over her glass, but Carrie skilfully removed it from beneath her palm and filled it.

'Good, let's drink to your happiness, and then I want to

181

ask your advice.' A third of her glass's contents went down Carrie's throat. 'We've found a good architect to help to re-design the cottage, and he and I have already paid a flying visit to the place. I like his ideas and he's fitting in with mine but we're not going to start work on the cottage until the autumn at least. But Bernie's set his heart on holding a party soon for some of the local folk so we can get to know each other. I need a list of people we should invite. No more than fifteen, I'd say, and even at that I hope the weather'll be kind and let us use the garden as well as those poky little rooms. We'll get caterers in, and of course you and your Duncan are at the top of the list. So,' she delved into her beautiful leather bag and produced a small notebook and an expensive-looking gold pen, 'let's get started, shall we?'

'I'm going back to the cottage – hop in and I'll drop you at your house on the way,' Carrie offered when they emerged from the pub. She seemed as right as rain despite drinking more than half the bottle of wine, but Helen, feeling distinctly light-headed, eyed the smart little sports car nervously.

'I'll walk – I've got a bit of shopping to do.'

'Okay.' Carrie hugged her, sketched a swift kiss about an inch from her cheek, and turned towards the car, then paused and turned back. 'Helen, let's do lunch often when I'm staying in Prior's Ford. It would be so nice to have you as a best friend again. You could introduce me to your friends; I'd like that.'

For a brief moment, so brief that Helen wondered after-wards if she had imagined it, timid little Carrie Wilson gave a familiar appealing look at Helen from beneath Carrie Alston's long lashes, then she was gone.

'We might be a bit dull for you, Carrie. You must meet lots of interesting people.'

'Oh I do, but mainly in the line of business. Sometimes I miss what you and I had. See you,' Carrie said before hopping into the car and zooming off.

On the way home Helen walked carefully, making a point of putting one foot before the other, and once there she went upstairs with the intention of starting work on the agony aunt letters, but found herself writing a letter to Lucinda Keen instead, based on her thoughts on the way home.

Dear Lucinda

I recently met a former classmate. She is now beautiful, glamorous, and confident while I'm dowdy, ordinary and timid. She has a successful career while I'm still trying hard, and hoping to get somewhere one day. She has loads of money while I never have enough. She is spending a fortune on a holiday home she will only live in for a small part of each year while I live in a council house that needs lots doing to it, and my family hasn't had a decent holiday for ages. Her husband thinks she is wonderful, and mine once thought the same about me but now we just seem to take each other for granted and the sparkle has long gone from our lives. What can I do about it?

She signed the letter 'Inferiority Complex (Mrs)', read it through, thought for a moment, then donned her Lucinda Keen hat and started on the sort of reply she would write if this letter was genuine.

Dear Inferiority Complex

If you have just recently met this perfect woman, can it be that you've fallen into the trap of accepting everything she says without question? You sound like a caring person who has to work hard and has been struggling to make ends meet for so long you've forgotten how to count your blessings. For all you

183

know your friend may also have her problems but isn't going to admit them to you or anyone else. Remember that you can't tell the contents of a book by looking at its cover. Concentrate on striving for a better life for yourself and the family you love and don't let anyone make you feel inferior.
   Lucinda Keen

About to delete both letters she changed her mind and typed them out to use in the next agony-aunt page. Writing them had helped her feel better about herself – and quite possibly they would help some other tired and somewhat depressed wife and mother. No doubt there were more of them around than there were Carries.

When she told Carrie she was happily married she had meant it. Perhaps, in the chaos of raising four children on never enough money, she and Duncan had lost sight of the warm glow they had once shared, but in Helen Campbell's world marriage was for good. Although Duncan was no longer the ardent young lover he had once been she didn't want to be married to anyone else other, if she were totally honest, than Brad Pitt. But he, alas, was out of her reach.

'And who knows?' she asked herself aloud as she pressed the save key. 'If I knew Brad as a real person rather than a dream I might well change my mind about him. Nobody's perfect.'

She went downstairs to make a mug of strong coffee and was about to carry it back upstairs to the computer when Jenny phoned. 'Just to say hello and how are you? We haven't seen much of each other recently, but that's because I'm learning how to take over from Ingrid.'

'How's it going? I keep meaning to look in at the Gift Horse but I've been busy too.'

'I think it'll be all right, but I'm getting butterflies as the time for her departure gets nearer. She's really anxious to be

184

with her parents, though. From what I hear, her mother's having a tough time.'

'Helen's son, Gregor, says Ella's not very happy about the move.'

'That's understandable, but I'm sure she'll settle down quickly. I expect they have female football teams in Norway. Maggie and Freya are going to miss each other. They've only recently become best friends and now they're being separated. But the good news is that Maggie's enjoying working in the Gift Horse at weekends and looking forward to being there full time in the summer, apart from when she goes to visit her grandparents. I've just realised,' Jenny said, 'that I might have interrupted your work with this call.'

'It's all right. I was making myself a black coffee following a boozy lunch in the Cuckoo with Carrie Alston. It was a walk down memory lane plus catching up. Her stepdaughters sound like a real handful.'

'I can sympathise with her there, having just been through the mill with Maggie. You can tell Carrie there's light at the end of the tunnel.'

'I wouldn't dare tell her anything. She's so confident, Jenny! But at the same time, I've got this feeling that all that glistens isn't gold – or is it glisters? She told me she adores Bernie and puts up with his daughters to keep him happy. I think she really meant it, though Bernie isn't my idea of the perfect husband.'

'To each her own.'

'I agree. I've decided that if I can't have Brad Pitt I'm happy to have Duncan. I know he isn't the most fantastic man in the world – Duncan, not Brad Pitt – but I wouldn't change him for Carrie's husband – or anyone else's.'

'You should tell him that when he comes home.'

'I'll make his favourite dinner. The best way to a man's heart is through his stomach.'

'You're full of clichés this afternoon. Is it a Lucinda Keen day?'

'You know me so well.'

'I do. And now I'm going to hang up and let you get back to your letter answering.'

Looking at the clock as she put the receiver down, Helen realised there wasn't much Lucinda Keen time left, so instead of returning to her old computer she began to plan Duncan's favourite dinner.

When the children arrived home from school they received a warm welcome from a mother ready to listen to what they had to say and willing to help with homework. When Duncan came home, tired and morose as usual, he was met with a hug and a kiss.

'What was that for?' he asked suspiciously, and then sniffed the air. 'Something smells good.'

'Beef olives, mashed potatoes and lots of gravy. Lemon meringue pie for afters. And this . . .' Helen gave him another hug and another kiss, 'is to say that I know I don't say I love you very often now, but I do. Love you, I mean.'

He was still wary. 'What have you been doing today to bring all this on?'

'I had lunch with Carrie.'

'The rich friend who's bought old Doris's cottage? How much did you drink?'

'Only two glasses.' It might have been three; she couldn't remember. 'Carrie had most of it, but she's used to wine with lunch. Stop looking a gift horse in the mouth, Duncan Campbell, and get washed – the soup's ready and your children are hungry.'

And she sang as she returned to the kitchen.

★ ★ ★

The phone conversation with Helen gave Jenny food for thought. Her friend had sounded so positive and so happy when she said of Duncan, 'I know he isn't the most fantastic man in the world . . . but I wouldn't change him for Carrie's husband.'

She knew what Helen meant. Once the first wonderful bout of passion – what could be called the Mills & Boon stage – ebbed as, sadly, it must do, it was all too easy to settle into the familiar comfy-slippers stage. Her love for Andrew had been rudely awakened the previous year when he had been diagnosed with cancer. Once he got the all clear and she was able to draw back from the brink of the terrible dark void that would have been her future without him, she had eased surprisingly quickly back into the comfy-slipper stage.

For the first time she realised that positive though he had been during his illness, he too had probably been standing on the edge of a dark void. Perhaps his sudden desire to make their partnership legal had been born then.

All at once she knew it was time to dismiss her own silly fears and put Andrew first.

23

When Andrew Forsyth arrived home at the end of a busy day he was surprised to hear that his wife was taking him to the Neurotic Cuckoo for dinner.

'Have I forgotten a special occasion?' he asked warily.

'No, I just thought it would be nice for us to have some quality time together.'

'All of us?'

'You and me. Maggie's agreed to see to dinner for herself and Calum.'

'Calum's choice, which means that it's beef burgers, chips and beans.' Maggie pulled a face, while Calum beamed.

'So change into something more comfortable. I've booked a table for seven,' Jenny said, and Andrew did as he was told.

'Are you absolutely certain there's nothing wrong?' he asked when they were settled in the Cuckoo's small restaurant. 'I'm assuming you want to talk about something important where the kids can't hear. Have you decided against taking on the Gift Horse when Ingrid leaves?'

'No, I think it should be interesting, and Maggie's been

189

doing really well there at weekends. I think she's needed to be needed, if you know what I mean. When she came here, to people she didn't know in a place she didn't know, all busy with our everyday lives, she must have felt like – like a spare part, I suppose. It was when you were so ill last year, horrible though it was for all of us, that Maggie began to feel useful and valued.'

'You could be right.' Andrew poured wine for them both as Gracie Fisher brought their first course.

'I phoned Helen this afternoon since we haven't seen each other for a wee while,' Jenny said as they ate. 'She was just back from having lunch with Carrie Alston – her school friend who's bought Doris Thatcher's cottage as a holiday home. She and her husband are planning a small house-warming party soon and she asked Helen to give her the names of people to invite. We're on the list.'

'Are we going?'

'We should, to back Helen up more than anything else. And I wouldn't mind meeting Carrie and her husband. Terribly successful and terribly wealthy, but I sense that Helen isn't comfortable with Carrie. Apparently she used to be a shy wee thing when they went to the primary school together, but now she presents herself as someone who's always been confident and the life and soul of the party.'

'She sounds pretty frightening to me.'

'And they've got twin teenage daughters who go to boarding school. His daughters by a first marriage. After telling Helen in front of her husband that the girls were sweet Carrie changed her tune today, possibly under the influence of the wine she was putting away pretty swiftly. She told Carrie in no uncertain terms that they're little horrors.'

'This is all beginning to sound too close to home for me,' Andrew said. 'Are you sure we have to go to their party?'

'We must, for Helen's sake.'

'All right, I'll go – for your sake, because I can tell that your nose is bothering you and you won't rest until you've seen this mysterious couple for yourself.'

As their main courses arrived and he poured more wine, he said, 'I'm glad you thought of this dinner. It's nice to be able to sit and talk about whatever we want without anyone else around. And nice to be able to enjoy a bottle of good wine in the knowledge that I don't have to drive home. We should do it again – p'raps twice a year? Grown-ups' quality time.'

'I'll drink to that.'

Jenny waited until they had ordered coffee before excusing herself and going to the Ladies. When she got back the coffee had arrived and she slipped into her seat and helped herself to sugar before pushing the bowl over to Andrew.

'I don't take sugar, you know that.'

'Yes, I do, but I just thought you might like to look at the bowl.'

'Why would I want to do that?'

'Well, if you don't find the bowl interesting, you might like to look at the hand offering it to you.'

'Jenny, is this some kind of a – Good Lord,' Andrew said, staring at the third finger of her left hand. While in the Ladies she had removed her wedding ring and replaced it with the ring he had given her at Christmas.

'Andrew Forsyth, will you marry me?'

'You mean it?'

'With all my heart,' Jenny said. 'I've been a fool, but now I've realised how silly I was to panic over the thought of another marriage. So – will you marry me?'

'Just you try to stop me!' Andrew told her.

*   *   *

191

'You know,' Jenny said as they walked back home, arms about each other, 'lots of couples renew their vows regularly. We could tell the children that's what we're doing.'

'No, we're going to tell them the truth. And we're going to tell the whole village the truth as well. No more lies or subterfuge, Jenny, and no thoughts of sneaking off somewhere for a secret ceremony. We're going to have a proper wedding in the church with Naomi officiating, if she agrees, followed by a party in the village hall with everyone invited. And Maggie's going to be your bridesmaid and Calum's going to be my best man.'

'How long have you been planning this?'

'Since Christmas. I knew I'd wear you down eventually.'

'You didn't wear me down; I just came to my senses.'

'Hang on,' he said as they reached the gate, 'there's something to be done before we go in to tell the kids. Take the ring off – go on.'

Puzzled, she did as she was told. He took it from her and then took her left hand in his and slipped the ring back on.

'There,' he said, and drew her into his arms. The kiss was romantic to start with, until Jenny spoiled it by starting to giggle.

'Sorry, but I feel like a teenager, kissing by the garden gate in the dusk. D'you think any of the neighbours saw us?'

'So what if they did?' Andrew said, and kissed her again, properly this time.

Maggie was watching television in the living room, the cat asleep on her lap.

'Where's Calum?'

'Getting ready for bed.'

'I'll call him down.' Andrew went into the hall.

'Is there something wrong?' An anxious frown drew Maggie's brows together. 'Andrew's not . . . ?'

192

'Andrew's fine, love. I'll let him tell you both,' Jenny said as Calum came thundering down the stairs and followed his father into the room.

'We've got news for you. Jenny and I are going to get married.'

There was a moment's silence, then Maggie yelped, 'What do you mean, you're *going* to get married?' while Calum pointed out, 'You've been married for ever. You've got me and that proves you're married.'

'Actually, old son, it doesn't. It's a bit complicated. You see, when your mum and I met each other we couldn't get married because she was already married, to Maggie's dad . . .' Andrew hesitated, glancing at Maggie who, surprisingly, took over.

'The thing is, Calum, your mum wasn't happy with my dad.' She got to her feet, dislodging the cat who, annoyed at being disturbed, stalked off to the hall. 'She went away on her own, then met your dad and realised that he was the person she should have married. So they pretended they were. But then my dad died, which means they can get married properly. D'you understand what I'm saying?'

'I think so. Does that mean I'm an orphan?'

'No, it means that you're—'

'Our son, and we were thrilled to bits when you arrived,' Andrew cut in swiftly, adding, 'and thrilled again when Maggie came to live with us because your mum had missed her very much. But now we're a proper family and we think it's time to have a proper wedding, so we've got engaged – show them your engagement ring, Jen.'

'So when are you getting married?' Calum wanted to know while Maggie tried the ring on.

'There's no big hurry – we've already waited for quite a while, haven't we, Jen?'

'For far too long. What about mid-September?'

193

'That's okay with me. We're going to do it properly, in church, with a big party afterwards in the village hall for everyone,' Andrew told the other two.

'Does that mean we'll have to dress up?' Calum grimaced.

''Fraid so, old son, because you're going to be my best man.'

'Oh, wow!'

'And I hope you'll be my bridesmaid, Maggie.'

'Only if I don't have to wear frills and ribbons.'

'Absolutely not,' Jenny said happily. 'It's going to be a special day for all of us and we're going to enjoy every minute of it.'

24

As before, Amy arrived unannounced. Clarissa answered the door to find her on the step, festooned with bags and with her suitcase on the path. Her clothes were the usual mixture of colours and patterns, but now her hair, previously red, was an interesting shade of sea-green.

'Here I am!' she announced, then, seeing her hostess's surprise, 'Oh dear, I've done it again, haven't I? I've forgotten to let you know I was comin'.'

'No, not at all!'

'Clarissa, I can tell by your face you're lyin'. I could've sworn I sent a card tellin' you I'd be back this week.'

'It might have got lost in the post. Come on in, it's lovely to see you.'

'And you. I've got more stuff in the car.'

'I'll help you. The bedroom's all ready,' Clarissa said as they collected Amy's bags and suitcases and struggled upstairs with them.

An hour later they were sitting at the kitchen table, surrounded by photographs. 'It was just the best time ever,'

Amy said enthusiastically. 'I met so many lovely people – I tell you, I'm in no hurry to get back home!'

'Stay here as long as you like.'

'I might do a bit more travellin' before I'm done, if you don't mind me usin' this lovely place of yours as a base.'

'Of course not.'

'So – what's been goin' on while I was away?'

'Nothing much, it's a quiet little village; that's what I like about it.'

'You sure nothin''s happened?'

'One thing – do you remember Jenny and Andrew Forsyth? They live in the River Walk estate near the river. Jenny's keen on crafts and she works in the Gift Horse.'

'Oh, I remember. Her husband was pretty sick last year – right?'

'That's right. Well, it turns out they're not married at all because Jenny was already married to an abusive husband when they met. She'd run away from him.'

'Doesn't she have a stepdaughter who lives with them?'

'Maggie, yes. But we all assumed Jenny and Maggie's father were divorced, which was wrong. Anyway, apparently Jenny's been widowed for years without knowing it, so they're going to have a proper wedding in the village church in September and we're all invited to the ceremony and to a party in the village hall afterwards. It's caused quite a lot of talk in the village about them living in sin, as some of the older gossips put it. Though I believe that under Scottish law a couple who've been together for a reasonable length of time can claim to be legally married.'

'Oh tosh, every community in every part of the world has its disapproving gossips.' Amy flapped a hand at her friend. 'They're just busybodies, but at the same time I suspect they're also the people who put a bit of spice and excite-

196

ment into community life. And a party's a party! So – what else?'

'Nothing I can think of.'

'Clarissa, you know what I admire most about you? You are a very honest woman.'

'Thank you.'

'You're welcome. But honesty can have its drawbacks and one of 'em is that you can't tell a lie without givin' yourself away. Somethin''s not right, and you're not tellin' me what it is. But I'll find out anyway.'

'Nothing's wrong, really.'

'So where's Alastair?'

'How should I know? We don't live in each other's pockets.'

'Maybe not, but it seems to me the two of you are pretty close to it. You've not even mentioned his name since I arrived. Have you fallen out?'

'Why should we?'

'I don't know, that's what I'm aimin' to discover. It might be that I was married all those years to a police officer,' Amy said thoughtfully, 'or it might be that I was born nosy, but I can always tell when somethin's wrong. And as soon as you opened the door to me, I knew you'd been frettin'. So what's been goin' on?'

Clarissa stared at her across the kitchen table, and Amy stared right back. For a moment British reticence and American openness met in a mental arm-wrestling match; openness, aided by a desire deep within Clarissa to seek help and advice, won.

'I'll be back in a minute.'

'I'll make more coffee,' Amy said.

When Clarissa arrived back downstairs she handed the envelope over without comment. Amy read its contents in a glance.

197

'So – someone's stirrin' things up, huh?'

'You could say that. Alastair got a similar letter.'

'Anyone else get letters like this?'

'About my friendship with Alastair? I hope not!'

'I meant, about themselves. Usually when someone decides to spread poison they really like to spread it.'

'Nobody's mentioned any letters to me.'

'Have you spoken to anyone apart from Alastair about this one?'

'Of course not. It's too – embarrassing.'

'If everyone else in this place thinks the same as you do there's no way you could know about other letters. I'm willin' to bet there are. What does Alastair think about it?'

'The same as I do – that these accusations are ridiculous.'

'What's so ridiculous about them? He's your best friend in the village, isn't he?'

'Yes, but only a friend. For one thing, I'm old enough to be his mother. There's a good twenty years between us.'

'So? Age has nothin' to do with the way folks feel about each other, and Alastair's crazy about you.'

Clarissa felt herself go red. 'Don't be silly, Amy.'

'I'm not the one that's bein' silly. Maybe it's time you decided to be honest with yourself.'

'I'm not going to talk about this any more.' Clarissa took the letter back, folded it with trembling fingers and had some difficulty in slotting it into its envelope. 'Alastair and I agree that this letter writer's just out to cause mischief, and we've decided to see less of each other for the time being, just in case.'

'That's up to you, but I don't see it's goin' to make any difference. What is it they say about absence makin' the heart grow—'

'I forgot to tell you we've got newcomers to the village,'

Clarissa interrupted. 'At least, one of them is. A couple from Berwick on Tweed, just over the border in England. Apparently the wife was born here and went to the local school. Her family moved away when she was about eleven and now she and her husband are making big changes to the cottage that belonged to Doris Thatcher.'

'So who's Doris Thatcher and why's she givin' up her cottage?'

'She was one of the oldest village inhabitants and she died, poor old soul. Apparently the Alstons plan to extend the cottage and use it as a holiday home. There's a bit of ill-feeling in the village about that – outsiders pricing property out of the reach of local people. Prior's Ford's never had a holiday home before.'

'If this woman and her husband can afford to make big changes to the cottage she sounds like a local girl who made good.'

'Oh, yes, they have their own business. Helen Campbell – I don't think you know Helen – says Mrs Alston was a shy wee thing at school, but now she's a glamorous career woman. She and her husband are holding a party next Saturday evening and I've been invited. I'm sure you'd be welcome too.'

'Sounds interestin', Amy said. 'I want to have a look at this local girl who's hit the big time.'

The following day, a Sunday, Naomi's sermon was based on 'love thy neighbour as thyself', and 'do unto them as you would have them do unto you'. When she had finished she looked round the congregation for a long moment before saying, 'And now I must raise a serious matter affecting some of our residents. Over the past two weeks some members of our community have been the victims of a malicious prank.' She paused as a shocked and somewhat excited murmur arose, and waited until it had died down before going on. 'They

199

have received unsigned letters making unfounded and untrue accusations against them. A few people have shown those letters to me, and my concern is that others may have received them and been too upset or alarmed to confide in anyone. To them, I say this – you are not alone, and you have nothing to fear from this letter writer because people who don't sign their names are not to be taken seriously. Should anyone who has received one of those letters feel the need to talk about it in confidence I am here and you can be safe in the knowledge that nothing said will go any further.' She took time to look round the congregation, row by row, face by face, before going on. 'Should the writer of those letters be among us this morning then I say to him or her on behalf of the good people of Prior's Ford – search your conscience and be aware of how much distress you are causing. If the village continues to be plagued in this way, further measures may have to be taken.'

She paused again while people stirred uncomfortably and heads turned to cast glances to either side.

Then at last Naomi said, 'Let us pray.'

'How did I do?' Naomi asked the Kavanaghs, who had attached themselves to the tail end of people leaving the service.

'I think you put it tactfully,' Robert said in reply, while Cissie nodded at the groups of people scattered around, all murmuring busily, and added, 'You've given them something to talk about.'

'And think about too, I hope. Even if there are no more letters, now the writer knows it's become public knowledge, that's a good thing.'

'D'you think the writer might have been here this morning?'

'Who knows, Cissie? It could be one of those holier-than-thou people with the view that they have a God-given right to tell others how to live their lives. If so, they were probably among today's congregation. Even if they weren't they'll hear about it by teatime,' Naomi said. 'I may well have quite a busy day tomorrow.'

'Talking about those weird letters?' Hector Ralston-Kerr asked cheerfully, joining them. 'I got one of them.'

'What on earth could anyone accuse *you* of?' Cissie asked, astonished.

'Not me – my great-grandfather. According to the writer he seduced half the women in the village during his lifetime. I wouldn't be at all surprised. My father told me he was a randy old devil. Bit late to fret about it now, eh?'

Spotting Stella Hesslet in one of the pews, Amy waved to her as she and Clarissa made their way slowly up the aisle towards the exit. 'Can we invite Stella to lunch?' she asked when the two of them had exchanged a few words with Naomi and moved away from the church door. 'I'd like to show her some of the photographs and brochures I collected, and I've got some more crosswords to test on her.'

'Of course, there's enough to go round.'

'Isn't Alastair coming to Willow Cottage today? I didn't see him in church this morning.'

Clarissa, too, had been watching for Alastair. 'He's probably working.'

'You do realise the two of you are just givin' in to this silly letter writer?' Amy started, then to Clarissa's relief she changed the subject. 'There's Stella now, talkin' to Naomi. We'll wait here to be sure to catch her before she hurries off.'

'She looks upset. I wonder if she got one of those letters?'

'If so, we'll find out.' Amy waved vigorously at the librarian. 'Stella, come back to Clarissa's an' have some lunch with us. There's enough for three.'

'If you're sure . . . ?'

'We are. I want to bore someone with photographs and brochures afterwards. Clarissa's seen them already an' she's dyin' to get some work done in her garden this afternoon.' Amy linked an arm through Stella's as the three of them set out to walk the short distance from the church to Willow Cottage. 'Are you all right? You looked upset when you were talkin' to Naomi just now. You've not had one of those nasty letters, have you?'

'No!' Stella said swiftly. 'I – I've spent the past two weeks in Whitby, visiting a friend. I only got back last night and I knew nothing about the letters until just now. It's horrible – I can't believe it!'

'I was surprised to see a stranger in the mobile library last week,' Clarissa said, anxious to move away from any more talk of the letters. 'I wondered if you were ill but she said you were on holiday. I spent a week in Whitby a few years ago, it's a lovely place.'

'Yes, it is. Alicia – my friend – runs a B&B, so I help out while I'm there. It's a great way to meet people,' Stella said, and suddenly blushed for no reason.

The blush didn't escape Amy's sharp eyes. 'Isn't it just? So – did you meet anyone nice?'

'Well – all the guests were nice.'

'And you didn't find one of those strange letters on your mat when you got home?' Amy probed, adding hastily, 'You don't have to say if you have, but Clarissa and I wouldn't breathe a word to anyone if the answer's yes.'

'No, I just got the usual bills and unsolicited catalogues. I'm so sorry for the poor people who got them, though. It's a horrible thing to happen in a lovely little village like Prior's Ford.'

'Let's hope that now Naomi's spoken out about it the guilty

202

party will take heed and stop it once and for all,' Clarissa said firmly as she opened her garden gate.

After lunch Clarissa escaped to the back garden, leaving the other two to look at photographs and talk about crosswords.

'Did you see how upset Stella was when we spoke about those letters?' Amy asked once their guest had gone. 'I've a feelin' she received one and doesn't want to admit it.'

'If so, I don't blame her because I want to forget about the whole business. Hearing it mentioned aloud from the pulpit was *horrible*,' Clarissa said fiercely. 'I just hope that whoever's behind it realises it's got to stop!'

'Don't you need to know who and why?' Amy asked. 'This sort of business is like an illness – the best way to cure it is by knowin' what caused it in the first place.'

'I don't care about the whys and wherefores, I just want it to stop.' To Clarissa's horror her voice wavered on the last word.

To her relief, Amy tactfully returned to the house and left her on her own.

25

Molly's visit seemed to Lewis – though not to Ginny – to pass too quickly.

'Can't the two of you stay on for another week?' he asked as he sat on the bed watching Molly pack her bag. Rowena Chloe was sitting on his lap, babbling out a story in baby-talk as she flipped the pages of one of her books, pointing to each detail in the pictures with an incredibly tiny finger. To Lewis, everything about her was incredible – her squirming, warm, solid little body, her red curls, slightly darker than Molly's, her wide hazel eyes, her curiosity in everything around her and the quick smile that lit up not only her chubby little face but the entire room.

'Time to move on, babes. My feet are starting to itch.'

When she and Lewis first met Molly was a backpacker, working in Linn Hall's kitchen. Motherhood hadn't changed her restless nature: over the autumn, winter and early spring months she and Rowena Chloe lived in Inverness with Molly's parents and sister while she worked wherever she could find a job in order to save for the better weather, when she set off on her travels, earning her keep wherever she could.

'Anyway,' Molly went on as she folded her daughter's little overalls and tucked them into the bag, 'this place is all right for a visit but there's not much happening, know what I mean?'

He didn't. For him, every day was filled with work in the grounds and plans for the future. He loved Prior's Ford and had missed it when he was away at university. He could never imagine being bored here.

'There's the Scarecrow Festival coming up. You enjoyed that last year.'

She shrugged. 'It was okay, but once was enough.'

'We could do with your help. Jimmy McDonald's come up with the idea of having scarecrows dotted all round the estate. He and Ginny are getting volunteers together to make them, and Ginny and Lynn Stacey are going to get the kids who visit to list the number of scarecrows they can find.'

'Sounds terrific – not! I'd far rather be in Portugal.'

'You're going abroad again this year?'

'Uh huh, with some mates, and we're leaving just before this festival of yours begins. Travelling's fun. Come with me, Lewis, let's see the world together before we settle down.'

'Darling, I can't possibly leave Linn Hall when there's so much to do!'

'Oh, don't be so dull! Surely Duncan and Ginny can look after things for a few weeks?'

'Not without me there too. Maybe I'll be able to go abroad with you once we've got the place up and running properly.'

'I hope you're listening to your daddy, Weena.' There was an edge to Molly's voice. 'He's finally promised to go travelling with me – and you can have the fun of pushing our wheelchairs around when it happens.'

'It'll happen – one day.'

'Probably the year my mum wins the millions she keeps talking about on the Lottery.' Molly came over to sit on the bed beside him, sliding an arm about his shoulders. 'D'you love me, Lewis?'

'You know I do.' The memory of the anonymous letter he had received tried to push its way into his mind and he slammed a door on it. He wouldn't believe what it said – couldn't believe it!

'Well, look at it this way. Us being in Portugal together would make me happy – and knowing that I'm happy would make you happy, wouldn't it?'

'Of course, but—'

'So we can be happy together in Portugal,' she finished triumphantly.

'It's not that simple,' he protested, baffled by her idea of logic.

Molly flounced to her feet. 'Lewis Ralston-Kerr, you're such a stick in the mud!'

'I'm trying to plan for our future.'

'What future?' she said and went out, slamming the door behind her.

'Oh, blast!'

'B'ast,' Rowena Chloe echoed, and Lewis kissed her soft hair with its special baby smell.

'You're my little girl, aren't you, and you're going to enjoy living here, you and me and Mummy all together always. Say yes for Daddy.'

Instead she stuck a finger in his eye and then, suddenly bored, said, 'Want down – want Muffin!'

It took some time to get down to the kitchen because the baby insisted on mastering the stairs by herself, breathing loudly with the effort while Lewis clung to her fist, terrified in case she pulled free and fell.

By the time they reached the kitchen Molly was back to her usual sunny self.

'Your mum's just agreed to let Weena stay here during July,' she said. 'My mum and dad want to go back to Spain for a month. You don't mind, do you?'

'Of course not, that's great.' Lewis was cheered by the prospect of spending more time with his daughter.

Molly would be fine once she'd worked off her love of travelling. And when they were married and Linn Hall was properly open to the public and earning its keep he would be able to afford family holidays abroad.

Then everything would be perfect – because it had to be.

As Naomi had predicted, several people sought her out over the next few days to talk about the unsigned letters they had received.

The first two came together – Alma Parr and Moira Melrose.

'We can tell you who isn't behind these disgusting letters,' Moira said as soon as they were settled in the vestry, where they found Naomi behind her desk, 'and that's most of the Rural members.'

'And the two of us, of course,' Alma put in. 'We each got one on the same morning and decided to put our heads together to find out who was behind them.'

'Did you?'

'Sadly, no, but we know who didn't write them. Our letters were written by the same person, so we got the Rural members to write down their favourite recipes, then we checked them all against the letters,' Moira said smugly. 'Almost all the members contributed and not one of them has the hand-writing on the letters.'

'That was very astute of you both.'

'We thought so,' Alma said, and the two former enemies smirked at each other. 'And now,' Alma went on triumphantly, 'we have the beginnings of a special Rural calendar for next year, with a recipe for each month.'

'Well done, ladies.'

'You don't need to see our letters, do you?'

'Absolutely not, Moira, that's no business of mine. Thank you very much for having the courage to come and speak to me. You can be sure that what you've told me will go no further.'

Alma and Moira, or, as Naomi now thought of them, Miss Jane Marple and Mrs Jessica Fletcher, assured her almost in chorus that they were only doing their duty by the village, and left.

Jess McNair came in later, laden with shopping bags, her face pinched with worry. She found Naomi in the church, reorganising Rita Billings's flower arrangements, which had been irritating her all through the previous day's service. Rita had a good heart and enjoyed 'keeping the church nice', as she put it, but colour combination wasn't her strong point. When Naomi heard the church door open she jumped guiltily away from the big vase she had been working on and then gave a sigh of relief at the sight of one of her favourite parishioners.

'Jess, come on in, it's lovely to see you.'

'Ye're sure I'm no' interruptin' somethin' important?'

'Not at all.' Naomi hurried up the aisle to take the bags. 'These weigh a ton! Come into the vestry, I've got a flask of coffee and I was just about to have a cup.'

'Not for me, pet. Ewan's over at the Cuckoo deliverin' the eggs an' he's collectin' me in a minute or two. I said I wanted tae give ye a recipe I'd promised ye.' Jess glanced nervously about the church. 'Are ye on yer own?'

'There's nobody else here. We can sit in one of the pews and if anyone comes in we'll hear them before they hear us. What's wrong? You look upset.'

209

'I've come about what you said yesterday – those letters.'

'Oh, Jess, don't tell me that you got one!'

'No' me, it was our Victor.' Jess delved into one of the bags and produced a sheet of paper. 'Here, read it for yersel'.'

The letter had been crumpled up and then smoothed out and folded neatly. Naomi noted as she ran her eyes over the few lines that the handwriting was similar to the other letters she'd seen.

'What did Victor say about it?'

'Och, he just crumpled it up an' threw it away. I picked it up after he'd gone.' Jess's eyes filled with tears. 'It's no' fair, Naomi! I know that him wantin' tae marry Jeanette's made things difficult for Bert and Ewan, but my Victor's surely got the right tae follow the path he thinks best? He didn't do it out o' badness and I'll no' have anyone say different!' She fumbled in her pocket for a handkerchief and dabbed at her eyes.

'Jess, I've seen a few of these letters and believe me, they're nothing at all, just silly empty accusations. I take it that Bert and Ewan know nothing about this?' Jess shook her head. 'I think that's wise. I'm telling you what I've told others about this matter – try to forget it.'

'Ye think so?'

'I do. I don't think we're going to hear about any more letters, not after they were mentioned from the pulpit. Whoever sent them must know by now that he or she has caused a great deal of unhappiness to those who received them – and raised a great deal of anger among the rest of our community. I think it's over.' She handed the letter back but Jess waved it away, shaking her head.

'I don't want it.'

'Then I'll make sure it's destroyed here and now.'

A car horn tooted outside and Jess gave her eyes one last

hurried pat with the handkerchief. 'That'll be Ewan. Dae I look like I've been cryin'?'

'You look fine. I'll take the bags,' Naomi said firmly. 'And mind what I said – you put that letter right out of your mind.'

'I will. Now that I've told you I feel better already,' Jess said as Ewan appeared at the church door.

'There ye are. I'll take those.' He relieved Naomi of the bags and watched smilingly as the minister hugged his mother.

When she was alone Naomi went to the vestry where she fed the letter into the small shredder donated by a parishioner before having her coffee.

26

It was fortunate that the weather was perfect on the evening of the Alstons' house-warming party. Although there weren't many guests the two small downstairs rooms were quite crowded and the garden took the overflow.

As all Doris's furniture had gone to auction, Carrie and Bernie had furnished the place with pieces from their own cabinet-making business.

'You make very attractive furniture,' Naomi told Bernie, 'and every piece suits this cottage perfectly.'

'That's because they were all chosen by Carrie,' he said proudly. 'I know how to make 'em, but she's the real genius when it comes to showing them off to full advantage. She's turned our showroom into a work of art, and she has a hand in the designing, too.'

'I'm impressed.' She ran a hand over a corner cabinet. 'This sort of thing makes my weird assortment of furniture look really untidy.'

'You should invite Carrie to have a look at the manse some

time. I'm sure she'd be able to recommend items from one of our own ranges.'

'I doubt if I could afford this beautiful rocking chair, let alone anything else.'

'I think we could manage to work out some form of discount for friends and neighbours.' He produced a business card from his blazer pocket. 'Another drink? I've set up a small bar in the other room.'

'We're camping in the place this year,' Carrie was explaining to a group when Naomi and Bernie arrived. 'I was so keen to spend part of the summer back in Prior's Ford that I persuaded Bernie to wait until the autumn before extending the place.'

'What d'ye mean, extendin'? It's a cottage, no' an accordion,' said Ivy McGowan, who had made a point of arriving early and grabbing the most comfortable chair.

'There now, Bernie, what did I tell you about Mrs McGowan?' Carrie, stunning in a sea-green silk trouser suit with a deep blue lacy scarf twined about her throat, gave a tinkling laugh and the ice in the gin and tonic she held tinkled an accompaniment. 'The jewel in Prior's Ford's crown!'

'That's what she always said,' her husband agreed. 'D'you remember my wife, Mrs McG?'

'It's McGowan, and o' course I mind her. A skinny wee thing that couldnae say boo tae a goose – but mind you, lassie, I always had the idea that there was a sleekit side tae ye. How else,' Ivy said, her gaze flicking from Carrie to Bernie and back again, 'would an ordinary wee village lassie make all this money ye're supposed tae have?'

Carrie had to struggle to keep the smile from slipping. 'That's thanks to Bernie. He's the brains in our business.'

'I wouldn't say that, love. You play your part.' Bernie Alston took his wife's free hand and kissed it.

'Dear heavens!' Ivy said in disgust while Andrew Forsyth asked hurriedly, 'What plans do you have for the cottage?'

'We're going to open it up on either side − this room will be the lounge-cum-dining room, twice the width it is at the moment. And the same thing's happening to the room at the other side of the passage. That will be the study, but it won't be as large as this room because we plan to widen the passage to make a much more attractive entrance hall with a small cloakroom. A decent-sized kitchen's going to be built on at the back, running along the whole width of the cottage and giving us some extra space upstairs. I love cooking, don't I, Bernie?'

'She's a fantastic cook,' he agreed, giving her a fond smile.

'Upstairs . . .' As Carrie indicated the ceiling the flared sleeve of her jacket fell back to expose a tanned forearm and a diamond bracelet, matching her drop-earrings, sparkling on one wrist, 'we'll have the bathroom and four bedrooms, one for us, one for each of the girls and a spare room for guests. Our room will be en-suite, of course.'

The listeners were stunned into silence, broken by Ivy commenting with glee, 'Oh my. Poor Doris was so proud of her wee cottage − she'd hate tae know what you're plannin' for it, the old soul!'

'I like to think she would be delighted to know it was going to have such an exciting make-over. My wife,' Bernie said proudly, 'could have been a top-notch interior designer if I hadn't found her first and claimed her for my own business. You should see what she's done with our proper home. Though I still think the spare room should be replaced by a dressing room for me, darling. As far as I'm concerned this place is going to be our little nest; just for us.'

'Bernie,' Carrie patted his cheek, 'is a typical man; he loves his home comforts.'

'What man doesn't?'

'You're not going to have much of a garden once you're finished,' Helen ventured.

'All we need is a paved area at the front and a nice patio at the back, overlooking the river,' Carrie said carelessly. 'And room for a garage at either side, of course.' She clapped her hands. 'Now it's time to eat, everyone. I'm afraid that due to the lack of space it's only a buffet, but the caterers were very warmly recommended. Please help yourselves.'

'And the bar will be open all night,' Bernie chimed in. 'Carrie, where are the girls?'

'Didn't you say they're in a boarding school?' Helen asked.

'Yes, but we arranged for them to spend the weekend here so they could see the house and meet our new friends tonight. They're still upstairs, getting ready. I'll hurry them up.'

'Are you sure she was at school with us?' Duncan Campbell muttered to his wife as Carrie went in search of her step-daughters while the guests, urged on by Bernie, descended on the long table packed with platters of food.

'Yes, but she didn't look anything like the way she does now.'

'She's landed on her feet, hasn't she?'

'I suppose.' Helen felt that Carrie was acting out a stage play, and she found Bernie's charm cloying. 'Enjoying yourself?' she asked, slipping a hand through her husband's arm, glad she was married to him and not to Bernie.

'Not particularly. We don't have to stay for long, do we?'

'We'll give it another hour and then go home.'

Carrie arrived back downstairs, assuring everyone the girls were on their way, but another half hour passed before the Alston twins finally arrived, both looking sulky. As first a few, then more of the guests caught sight of them, conversation petered out. Bernie, behind the side table set up as the bar, glanced up to see why silence was falling, then bounded to the door to meet his daughters.

'And here they are at last – my little girls! Come and be introduced to everyone, darlings. This is Maureen, the elder by thirty-six minutes, and this is Rhona. And these, my lovelies, are our new neighbours.' He put an arm about each of them, ignoring their attempts to wriggle free. 'Say hello, Rhona – Maureen.'

Maureen, whose long blonde hair fell to her shoulders, wore an orange tight-fitting top with a neckline that plunged almost to the broad belt of her knee-length black frilly skirt. 'Good evening, everyone.' She spoke like a little girl and her smile was sugar-sweet. Her outfit was finished off with black stockings and black high-heeled shoes.

'Hi,' Rhona snapped, glowering. Her fair hair was shorter than her twin's and piled on top of her head in a mass of curls. She wore a black satin top with a stand-up high-necked collar over tight blue denim jeans. Both girls were immaculately made-up with eye-shadow, mascara and lip-gloss, and their eyebrows were carefully shaped and pencilled. Maureen's make-up was strong, with red lips and blue eye shadow, while Rhona's was very pale.

'Just in time to help me make sure that our guests have all the drinks they need,' Bernie said jovially.

'I expect they can make sure of that for themselves,' Maureen told him irritably.

'Of course they can, but it's our place as hosts to look after them.'

'*We're* not hosts – it's not *our* party.' Rhona's sweetness gave way to a sulky frown. 'We want to go out. This place is so poky I can scarcely breathe!'

'Now now, you're getting a weekend off school to help us look after our new neighbours, not to go wandering off goodness knows where on your own.' Bernie's smile was still there, but there was an edge to his voice that made his daughters do as he wished, though with bad grace. Carrie meanwhile moved from group to group briskly, trying to keep the conversation going.

'We're all looking forward to attending our first church service tomorrow morning,' she told Naomi.

'You'll be very welcome.'

'Her – going to church? That'll be a first,' Clarissa heard Rhona mutter to her twin as the two of them brushed past.

In the corner that she had made her own, Ivy McGowan was telling Cynthia and Gilbert McBain and Kevin Pearce and his wife Eleanor about the unsigned letter she had received.

'But, Ivy dear, it can't possibly have come from Doris Thatcher,' Eleanor was protesting. 'Dead people don't write letters.'

'I'd put nothin' past that one,' Ivy said obstinately. 'Who else would write such a nasty letter to me? Did you get one?' Then, as the Pearces both shook their heads, she turned to the McBains. 'Or you two?'

'Certainly not!' Cynthia was shocked by the very thought. 'Gilbert and I have never in our entire lives done anything wrong!'

'Neither have I, I'll have you know. Those things Doris accused me of in this letter – she was guilty of 'em herself, I can tell you that for nothin'. Oh, the letters I could have written to folks in the village about her in her younger days don't bear thinkin' about! An' don't you go tellin' me that we shouldnae speak ill of the dead,' she added to Naomi, who had joined the group.

'I wouldn't dare, though I don't see much point in running down people who can't defend themselves.'

'What about me? I can't defend myself against that letter,

218

can I, when the writer's dead! I'm willin' tae bet you've had a lot of folk comin' to tell you they've had letters too, after you speakin' out about it from the pulpit last Sunday.'

'You know perfectly well I can't say anything about that, Ivy,' Naomi chided the old woman as Cissie Kavanagh, alerted by a quick glance from the minister, arrived.

'Ivy, Robert and I are off home now; why don't you come in our car? Robert brought it specially to save you the walk.'

'Poor little Doris – if she knew about all the changes the Alstons are planning for her lovely little cottage she'd be broken-hearted,' Naomi said as she left the party two hours later with Clarissa and Amy.

'The garden's an absolute delight; tonight was the first time I had the chance to walk round it. She must have spent hours sitting on that pretty little wooden bench watching the river, and listening to the sound of the water. So soothing,' Clarissa said enviously.

'Yes, she did, especially as she got older. She had one of the prettiest gardens in the village. She was widowed by the time I came here, but I was told that she and her husband both enjoyed gardening and often took top prizes at horti-cultural shows, with Doris specialising in flowers and Mr Thatcher growing wonderful vegetables. After he died she was too frail to keep it going on her own but neighbours helped her keep the front garden pretty and the back garden product-ive. Many's the basket of vegetables I got from her, and I wasn't the only one. She was always very generous at Harvest Festival. And now her home's going to become nothing more than a large extension with a patio at the back and a garage at either side! I do hope her spirit doesn't know about this.'

'If it does, it'll haunt the new owners, and serve 'em right,' was Amy's opinion.

'Please don't say a thing like that,' Naomi pleaded, 'it sounds too like Ivy with her nonsense about Doris writing letters from beyond the grave. In any case, the woman had such a sweet nature that I can't see her spirit haunting anyone.'

'Mrs McGowan can't be serious about that,' Clarissa put in.

'Of course not, but the two of them were at loggerheads for so long that if World War Three started tomorrow Ivy would insist it was Doris's fault.'

'I wasn't struck on our hosts this evening – or their daughters. Did you hear the way they spoke to their father? And the way they looked at their mother? To be honest, I doubt if any sweet-natured spirit would want to haunt those dreadful kids,' Amy declared. 'If I'd anythin' to do with them they'd get a good swift kick right up their—'

'Stepmother,' Clarissa interrupted hastily. 'I mean, I understand that Carrie's the twins' stepmother.'

'And I reckon there's no love lost between them and her,' Amy added. 'I caught one or two glances between the three of 'em durin' the evenin' and there was nothin' motherly or daughterly about 'em, I can tell you.'

'Their father clearly dotes on them, so no doubt Carrie's hands are tied as far as the girls are concerned. According to Helen Campbell she was a shy wee thing when she lived here. It's hard to believe, now.'

'She might just be trying too hard to impress people,' Naomi suggested.

'I'd say sly rather than shy. In all the years I spent deliverin' babies I've met a lot of women, an' I find my first impressions are usually the right ones. I'd watch out for those Alstons if I were you. They're not what they seem.'

'Whatever they may be they have the right to make whatever changes they wish to Doris's former home,' Naomi said as they reached the manse gate. Then she added wistfully, 'Even if the rest of us don't like what's happening.'

'I'm going to Dumfries for a day's shopping,' Clarissa announced on Monday. 'Want to come along?'

'I think I'll pass on that one. Stella's got the day off and she's invited me to tea this afternoon. I said I'd take some of my new crosswords for her to try out, and I'm just goin' to wander round the village this mornin'.'

'It's a nice day for a walk,' Clarissa agreed, reaching for her car keys.

Amy's walk took her to Jasmine Cottages. The row of small houses had been built over a hundred years earlier with stone from the old granite quarry and the walls glittered in the sunlight. Hanging baskets and window boxes were packed with Busy Lizzies, fuchsias, begonias, geraniums and trailing blue and white lobelia, while the front door steps and the pavement along the entire row were spotless.

There was no answer when she knocked on Ivy McGowan's door, so she went round to the back to find everyone gathered outside Ivy's back door in a variety of folding seats, benches and deck chairs. This being Monday, the washing lines were filled with laundry flapping in the warm, drying breeze.

The newcomer was immediately made welcome, a seat found for her and a cup of tea thrust into her hand, while a plate of Cissie Kavanagh's freshly made pancakes, the butter melting into their warmth, arrived on the folding table by her side.

Nobody asked why she was there. Instead, they all went on with their discussion, which happened, to Amy's satisfaction, to be about the poison-pen letters.

'Correct me if I'm wrong,' Ivy said in a voice that didn't expect to be corrected, 'but it seems there's been no more

221

letters since the minister spoke out against them from the pulpit. When she came here to see the one I got I asked her to do whatever it is that preachers do to banish bad spirits, an' it seems to me that speakin' out last Sunday as she did, right there in the church itself, did the trick. Doris took the hint.'

'You seriously think Naomi exorcised Doris Thatcher's spirit?' Charlie Crandall asked. 'But that's—'

'The thing is,' Hannah Gibbs cut in swiftly, 'the letters seem to have stopped. I think we should just leave it at that and be thankful.'

'Hear hear,' Robert Kavanagh boomed, helping himself to another pancake.

'Ivy might have something, though,' Dolly Cowan said excitedly. 'When they auctioned off the contents of Doris's house I bought a sweet statuette of an angel and put it on a little table in our living room. And every morning it seems to have moved slightly in the night, doesn't it, Harold?'

'So you say, dear.' Her husband sounded doubtful.

'It definitely does. I have to put it back in its proper place every morning. D'you think,' Dolly's large blue eyes grew even larger with excitement, 'that Doris could be moving it every night as a sort of sign that she's still with us in spirit?'

'If she is, she'd be more likely to throw it at you, not just move it.'

'Oh, Ivy, I don't think Doris would do such a thing,' Cissie protested, adding as her husband raised an eyebrow at her, 'Not that I believe she would move things around either.'

'Where is this table holding the statuette?' Robert wanted to know.

'Right by the front door.'

'There you are then, it's probably vibrations caused by one

222

of those lorries that go through the village early in the morning. Or one of your dogs banging against the table as it passes.'

'Mini and Maxy sleep in the bedroom with us, don't you, my loves?' Dolly cooed to the two poodles lying at her feet. They looked up at her adoringly.

'Or the table might be slightly wonky, making the statuette slide very slowly,' Muriel Jacobson suggested. 'You should check that out, Harold.'

'I've got a spirit level you can use,' Charlie offered.

'No, leave it,' Dolly said. 'I like to think that Doris is saying good morning to me.'

'Never heard so much nonsense in me life,' Ivy snorted. 'Cissie, got any more tea in that pot?'

'Plenty.' Cissie refilled the old woman's cup and then poised the teapot over Amy's empty cup. 'More for you, Amy?'

'No thank you, I've just recalled an errand I promised to run for Clarissa.'

Amy, who had been quieter than usual but who had listened intently to everything said, made her farewells and departed, well pleased with what she had found out. Sometimes, as her husband Gordon had told her more than once, listening made more sense than talking.

It was certainly much more interesting – and informative.

27

'I feel like someone in one of those programmes on the telly,' Jimmy McDonald said breathlessly but enthusiastically. 'You know, the ones where folk explore away out in the wild where no man has gone before, apart from tribes with blowpipes.'

'We don't need blowpipes in Scotland, we've got midges.'

'Not at this time of day, Lewis.' Ginny paused, bent over with hands on knees in an attempt to catch her breath. The three of them had been using a staircase of large flat stones set into the hill behind Linn Hall, close to the dry channel that had once been a series of gentle waterfalls. Muffin had started with them, but had quickly rushed ahead and kept darting out of bushes to check on their progress before vanishing again.

'Someone,' Ginny said now, 'went to a lot of trouble to make this place accessible.'

'I can't think why.' Lewis paused on a flat stone, turning to look down at her. 'Who would want to climb all the way up here?'

'For the view?' She flapped a hand at what could be seen

225

of the estate, the village below it, and the fields beyond. 'It's wonderful!'

'You'd have to be fit to get high enough to enjoy it.'

'You can put in proper steps with railings, and water-loving flowers to edge the falls all the way down to the gardens once we clear the dam. Prune back the bushes and trees to open up the view and have some seats at the top – a little picnic area, perhaps.'

Looking down the overgrown hill – all at once seeing through her eyes what it could be like – Lewis marvelled at the ability she possessed to look at chaos and see a way to introduce order and beauty. She had done it with the kitchen garden, now packed with fruit, vegetables and herbs, and with the old stables, for years used as a dumping ground for unwanted items. He wondered, not for the first time, if he could find enough money to keep her in Prior's Ford until the estate was under control. He wished Molly could see his rundown, impoverished and dearly loved home as Ginny did – then as the thought of Molly reminded him of the malicious letter a pain seemed to lance through his heart.

'Hey,' Jimmy called down to them, 'I've arrived! I'm king of the castle. There's a load of branches and stones up here needin' tae be moved!'

The mind-picture of the boy trying to heave at a fallen branch and sending an avalanche of stones down the hill towards them swept all thought of the letter and Molly from Lewis's mind. 'Don't touch a thing until we get there,' he roared. At the same time Ginny was shouting, 'Get back from the edge, Jimmy, you could fall!'

'Is this all yours as well?' the boy wanted to know when they joined him at the top of the hill, receiving a rapturous welcome from Muffin.

'It goes back for the best part of an acre then meets up with farmland. That's our boundary.'

'Geez! Imagine havin' all this tae play in!'

'It was great,' Lewis agreed, grinning at the memories.

'Can I have a look?' Jimmy wanted to know, and when Lewis nodded he went whooping off among the trees, Muffin bounding along after him.

Ginny was already getting down to business. 'We need to work backwards, from the lake to here. Clearing the dam has to be the final part and before we do that we must dig beyond it because the river's—'

'It's really just a burn.'

'Okay then, the burn's forgotten that it's a riv— a burn and it's turned itself into a marsh. With any luck we could have it restored to its proper route and running downhill by next summer.' She dug into her anorak pocket, produced a small digital camera and began to photograph the blockage from all angles.

'You think of everything, don't you?'

'The camera, you mean? I've been taking pictures of the work going on at the lake, and other parts of the estate. One day you'll be able to show visitors a record of the way you've turned the grounds back to their former glory.'

'With a lot of help from you.' Lewis perched on a boulder and looked down at the village roofs below. 'Cam and I and some of the other boys from the village had some terrific times up here. There's a wee summer house back there some- where that we used as a gang hut.' He gestured with a thumb towards the tangle of undergrowth behind them.

'I wish I could have been part of your gang. I had such a dreary childhood, being trailed around from place to place by my mother or left in London with the housekeeper of the moment while she was filming or touring in a stage play.'

227

'You've grown up to be remarkably normal, given that sort of childhood.'

'Normal comes naturally to me. That's what infuriates my mother about me; she hates having a normal daughter. Smile, please.'

'Don't.' He waved the camera away. 'I'm not in the mood.'

'Something wrong?'

'Just wondering if we're ever going to get this place back to the way it was.'

'Of course you will – you've done wonders already.' She waited until he had turned to look downhill again before taking a quick picture, then moved to a new position and started on another series of photographs. 'I can't wait to see the water falling down the hill again. D'you remember that?'

'Not really. I think there was a slight trickle but no more than that. To tell the truth, I might even have had a hand in damming it completely. Me and Cam.'

'Vandal! Your father's been really helpful over these old photographs; we're beginning to map out quite a few areas of the garden as they were.'

'He's having a great time. I've never seen the old man so animated.'

Ginny grinned at him. 'With some people it's a matter of finding a subject to get animated about. Right, that'll do for the moment.' She got up and rubbed at the damp, dirty marks on the knees of her trousers. 'Jimmy? Time to get back to work.'

Amy opened a tin of soup and made a sandwich, then ate her lunch in Willow Cottage's back garden, eating with one hand while swiftly mapping out a new crossword with the other.

Promptly at three o'clock she arrived at Stella's house to receive a warm welcome.

'It's such a lovely day I thought we'd sit outside.'

'Sounds great. Clarissa's gone shopping so I've been workin' on a new crossword in her back yard. I've brought it for you to have a look at.'

'Good. It's so lovely to know I'm the first to see some of your crosswords, Clarissa,' Stella said as she led the way through the house.

'Oh, you've been very helpful. In fact, when I get back home I plan to keep sendin' batches to you.'

'I'd be delighted. Afternoon tea first?'

'Sounds okay to me.'

Stella's garden, like Clarissa's, was a pleasure to sit in. An old willow cast its shade over the table where they sat, and the air was perfumed by the rose bed nearby. Bees murmured contentedly as they went about the business of collecting pollen and birds sang their distinctive songs in the trees in neighbouring gardens.

When Amy had finished her tea she moved her chair from the shade; eyes closed and head tilted, she tipped her face up to catch the afternoon sun's warmth. 'This is so peaceful!'

Stella nodded. 'My grandmother had a framed piece of embroidery in her living room when I was a little girl. It said, "Nearer God's heart in a garden than any place else on earth". She'd embroidered it as part of her bottom drawer just before she got married. There were flowers all round the borders – blue love-in-a-mist, pink hollyhocks, yellow and crimson roses – the sort of flowers my grandfather grew. I thought it was beautiful and I loved the words. I wish I'd got it when the house was broken up – I don't even know what happened to it. I hope it wasn't thrown out.'

'The sound of those bees could just lull me to sleep.'

'Why not? Have a nap while I take the dishes in, then I can settle down to the new crosswords.'

229

'It's too nice to sleep. I'll wander round and admire your garden,' Amy said, getting to her feet. When Stella returned she found her guest on her knees by a vegetable bed.

'Found a few weeds – I just can't help interferin' with other folks' business.' She got to her feet. 'Where do I put them?'

'In the bin. I'll do it.' Stella held out her hand but Amy shook her head.

'No sense in us both havin' to wash. You start on the crosswords and I'll get rid of those, then use your bathroom.'

She returned, clean-handed, ten minutes later to find her hostess working busily at the first crossword. Amy settled herself down again on the comfortable sun lounger and lay back to let the sun caress her face.

Birds sang, bees hummed, the old tree's leaves rustled now and again as a gentle breeze rippled through it. A plane passed overhead, unnoticed by either of the women because it was too high to be heard. It recorded its passing in a double white line that scratched across the blue background, then gradually rippled out to either side and began to dissolve slowly.

After a while Amy yawned, stirred and said without opening her eyes, 'How're you doin'?'

'I've finished the first one. Want to look at it?'

'No need, you'll have got it all right. Darn it, Stella Heslett,' Amy said drowsily, 'I'm just glad the folks who read the papers that publish my crosswords aren't as smart as you are.'

'It helps if you love reading. Ah – I'm a bit stuck now.'

'Uh huh? What is it?'

'Three words, three letters then three again, then five. "Enacted he be." Sounds as though it might be something about Shakespeare, but I can't think what. Or it could be an anagram.'

Amy said nothing, and Stella scribbled on the notepad by

her side for a few minutes before shaking her head. 'It looks as though I'm stuck.'

'I did that crossword while I was havin' my lunch in Clarissa's back yard earlier,' Amy said drowsily. 'That's where I got my inspiration.'

'Something in a garden with three words.' Stella did some more scribbling. 'Now I've got the first word ending in "e", and the middle letter in the last word is "n" but I think I'll have to give up.'

'I'm pleased to hear it. Want a clue?'

'I think I need one.'

'Then listen.'

After a pause Stella said, 'You told me to listen and then didn't say anything.'

'I didn't say listen to me. Just – listen.'

There was another, longer pause before Stella exclaimed, 'The bees, not the birds. Bee – there isn't an "s" so it can't be plural – no – *the* bee?' She scribbled again, and said, triumphantly, 'The bee dance!'

'Well done.'

'Not really, I needed a good strong hint.'

'Is that you finished?'

'I've still got another anagram. "She tells tales." Two words, first six letters then seven letters. A writer, perhaps?'

'Could well be – but on the other hand . . . possibly not.'

'Mmm. Third letter of the first word is "e" and last letter of the second word is "t". You're very good at laying out crosswords where filling clues in doesn't often help with other clues.'

Amy chuckled. 'It's my speciality, honey, drives folks mad.'

'I don't know how you do it.'

'It's like ridin' a bike – once you've got the hang of it you never lose it. You just have to keep practisin' until you get there.'

Stella scribbled, thought, scribbled again, while Amy enjoyed the sun's warmth. Finally the librarian said in frustrated tones, 'It's no use, I just can't get it!'

'It's actually pretty easy.'

'Once you know what it is. Amy, you're such a tease! I give in.'

'Sure you don't want another five minutes?'

'My brain's turning to mush. *Please* put me out of my misery,' Stella begged, laughing.

'Okay, if you're sure.' Amy Rose sat up on the sun lounger, swinging her skinny legs down to the ground. 'Hand your notebook over.'

Stella did as she was told and watched as Amy printed out the clue – 'she tells tales' – and wrote two words beneath them. Then she handed the book back.

'There you are. Puzzles and conundrums are always easy once you know the answer.'

Smiling, Stella looked down at the two lines Amy had written. The smile froze and then began to disappear slowly – like the Cheshire Cat's in *Alice in Wonderland*, Amy thought – as she read 'she tells tales' and below it, in strong clear letters, 'Stella Hesslet'.

Slowly, Stella looked up. 'You know,' she said, her voice so low that Amy only just caught the words, 'you know it was me.'

And she burst into tears.

28

'Drink this coffee – drink it,' Amy insisted when Stella shook her head. 'It's got whisky in it – it'll make you feel better.'

Stella had finally finished crying, and was now curled up in a ball on her living-room couch, arms locked about her knees, her body shaking. 'I don't want—' she started to say, then lifted a face covered in wet red blotches. 'I don't have any whisky in the house. Where did you get it?'

Amy withdrew an empty miniature bottle from her skirt pocket. 'I always carry one just in case. I didn't put the empty bottle in your bin because I reckoned you wouldn't want the garbage men to think you're a solitary drinker. Drink it, it won't hurt and it might help.'

Slowly and reluctantly Stella released her legs and straightened until she was sitting up properly. Amy carefully put the mug, wrapped in a clean tea-towel, into her shaking hands and curled her fingers round it. 'I've wrapped it to make it easier to hold. Here' – she crossed the room and returned with a bean tray, which she settled on Stella's lap – 'just in case you spill any. Not another word from either of us until that mug's empty. You've only got half the whisky by the way; I have the other half,' she remarked as she picked up her own mug from the small table where she had placed it. 'Not because I need it, just because I'm partial to coffee with a kick.'

Stella took a tentative sip and wrinkled her nose at the taste, but aware of Amy's watchful eye did as she was ordered. By the time her mug was empty the shaking had eased.

'Good girl.' Amy, her own coffee long finished, took a handful of tissues from the box she had found and placed by the couch. 'Wipe your face and blow your nose,' she instructed, 'and then we can have a talk. Okay?'

'How did you know it was me?' was Stella's first question when she had again followed orders.

'I didn't, until this mornin'. I made the crossword up while I was havin' my lunch. I figured that if I was wrong about you I could say that "she tells tales" was a joke. But I was pretty sure I was correct. It felt right,' Amy said comfortably.

'I didn't write the letters.'

'I know you didn't. I've got letters you wrote to me when I was travellin' and I've seen one of the anonymous letters, and the handwritin''s completely different. You didn't write 'em, you just posted 'em. Don't tell me,' Amy added hurriedly as Stella opened her mouth to speak. 'Let me tell you how I worked it out, to see if I was right. This mornin' someone in the village told me about an ornament she bought when Doris Thatcher's possessions were bein' auctioned off, and I'd already heard that old lady Ivy McGowan insistin' the letter she got came from the same Doris Thatcher. Well, nobody's ever heard of a spirit buyin' stamps an' postin' letters, so nobody believes Mrs McGowan. Then I thought – what if she's right? What if this Doris did write the letters an' someone else posted 'em? But how could that person have got hold of 'em? Then I recalled one time you invited me an' Clarissa here for supper,

234

an' I admired your taste in furniture because I like the same sort of thing. You told us you like old furniture an' you took us round this house because everythin' you have here has a story about what antique shop you bought it from, or what auction sale. You said the big old wardrobe in your bedroom an' that lovely little round table beside your couch used to belong to an old lady who'd lived in the village. I'm guessin' that the wardrobe has a secret drawer somewhere?'

'Inside the big drawer at the bottom, away at the back. I found it when I was giving the wardrobe a thorough clean. I thought I was doing the right thing,' Stella wailed. 'I knew Mrs Thatcher well – I took books to her every week. She was such a lovely old lady who would never say a bad word against anyone. There was some ancient quarrel between her and Mrs McGowan, everyone knew that because Mrs McGowan never made any secret of it other than what caused it, but even so Mrs Thatcher just smiled and never said a word against Mrs McGowan.'

'A very good way of retaliatin' against an enemy.' Amy nodded. 'It must have driven Ivy McGowan mad, never gettin' the chance to have a good stand-up row and never havin' folks sorry for her because Doris bad-mouthed her.'

'The letters were addressed and sealed, and knowing how nice Mrs Thatcher was I thought they must be letters she wanted people to get after her death. I thought because she had died suddenly in the village hall she hadn't had time to leave them where they could be seen, or ask anyone to post them for her. So I did it. And then a colleague at work asked me to switch holiday dates with her and I went off to Whitby and I didn't hear about the letters until I got back.'

'You looked so upset that day the preacher talked about them in church that I thought you'd had one as well. I was waitin' for you to tell me about it and when you didn't, I guess that was another little piece put into the jigsaw. You weren't upset because a letter had caused you grief, but because, without meanin' to, you'd caused grief to other people.'

'I've not slept well since then. I'm glad you've found me out, Amy. Now I can go to the police and confess what I've done.'

'Oh, I don't think you need do that, Stella. You did what you did in good faith, and I suppose you posted all the letters you found? Folks are beginnin' to think the letters are over an' done with, an' so they are,' Amy went on as the librarian nodded, 'and I'm certainly not goin' to tell a soul, not even Clarissa.'

'I don't feel right about keeping quiet now you know. I deserve to be punished.'

'You have been, since you found out what the letters were like. You thought you were doin' a good turn and if you come clean you'll probably lose your job and have to move away from here. I reckon that old Doris has done enough harm without causin' even more, don't you? It's over, Stella, let it be. Y'know, I wish I'd met this Doris. She sounds like one helluva woman,' Amy said enthusiastically, 'havin' everyone thinkin' what a sweet old soul she was when all the time she was gettin' her kicks by drivin' Ivy crazy an' snoopin' on folks an' writin' nasty things about 'em. Stella, I should thank you.'

'Thank me?'

'Uh huh. When my Gordon was alive he sometimes talked to me about the police work he was doin' – oh, I know he shouldn't have but it never went any further – an' often I was able to come up with new ideas. Women have a different way of lookin' at things. To me it was like workin' out a really tough crossword. More than once he got praised up for solvin' a case he'd had the sense to share with me. Since he passed away I've missed those cases of his an' it's been just great to have another to chew on.' She paused, and then chuckled. 'You know what? I just heard Gordon say, clear as a bell, "Dammit, Amy Rose, is that you pushin' your nose into other folks' business again?"'

Amy had told Stella the letters hadn't done much damage, but that wasn't true. Two people she had come to care for had been damaged and she had to do what she could to help them.

So instead of returning to Willow Cottage she walked out of the village, past the old priory ruins and the quarry, where a group of children were making the most of the play area, before turning off the road and heading across the fields towards Alastair Marshall's cottage.

The door was wide open and he emerged at her call, a paint brush in one hand. 'Hi, Amy – love the hair, what a fantastic shade of green!'

'I'm quite pleased with it myself.' She had to tip her head back to look up at him. 'Have you gotten taller while I've been away or have I shrunk?'

'I stood out in the rain for too long the other day.'

'That could do it. Am I glad you're home, because walking on a day like this has given me a hefty thirst.'

'And as it happens I was getting myself a shandy. Care to join me?'

'I most certainly would!'

'Sit yourself down.' He nodded in the direction of two old deckchairs and a rickety table set in the knee-high wilderness that had once been a lawn, and disappeared into the dim interior to return with a filled tumbler in each hand.

She watched his approach with approval, not just because of the full glasses he bore but also because he wore nothing but a pair of faded jeans that had been cut off just above the knee. He was slim, but muscle lay beneath the smooth skin flushed by the sun's heat. It was a while since she had seen such a fit and attractive young male, she thought with a stab of nostalgia for the past.

'So what brings you here, if I may ask?'

She tasted her drink, then took a hearty slug before replying. 'Clarissa's shoppin' and I got bored on my own. Actually, that's a lie. I came to see you because you haven't visited Clarissa since I've been back an' she scarcely mentions your name. It's botherin' me.'

'We've both got things to do.'

'Let's cut to the chase, Alastair. Clarissa showed me the anonymous letter she got, and I know you got one as well, both of 'em about your friendship.'

'If you want to see mine you can't because I destroyed it. It was stupid mindless rubbish.'

'If that's so, why have you and Clarissa let the letters get to you so badly? If there was no truth in what they said you'd have shrugged 'em off and gone on with your friendship. Cards on the table time, Alastair,' she went on when he stared at his half-finished drink and said nothing. 'The letters might have been malicious, but there was some truth in 'em, wasn't there? I'm good at sussin' folks out right from the start, an' I'm not often wrong. I knew how you two felt about each other from the first evenin' I arrived in Prior's Ford and I've not changed my mind one whit.'

'Don't be daft!'

'Don't you be, either. Sometimes folks just belong together an' age has nothin' to do with it. Maybe the time's come for you and Clarissa to sit down and have a good honest talk. Get the truth out in the open.'

'And lose her entirely?'

'I don't think that'll happen because I know she's missin' you

238

as much as you're missin' her. You might at least find a way to mend a friendship that means an awful lot to you both.' He glared at her, his mouth a thin closed line. 'Okay, I've said what I came to say and I guess I've outstayed my welcome.' She drained her glass, set it down, and got to her feet. 'Thanks for the drink,' she said, and left without looking back.

She hadn't come away from their encounter empty handed, so to speak. Although he hadn't realised it, Alastair's 'And lose her entirely?' had confirmed her belief that what he felt for Clarissa was much more than mere friendship.

'I know, Gordon, I know,' she said aloud as she approached the stile. 'I should mind my own business. But sometimes things just have to be said, know what I mean? Once said an' heard they can't be forgotten. With any luck he'll find the courage to do what has to be done. And if not – well, Gordon, at least I tried.'

All too soon for Helen and Jenny the school summer holidays arrived and the time came for the MacKenzies to leave for Norway. Ingrid, Peter and their daughters had become greatly liked members of the community, and almost everyone turned up for the farewell party in the village hall, including the Alston family, who were spending the weekend in their holiday cottage. They swept in as though the party was being held for them: Carrie in a silky black trouser suit, the trousers flared and a scoop-necked white silk blouse beneath the open jacket, Bernie in a beautifully cut shirt over tailored jeans. The twins were dressed in much the same way as they had been at the house-warming party, and with the same detailed make-up, Maureen in bold colours, Rhona in pale colours.

'The professional country-dweller look,' Andrew commented under his breath as Carrie and Bernie toured the hall, shaking hands with everyone and introducing themselves, seemingly

239

oblivious to the fact that they were being given a cool reception by quite a number of the villagers. 'They could have stepped from a glossy magazine photograph of the landed gentry enjoying some country pursuit.'

'Or from one of those old middle-class English films,' Duncan Campbell said sourly. 'As for these two . . .' he nodded in the direction of the Alston twins, who had moved straight to where the young people had congregated, 'they're goin' tae cause trouble in the village, you mark my words.'

'They look tasty,' was Cam Gordon's opinion.

'That's just what I mean. They're what's called jail bait, Cam. You keep well away from them; they could get you into a lot of trouble.'

'I'll bet!' Cam said enthusiastically, picking up his glass of beer and heading towards the twins.

'Some folk,' Duncan said in disgust, 'never learn.'

'I wouldn't worry,' Jenny told him. 'Bernie seems to be keeping a close eye on his girls and I pity the man who crosses him.'

Ingrid and Peter had hired a disc jockey, and while the younger element took to the dance floor in the larger hall most of the adults retired swiftly to the smaller hall where they could talk without having to shout over the music.

Carrie and Bernie danced together frequently. She tended to return to the smaller hall between dances, while he stayed to watch the other dancers, a glass always in his hand and a benign smile on his somewhat florid features, but his heavy lidded eyes rarely straying from his daughters. Occasionally he made one or the other dance with him, something they did with a clear ill-grace.

When they all left halfway through the evening the atmosphere seemed to lighten.

'I don't care to speak ill of people I don't really know, but

I wouldn't want my children to become too friendly with those girls,' Ingrid told her friends. 'They're a lot older than their real age. What is it that people say? As if they've been here before?'

'Maggie thinks they're weird,' Jenny admitted.

'Freya tells me that they have nothing good to say about the village, the cottage or their father and stepmother.'

'That might be their mother's influence,' Helen volunteered. 'From what Carrie's told me the twins spend most of their time with her in the school holidays. Since Bernie left her for Carrie, I could understand her trying to turn her daughters against their father's second wife.'

'They came into the store today,' Marcy said, wrinkling her nose in distaste, 'and looked round the place as if it was cheap and nasty. Sniggered a bit and tried to flirt with Sam, but he wasn't having any of it so they bought a Mars Bar each and sauntered out. I was relieved to see them go.'

Helen nodded. 'I know – I was there at the time. I'm just glad that my Gregor's too young to be of interest to them – he is, isn't he?'

'Yes, he is, but by the way he's staring at them I'd say he's hovering on the verge of discovering that girls aren't all football mad like my Ella. Don't worry, Helen, I doubt if that family will be in the village for long. They are not our type,' Ingrid finished firmly.

'Carrie was born here,' Helen pointed out, trying hard to protect her friend.

'Perhaps, but living with people like that man and his daughters has turned her into one of them. The leopard has changed its spots.'

'She's certainly nothing like the little girl I knew,' Helen admitted.

'Whereas you're still the same lovely person you always

were. I am going to miss you all so, so much!' There was a sudden and most unexpected tremor in Ingrid's voice. She blinked her blue eyes rapidly and then gathered the three of them into a general hug.

'I wish you could at least have waited for next week's Scarecrow Festival!' Ingrid was holding them all so tightly that Marcy's voice was muffled.

'So do we, but my parents can't manage for much longer without us.' Ingrid released them in order to grope for her handkerchief. 'It's so *difficult* to leave good friends. And I've just realised lately that it's also difficult,' she added with a shaky laugh as she dabbed at her eyes, 'being part Norwegian and part Scottish. I hadn't realised how much I love Scotland until now!'

'We're going to miss the MacKenzies so much,' Jenny said later as she and Andrew prepared for bed, 'especially me. I'm still not sure that I'm going to manage to keep the Gift Horse going without her.'

She waited for some much-needed encouragement, but instead there was silence.

'Andrew?' She glanced into the dressing-table mirror to see him sitting on the bed, studying the sock he had just taken off. 'What's wrong with it?'

He jumped slightly. 'What's wrong with what?'

'That sock you're so interested in.'

'Oh, that.' He tossed it onto a chair and began to pull the other one off. 'Nothing. I was just thinking about something else. Something that – oh, it's nothing.'

'You've got me curious now.'

'It's best not to say because I'm probably wrong. I thought I was at the time, but tonight I'm beginning to think I was right after all.'

'Now you've really got me curious. Tell me what it is!'

'It's Helen's friend, Carrie. Last week when I was late home because I had to go to that business dinner in Dumfries, I thought I saw her in the hotel bar.'

'With Bernie?'

'That's what's bothering me. She was with a man, but it wasn't her husband.'

Jenny spun round on the dressing-table stool to stare at him. 'Are you sure?'

'I wasn't at the time, so I decided it must just be someone who looked like her. I've only seen her once, at that dreadful party they held when they first arrived. But tonight in the village hall I realised it *was* her. She was wearing the same clothes and the same earrings – those big chandelier things.'

'You're quite sure that she wasn't with Bernie?'

'Positive. I got a good look at both of them this evening.'

'Perhaps she was attending a business dinner too. She told Helen that she deals with the sales side of their business and that probably means a lot of socialising.'

'Jen, I can assure you that what I saw had nothing to do with business. As I said, they were in the hotel bar and they were being very affectionate towards each other. They left just before we were called to the dining room, hand in hand and heading towards the lifts, not the exit.'

'That's strange, because according to Helen, Carrie swears that Bernie left his wife because he adores her, and she adores him.'

'Well, whatever she was there for and whoever she was with it's none of our business. Best to keep quiet about this.'

'I've no intention of saying a word to anyone, including Helen,' Jenny told him.

But keeping quiet about what Andrew had seen didn't stop her from wondering what Carrie Alston was up to.

243

29

The second Prior's Ford Scarecrow Festival went smoothly, with none of the petty vandalism that had almost spoiled the previous year's festival. The weather again was kind and visitors flooded in. Jenny and Maggie were worked off their feet at the Gift Horse and so many people visited the Neurotic Cuckoo that Gracie Fisher and her daughter Alison had to keep dashing across to the store for more groceries to meet the demand for pub lunches.

Linn Hall's first proper Open Summer was an impressive success. Lewis had dreamed of opening the grounds to the public for years, and at last he had proved to his parents and to their bank manager that the venture could be a success. Only one thing marred his happiness that July – Molly's absence. It was wonderful to have Rowena Chloe at the hall, but despite his hopes that Molly would change her mind and hurry back from Portugal to be with him and their daughter for the Scarecrow Festival all he got were occasional postcards, generally with 'Hi, babes, having a fantastic time' scrawled across them, and the rest of the space covered with kisses for him and Rowena Chloe.

'She won't even stay in this country for the sake of that lovely little girl of hers,' Jinty McDonald said in disgust to Ginny. 'What sort of a mother is that? I found it hard enough to leave my wee ones with a babysitter for an hour when I had to. I wish Lewis had found someone more deserving than her, I really do!'

'You can't choose who you fall in love with.'

'You sound very knowing.' Jinty raised her brows. 'Speaking from experience?'

'In a way – I was thinking about my mother and father. They were like chalk and cheese from the start, from what I've heard.'

'Well, I'm glad they got together because if they hadn't, you wouldn't have happened – just like that lovely little Rowena Chloe.'

Nobody knew that Lewis himself was beginning to have real doubts about Molly's ability to settle down to life at Linn Hall. The suggestion in the poison-pen letter that he might not be Rowena Chloe's father and the phrase, 'Most of the village think otherwise' kept coming into his mind when he was with the little girl. He adored her and her mother, and he kept telling himself the letter was no more than a pack of vicious lies, that Molly was true to him and Rowena Chloe was his flesh and blood.

On several occasions he took the letter from its hiding place with the firm intention of tearing it into tiny bits and forgetting it, but each time he ended up reading it again, and each time the pain it caused was worse. For some reason beyond his ken he always folded the letter and put it away again after reading it, unable to destroy it. If Amy Rose had known the way the unknown writer's words were affecting him she would have told him that was why such missives are called poison-pen letters – because the writer's pen has been dipped into a

246

poison that would, if allowed, spread its venom slowly and relentlessly through the victim.

The Alstons were very much in evidence during the Scarecrow Festival. Carrie and Bernie, he dressed like a country squire and she in floaty floral prints, made a point of touring the village and going into rhapsodies over every single scarecrow during festival week, with Bernie's twin daughters in sulky attendance.

In the evenings Rhona and Maureen were always to be seen on the village green, where the local teenagers tended to gather.

'They've got the young lads all of a tizzy,' Jinty reported to Fliss. They and the women helping them had been kept busy providing refreshments for visitors and now the two of them were taking advantage of a quiet moment to have a seat and a cup of tea in the yard outside the kitchen door. 'I'm keeping a close eye on my boys, I can tell you.'

'They're not really village folk, are they?' Fliss had been quite intimidated by Carrie and Bernie when they came to Linn Hall earlier in the week. Following a tour round the grounds they had swept into the kitchen, where they did their best to persuade her to show them round the rest of the house.

'We have our own business, you know – hand-made furniture of the very best quality,' Carrie had informed her. 'Naturally, we're interested in fine old houses like yours. You must have some lovely furniture. Couldn't we have a little peep?'

'Well, I – we're thinking of opening part of the house to the public, but not yet.'

'But with us being in the furniture business, we're not like the other visitors,' Bernie had coaxed her. 'It would be an honour to be taken on a personal tour by the lady of the house.'

Fortunately for Fliss, Jinty had come to the rescue. 'There's still a lot of renovation work to do on the house and

Mrs Ralston-Kerr's far too busy to show anyone around,' she had announced flatly. 'Is it coffee or tea you want?'

'Is the coffee ground?'

'Instant.'

'In that case,' Carrie said, 'I think we'll have tea.'

Before they left Bernie gave Fliss his business card, assuring her that if any new furniture was required for the house during its renovation his company would be able to assist, while Carrie invited the Ralston-Kerrs to visit their holiday cottage to admire the way they had furnished it from their own show-room. 'My mobile number is on the back of the card – do come, we'd love to see you again when there's time for a proper chat!'

'They're definitely not village folk,' Jinty said now, 'though Carrie was, at one time. Such an ordinary, quiet wee thing she was. Moving away from Prior's Ford's ruined her completely.'

As had happened on the previous year, Kevin Pearce won first prize for the best garden scarecrow, a striking Abraham Lincoln sitting in sombre splendour on a rustic garden seat.

'I've taken a photograph of it so I can show it to the chil-dren when the school term starts,' Lynn Stacey told Ginny during one of the suppers that had become a regular weekly event. 'It's a good way of teaching them about old Abe. Last year Kevin did an excellent Florence Nightingale – d'you remember the fuss he made when the village was vandalised and she went missing? Such a pompous man, but I'm glad she turned up in time to win the prize because he really did deserve it. By the way, you and Lewis and Duncan have made an incred-ible difference to the gardens. I loved the little scarecrows tucked away in corners so that we came on them unexpectedly, and I saw a lot of people taking the time to read the notices telling them about the flowers and plants.'

'I'm really grateful to you for all the help you've given me with the photographs and cataloguing.'

'It's been fun. I'm looking forward to seeing the lake and the pond back in business. Next year, d'you think?'

'Fingers crossed. Actually – can you keep a secret?'

'Absolutely.'

'Good, because I'm desperate to tell someone,' Ginny confessed, her eyes glowing. 'The estate made even more money than the Ralston-Kerrs had hoped for during the festival week, and Lewis says that if they find, at the end of the season, that they've made enough to pay me a wage, they'd like me to stay on over the winter. That would mean being able to keep working on the lake in good weather.'

'That's fantastic!'

'I know. I've told him I won't be looking for lots of money because I've not got any plans for the winter anyway.'

'What about having a really good holiday abroad – visiting your mother in Spain if she's still there over the winter.'

Ginny wrinkled her nose. 'She will be. The first six episodes of her sitcom are going to be televised in October but they've been given another series already. They start filming in November. But I had more than my fill of sitting around while she was working when I was growing up, and I've never cared for holidays. I'd far rather stay on in the village now I've got my snug little home on wheels. To tell you the truth, I'd be willing to work here over the winter for nothing.'

'Don't tell the Ralston-Kerrs that,' Lynn said firmly. 'You work very hard and they're fortunate to have found you. I don't believe you value yourself as highly as you should, Ginny Whitelaw.'

'I wish you would tell my mother.'

'One day I might get the chance to do just that,' said Lynn, who knew enough about psychology to realise that Meredith Whitelaw had never made her daughter feel worthwhile.

All Ginny could think of was the pleasure of spending the entire winter, as well as next spring and summer, in Lewis's company.

'I'm so glad,' Naomi said warmly, 'that you're involving Calum and Maggie in this wedding.'

'We both felt it was their day as much as ours.'

'Are any other family members going to be here for the occasion?' the minister asked, and saw a shadow cross Jenny's face.

'No. My parents and my sister and her husband all live in America, and they feel it's too far to come. As for Andrew's parents – to tell the truth, Naomi, like everyone else until recently they were under the impression we were already married. They're rather old-fashioned in outlook and Andrew says that if they found out the truth they'd probably not come anyway. They would feel he'd shamed them – and lied to them into the bargain.'

'Ah. Never mind,' Naomi said comfortably, 'sometimes friends can be closer than blood kin, and I'm sure the villagers will help make your wedding a family affair. I can't tell you how much I'm looking forward to it.'

'Me too.' Jenny brightened up. 'We're all going to Edinburgh on Saturday to buy our outfits.'

The front door opened, banged shut, and Maggie called, 'Jenny?' from the hall.

'In here, love. Naomi's come to discuss . . .' Jenny's voice tailed off as Maggie stamped into the room, her face like thunder. Both the entrance and the expression reminded her painfully of the terrible year they had gone through when Maggie had first arrived in the village, deeply unhappy and determined to make everyone else unhappy too.

'What's wrong?'

'Did you have to make such a fuss about this wedding of

yours? Couldn't you have gone away somewhere and done it quietly and saved me all this embarrassment?'

'Hello, Maggie.'

The girl swung round to see the minister sitting by the bay window. 'Oh – I didn't see you there,' she said lamely, flushing.

Naomi's rich laugh rang out. 'That I can't believe! I'm going to have to overhaul my wardrobe. You think this is a mite too conservative?' She smoothed her hands over her ankle-length skirt, a vivid green splashed with large blue and red flowers. 'So – Jenny was just telling me the wedding's going to be a real family occasion. Aren't you looking forward to it?'

'I was, until – Naomi, don't you think they should just get married quietly without anyone knowing about it?'

'Why should we? Who's been talking to you?' Jenny wanted to know.

Maggie's shoulders slumped. 'Lesley Thomson told me her gran says it's bad enough that you two were living in sin all those years, without shouting about it all over the village and expecting everyone to congratulate you just because you've decided to do the right thing at last.'

'And no doubt,' Naomi said calmly, 'Lesley Thomson's gran doesn't approve of me agreeing to have the ceremony in my church?'

'Well – yes.' Maggie's anger was beginning to deflate.

'I thought as much. The next time you see Lesley, sweetheart, you point out to her that Jenny and Andrew may have broken God's rules by living together outside the bonds of matrimony, but they're showing true penitence now by making their very happy and strong union legal and acceptable in the eyes of the law and the Church. And make sure that she and her gran know your parents have asked for donations to a charity for cancer research instead of wedding gifts. As for me – I'm the one who decides who has the right to be married in my church, though

251

of course I never make that sort of decision without having a word with Him upstairs. We mulled it over and we're both agreed that we're very happy to be involved with this particular marriage.'

'You're really sure we're doing the right thing?'

'Absolutely. Jenny,' Naomi peered at the small table by her side, 'do you have any more of those lovely little chocolate biscuits?'

'There's still half the packet left.'

'Good, cos there's only one left on the plate and while I'd love to claim it I feel Maggie needs a good chocolate binge to get the taste of Lesley Thomson's granny's disapproval out of her mouth.'

'I'll fetch them, and a mug for myself,' Maggie offered eagerly.

'I think the situation's been diffused,' Naomi said placidly when the girl had gone.

'That dratted old woman!' Jenny fumed.

'Don't worry about her. Mrs Thomson's one of the pillars of the church, but she and Ivy McGowan are as well matched as a pair of china dogs on a mantelpiece. I often think,' Naomi said, picking up the lone chocolate biscuit, 'that regular church-goers fall into three categories. One group is like you and Andrew – genuine Christians who actively practise what Christ taught us about compassion for others, another consists of poor souls who don't know how to make friends and see church activities as their only way of meeting other people, and the last group are doing their Christian duty while wearing invisible badges that proclaim, "I'm a better person than anyone else because I attend church." I welcome all three, but I prefer your group – though I have to admit that sometimes I enjoy the ones with the badges. They don't know it, bless them, but they make me laugh. Oh, good girl,' she went on as Maggie arrived, a mug in one hand, a packet of biscuits in the other and the cat close to her heels. 'Now you can tell me about the bridesmaid's outfit you plan to buy on Saturday.'

252

30

From where he and Wilf McIntyre were working in one of the top fields Bert McNair could see down to the farmhouse roof then beyond, along the length of the rutted lane to the main road and the field he had signed over to his elder son, Victor.

The field he had been tricked into signing over, he thought savagely as he paused for a breather, scrubbing sweat from his forehead with a sinewy forearm. The field that had been meant for a holiday caravan park but was now being turned into a small housing estate.

'I wish I'd smothered the bastard at birth,' he growled.

'Ye don't mean that, Bert.' Wilf knew immediately who his employer meant. 'You an' Jess were proud as punch the day Victor was born an' rightly so. He's just not cut out for farmin'. Mebbe ye should have let him go his own way earlier.'

'Ye could be right. With luck he might have gone off somewhere else instead o' meetin' up wi' a town lass an' gettin' fancy ideas intae his head.'

'There are town lasses everywhere same as country lasses,

and it's no' as if that field's good for grazin' or crops, ye have tae admit that.'

'Even so it hurts me tae see land goin' under concrete. It's happenin' all over the country now; soon there won't be any greenery left. Nothin' for the eye tae see but ugly wee boxes like that lot down there,' Bert nodded at the building site, 'that'll cost more than ordinary folk like us can afford. I'll tell ye this, Wilf, I'll make damned sure that not another inch o' Tarbethill land goes that way, and I've made Ewan promise me it'll no' happen in his lifetime either!'

'Ye cannae dae more than that. We're goin' tae need more wire here,' Wilf pointed out. The two of them were strengthening weak spots in the fencing.

'I thought we'd brought enough wi' us.'

'It's an old fence; there's more weaknesses than we realised. I'll go down tae fetch it,' Wilf offered, but Bert shook his head.

'I'll dae it while you finish that stretch. Ye've enough left tae keep ye busy till I get back.' It was a hot early-August day, and Bert needed a break. His eyes weren't as good as they used to be and he tired easily – not that he would admit as much to Jess because she would only worry, and nag at him to go and see the doctor.

'Take the flask wi' ye,' Wilf said without looking up from his work. 'It's dry as a bone and so am I.'

As Bert set off downhill towards the farm buildings and got nearer to the main road he could hear the sound of machinery from the field being turned into a collection of fancy box-like houses for yuppies. The noise of it, cutting through the summer air, set his teeth on edge and brought back all the bitterness of Victor's betrayal.

It was true what Wilf said: the field had been of little use apart from being used for the occasional village festivity, but he hated to think of boulders ripped from the earth that had held them safe for thousands of years, healthy trees with years of life still in them tossed casually aside to die slowly and, worst of all, the life-giving earth being smothered for ever beneath concrete. And his torment wouldn't end when the building work was completed. Every time he left the farm from now on he would see the houses, each no doubt with a car in the drive, washing in the back gardens and women chatting at front doors and over fences. The modern world was going to be no more than the width of the road away from Tarbethill land, the small estate squatting opposite the end of his lane like an alien enemy camped in preparation for an all-out attack. Although he would never admit it to his wife, his son or Wilf, Bert lived in fear of the day when the builders of boxy houses, possibly led by Victor, his own flesh and blood, might find a way to move across the road and take Tarbethill itself.

Suddenly anxious for the sight of Jess and the calming sound of her voice he took the Thermos to the house before collecting the wire. The kitchen, filled with the smell of freshly baked scones cooling on a wire rack, was empty and when he opened the inner door and shouted his wife's name there was no answering call. For a moment he was puzzled before remembering that she had promised to help Ewan in the cottage.

Bert tutted, for her absence meant that there would be no tea to take back to Wilf. He would no more have thought of making tea for himself and Wilf than he would have expected Jess to do the ditching and fencing: there were jobs that only men could do and jobs that only women could do and that was the way things were and always should be.

He went to the kitchen sink instead and turned the cold-water tap on. Taking a mug from the draining board he filled and drank it three times before giving a long drawn-out sigh of satisfaction, wiping his mouth with the back of one hand.

'Aaaahh! That's better.' He filled the Thermos with water

255

and turned to take some scones from the wire rack, then stopped at the sight of Old Saul, stretched out as usual on the rug before the fireplace.

As usual – but not as usual. The old dog hadn't lifted his head when he'd come in, or even thumped his tail feebly in recognition of his master's voice when he called for Jess.

'Saul? C'mon, boy.'

The dog didn't move, and when Bert, his heart leaping into his mouth, bent and touched his ribs they were warm, but still. The old dog's eyes, only half lidded, were blank windows in an empty house.

'Saul . . .' Something unpleasantly soft seemed to swell and then break in the farmer's throat. Without warning scalding tears filled his eyes and fell onto the dog's furry body. He hadn't cried since he was a bairn at his mother's skirts – couldn't even remember what crying felt like – but all at once an outpouring of grief gripped him.

Saul was the fourth generation of his family born at Tarbethill. Bert himself had trained him and he had turned out to be the best farm dog ever. He was an integral part of Bert's younger, stronger days, the days when he felt certain that with the help of his two growing boys he could rebuild the ailing farm into a worthy inheritance for them to take over. Time had treated him and Saul cruelly. It had leached the strength from their limbs and aged them while rules and regulations, laws and animal diseases had gnawed away at the land, refusing to let it flourish as it had done before.

Bert bent slowly from the waist, grunting with the effort. By the time he had gathered the dog's body into his arms he was breathless. 'Come on, old lad,' he said, blinking back the last of the tears, 'this isnae the place for you. Ye're a workin' dog, an outdoors dog. I'll take ye tae where ye belong.'

Once in the barn where Old Saul had slept from puppyhood

until he became too infirm to withstand the cold nights, Bert settled the body carefully on a pile of straw then sank down beside him. The current farm dogs were a bitch, sired by Old Saul, and her son. Bert had trained them himself, but good though they were neither was a patch on this old dog.

'There's none to match you, eh?' One hand stroked the animal's head rhythmically. They had shared the golden years, the years when cows from the Tarbethill herd, three times the size it was now, were known throughout Dumfries and Galloway as award winners and their calves always fetched good prices at the market. But the descendants of those dairy herds, every one of them Tarbethill-born, had perished in the foot and mouth epidemic, some stricken by the disease while others, seemingly healthy, had to be killed as a precaution. Like the other farmers, the McNairs had had to start over again at a time when the European market's power over Britain's farmers put paid to any hope of bringing back the good days.

'We're both the last o' the breed, eh?' he said to the un-heeding dog, then gave a heavy sigh and scrambled to his feet. Wilf would have to get on with the fencing on his own, for Bert had more important things to do now.

Into the house he went, through the kitchen, pausing only to take the key to the locked hall cupboard from the small dresser drawer where it was always kept.

'What d'you want?'

'That's a fine way tae welcome yer brother.'

'Can ye blame me?' retorted Ewan, who had been mowing the small patch of grass in front of the farm cottage when Victor appeared at the gate. 'Every time ye set foot on the place ye get Dad intae a bad mood.'

'He's up at the top field. I saw him an' Wilf from across the road so I took the chance tae see Mam.'

'She's here, puttin' the cottage tae rights. We've just had our first lot o' holiday-makers an' they liked the place well enough tae book in for next year. There's another lot comin' at the end o' the week.'

'So it's worked out after all? Well, good for you. I'll just nip in for a word an' be well away afore Dad comes back,' Victor promised and Ewan returned to work, pleased to have had the opportunity to boast to his brother about the cottage's success. Their first holiday-makers, a young couple with two children, had been delighted with the place, and with living on a farm. The children had been fascinated by the wormery and had helped Jess collect eggs and feed the hens while their parents, townspeople, had enjoyed the slower pace of village life. They looked like becoming regulars.

Ewan was still glowing over the success of a project that his father and brother had both scoffed at. Whistling, he finished the lawn and trimmed the edges.

Even with the noise from the building site opposite the farm lane the gunshot was clearly heard at the cottage and in the top field where Wilf awaited Bert's return with the roll of wire.

Ewan paused in his work as his mother appeared at the open door, a duster in her hand.

'What was that?'

'Mebbe Dad's seen a fox,' Ewan suggested as Victor appeared behind his mother. Jess shook her head.

'He didnae take the shotgun out wi' him. Anyway, it sounded . . .' She paused and then said, a tremor in her voice, 'It sounded closer.'

The fear he saw in her eyes turned his heart cold. 'I'll go and look. You wait here.'

'I'll come with ye.'

'Victor . . .'

His brother nodded. 'You go on, Ewan, Mum an' me'll wait here.'

'I'm goin' wi—'

'Stay here!' Ewan almost shouted at her, then he was out of the gate, pulling it shut behind him.

Jess shook Victor's hand off. 'I'm *goin'*!'

'We'll go together, then.' Much as he longed to catch up with Ewan he forced himself to keep to her pace. It was easier than he had expected, since his legs seemed to have turned to rubber. Like Ewan, he was chilled by Jess's reaction to the gunshot. It was as though she already knew something they couldn't, or didn't, want to grasp.

On the hill above, Wilf, too, was on his way to the farmhouse, scattering cows and sheep heedlessly and scrambling over walls and fences.

Reaching the farmyard, Ewan found the kitchen empty and the inner door, usually closed, ajar. He went through it then skidded to a halt in the hall as he saw the open, empty cupboard where the shotgun was kept. Spinning round, he ran back to the yard, shouting his father's name as he plunged into the barn.

The sudden transition from sunlight to darkness half-blinded him, then as his eyes adjusted he saw his father slumped over Old Saul, both of them motionless. The shotgun lay close by and in the dim light he made out bloody patches on the dog's grey fur.

'Ewan? Bert?' Jess called as she and Victor rounded the farmhouse. Seeing Ewan appear at the barn door she stumbled towards him, one hand pressed tightly to her heart.

'Victor, take Mum intae the kitchen.'

'Where's yer father? Is he in the barn?'

'Aye, but don't go in there.' He held out an arm to block her way. 'Go tae the house, Mum.'

31

For the first time in his life it was Ew
his mother sat in one of the fireside
idle in her lap for once, her dry eyes f
opposite.

He had dialled 999 and asked for a
ising that his father had no need of
his voice shaking, 'An' mebbe I shoul
the shotgun's there. I think there's bee

The operator assured him that all
now he was spooning leaves into a t
to heat. Wilf, who had arrived at a run
by the door, having been ordered ou
who insisted on being alone with th

'Alice,' Jess said suddenly. 'Ye'll nee
has tae be here.'

'I'll phone her when ye've got yer

'I can do the tea.' Jess put her ha
chair, started to lever herself up, the
the empty hearthrug. 'Where's Old S

She looked past him to the barn doo[...] falling on that side it was nothing but [...] whatever was within from her sight. [...] Victor and headed towards it. Ewan [...] his arms round her to prevent her fro[...]

'He's in there, isn't he?'

'Aye, Mum,' Ewan said, 'he is. Co[...] need tae telephone someone.'

'He cannae be left on his own.'

'I'll stay with him,' Victor said. 'Go [...] right, ye have tae fetch help.'

To the relief of both her sons she [...] lead her to the house.

'He's – he's in the barn, Mum, with Dad.'

'What were they doin' there? Bert was supposed tae be in the top field.'

'Bert came down tae fetch more wire,' Wilf volunteered, 'an' tae fill the Thermos up again. There it is by the sink.'

Jess noticed him for the first time. 'There ye are, Wilf. Come on in, man. D'ye want some tea? I'll make fresh, an' there's scones . . .'

'Water'll dae me fine, Jess.' The farmhand went to the sink, where he held the mug Bert had drunk from beneath the tap and emptied it in loud gulps before sluicing his face with double handfuls of water.

'I think,' Ewan said through dry lips, 'that Old Saul died an' Dad found him an' carried him tae the barn for some reason.'

'He'll no' have wanted the dog tae lie in the kitchen,' Jess said dully. 'Old Saul was an outdoor dog. A workin' dog, the best Bert ever had.'

The tea looked black enough when Ewan poured it into a mug. He added milk and then, recalling that sweet tea was supposed to be good for shock, added three heaped spoonfuls of sugar. As an afterthought, he shot a swift glance at his mother and seeing that she was staring down at her lap he fetched the bottle of brandy kept on a high shelf in case of emergencies and poured a good dollop into the mug.

When he handed it to Jess she looked at it as though she couldn't think what to do with it and he had to wrap her hands round the mug and make sure she was holding it firmly.

'Drink that, Mum, while I go and phone Alice.'

'There's the ambulance arrived,' Wilf said as Ewan went through the inner door. 'I'll go out tae them, Jess.'

*　　*　　*

'I'd been hoping to be first on the scene,' Constable Gloria Frost complained as the police car arrived in the farm yard. 'Before anyone messed any evidence up. I told you I should have driven.'

'There's nothing wrong with my driving,' Neil White snapped.

'That's open to debate.'

Neil bit back a response he knew he would regret later – Gloria would see to that. He'd had a miserable shift so far that day. Because they were keeping their estrangement from their work colleagues, when they were on the same shift they arrived together and left together. Neil was staying in a bed-and-breakfast establishment only a few streets away from the house they had bought together before their marriage. When he picked her up that morning she had been in such a bad mood that by the time they arrived at the station he was seriously wishing he could stop the car and make her get out and walk.

'Park over there,' she ordered him. As they got out of their vehicle the ambulance driver and the female paramedic emerged from the barn. The woman spread her hands out and shook her head.

'Nothing we can do here, love,' the driver said when the police officers reached them.

'Yes there is.' Gloria jammed her hat onto her blonde hair. 'You can stop calling me "love". Try "constable".'

'I don't think I'll bother,' he grunted as he made for the ambulance.

'Afraid it's a police matter,' the paramedic said. 'The poor man's beyond our help. Over and out.' She winked at Neil before following her driver.

Catching the wink, Gloria tutted and shot an angry glance at Neil before turning to see a burly, grey-haired man crossing the yard.

'I'm Wilf McIntyre, the farmhand. Bert and Jess – the McNairs,' Wilf stumbled on, his voice shaking, 'they own the place. Bert's – he's in there wi' his son Victor. Jess's in the kitchen, an' their other son Ewan's phonin' his sister in England tae tell her what's happen—' His voice suddenly broke on the final word and Gloria put a hand on his arm.

'It's all right, Mr McIntyre, we're here now. Why don't you go to the farmhouse and get yourself a nice cup of tea? We'll talk to you in a wee while.'

'I'd best make sure the milkin' shed's been put to rights,' Wilf mumbled, and headed off.

The barn was eerily silent in the special way that death scenes usually were. A young man stood near to the entrance as though guarding the bodies of the elderly man and the dog. He didn't appear to be aware of their arrival and when Neil said, 'Victor McNair?' he swung round on them, fists clenched and eyes fierce.

'Who are you?'

'Constable White, and this is Constable Frost. You've not touched anything in here, have you?'

'Of course no'. I watch *The Bill.*' It was what they all said these days. As his eyes adjusted to the shadowy barn Neil saw the wet shine of tears on the other man's cheeks.

'Could you just wait outside the door for a minute, Mr McNair?' Gloria asked. 'Messy,' she went on when they were alone. 'You have a word with the son and make sure nothing's been touched. I'll call the police surgeon and CID, then speak to the people in the farmhouse.'

On the way to the house she met another young man heading for the barn.

'I'm Ewan McNair. My dad – he's dead, isn't he?'

'I'm afraid so, Mr McNair. I've called in the police surgeon and CID.'

'What d'ye mean, CID? It was an accident, surely. Or mebbe

264

he did it himself. We've been havin' a struggle tae keep the place goin', an' it's been gettin' him down . . .' Ewan, realising he was beginning to gabble, stopped and ran both hands through his hair in confusion.

'It's the way things are done, Mr McNair. We always have to call in CID in the case of sudden death, especially where firearms are involved. They'll want to take photographs of the scene and bring in a firearms expert to have a look at the shotgun.'

'We've got a licence for it.'

'I'm sure you have, but we need to find out if it went off by accident while your father was carrying it. I'm sorry, but we have to make certain we've got all the facts right. Who's in the house?'

'Just my mother. I've phoned my sister tae tell her, but she lives in England. She'll no' get here until tomorrow.'

'I'll look after your mother. Neil – my colleague – is having a word with your brother. He'll want to talk to you, too,' Gloria said, then continued across the yard, speaking into her radio as she went.

Neil, emerging from the barn, watched his estranged wife's neat backside swaying beneath the skirt of her uniform, then was pulled back to the matter in hand when Victor McNair said, 'I suppose you're used tae this sort o' thing.'

'It's not my first death, but it's never easy to see the end of a life.'

Victor opened his mouth to reply, then closed it again, shook his head and rubbed the back of one hand over his face as Ewan joined them.

'Alice is comin' tomorrow,' he told his brother, and Victor nodded.

'That's good. Mum'll need her.'

★   ★   ★

The police surgeon arrived first. Gloria had still not come out of the farmhouse, so Neil left the man to his work and went in search of her, pausing in the open doorway to look round the flagged kitchen with its big range, its Welsh dresser holding rows of patterned plates and a table large enough to seat at least ten people comfortably.

Gloria was sitting on a chair she had pulled out from the table, hat off and tunic unbuttoned. She was almost knee to knee with a woman Neil took to be the farmer's wife – his widow now – her slim strong hands clasping the other woman's work-swollen reddened hands tightly. Gloria was talking softly, intently, and Neil hesitated, reluctant to intrude on the two of them during what seemed to be a very private moment.

Suddenly Jess McNair became aware of him. 'Come on in, son. Ye must be starvin' an' I never even thought o' bringin' out some tea for ye, an' somethin' tae eat.' She struggled to her feet, releasing herself from Gloria's fingers. 'Sit down at the table, the two o' ye. I've got some nice sliced ham in the larder an' there's home-made bread an' scones for after . . .'

'I'm all right, Mrs McNair, don't worry about me. Gloria, the doc's arrived.'

She snapped into duty-mode immediately, getting to her feet, sliding the chair beneath the table, putting her hat on and buttoning her tunic in what seemed to Neil to be one smooth movement. He had never managed to figure out how women could do that. Watching her get dressed in the mornings had been one of his pleasures, he recalled, then suddenly realised she was frowning at him and had to work hard to push the memory from his mind.

'I have to go now, Mrs McNair, but your minister'll be here any minute. Will you be all right on your own until then?'

'Of course I will, pet. Thanks for yer kindness, ye've been wonderful.'

266

'That's part of the job,' Gloria almost said but managed to change it in the nick of time to, 'That's all right, Mrs McNair. You take care now.' It *was* part of the job, but there was something humbling about the older woman's strength and dignity in the face of the horror that had suddenly and cruelly confronted her. Being with her, speaking to her woman to woman, had been a very special thing. Gloria cleared her throat and nodded briskly before hurrying out.

'She was just wonderful – just wonderful,' Jess said to the handsome young constable. 'Ye're lucky tae be workin' wi' such a kind lassie, son.'

'Aye, I am.' He knew how wonderful Gloria could be when she wanted to, but it had been a long time since she had wanted to be wonderful with him.

She was waiting for him outside the door, one foot tapping the ground.

'What got into you just now?'

'What d'you mean?'

'You were standing there looking like a fish that'd just been landed.'

'I was just – she's such a nice woman. It's a shame what's happened to her.'

'She'll get through it – she'll have to.' Gloria had abandoned all-woman and returned to all-business. 'For goodness' sake, get a grip. On days like this I wonder if you'd be better leaving the force and moving to some other job entirely.'

'Dream on,' he said as she made for the barn. Following her, he realised that he was doing it again – staying a couple of steps behind her in order to watch the way that neat backside of hers moved beneath her skirt. He lengthened his pace at once, telling himself as he caught up with her that he would have to lose the habit before people at the station began to notice.

They had almost reached the barn when a noisy car engine could be heard, and they both paused and turned in time to see a small car bounce into the yard. The driver's door opened and a large dark-skinned woman who apparently bought her clothes from Rainbows R Us popped out like the cork from a bottle of champagne.

'Who on earth's that?'

'The local minister, I presume.'

'That,' Neil said incredulously, 'is the minister?'

'Oh, well done! In only four words you've managed to be both sexist and racist. That's got to be a personal best!'

'I didn't . . . I was only commenting on her bright clothes,' he protested as Naomi disappeared into the house. 'I didn't realise that ministers dress like that.'

'Why shouldn't they? Clergy are people, aren't they?'

'So are police officers, I believe, but it's been a while since you've behaved like a person to me except at the station where the others can hear you. Gloria, why can't you—'

'Oh, stop whinging,' she hissed at him and led the way into the barn.

The CID arrived as the police surgeon was completing his examination, with the firearms expert close on their heels. The yard began to look like a parking lot, annoying the hens who were used to having the area to themselves. Car doors were left open and their radios could be heard chattering or crackling with static. Officers, male and female, some in plain clothes, came and went around the barn and in and out of the farmhouse.

Once Naomi had arrived Wilf hurried home to return with his wife, Maisie, a large basket filled with food over her arm. When they had assured themselves that Jess was in good hands Ewan and Wilf started to prepare for the milking.

'I'll come with ye,' Victor said.

'Are ye sure?'

'I cannae stand tae watch all these strangers takin' over my dad like that. He'd hate it!'

'He doesnae know about it, man. He's at peace.'

'Even so,' Victor started to say, then, as a long low vehicle with darkened windows arrived in the yard, 'What the hell's that?'

'We'll be finishing up soon,' one of the CID officers said from the barn door. 'Officers will be back tomorrow to take statements. Perhaps you should go to the house and tell the people with your mother to keep her away from the windows. We're taking your father away now.'

'But my mother'll want him tae rest here, in the house,' Victor protested.

'I'm afraid that won't be possible. There has to be a post-mortem.'

'Ewan . . .'

'You go to the milking shed, Victor, and me an' Wilf'll bring the beasts in once I've had a word with Naomi an' Maisie,' Ewan said quietly, and after a moment, during which it seemed that Victor was going to be difficult, his shoulders slumped and he headed towards the milking shed without another word.

32

When the milking was over and everyone had gone Jess and her sons picked at some food, then Victor got up to go.

'I'll be back in time tae help wi' the milkin' tomorrow, Ewan. An' I'll be here all day because there's the – there's things tae be arranged.'

'D'ye want tae stay the night? Your room's all ready; I keep the bed aired.'

'Thanks, Mum, but Jeanette an' her parents'll be wantin' tae know how things are. D'ye want me tae bring Jeanette with me tomorrow – or her mother? I'm sure they'd be happy tae help.'

'If ye don't mind, son, I feel easier wi' folk I know well about me just now. I'll get tae know your Jeanette an' her fam'ly soon, but just now's . . .'

'I know, an' they'll understand.' He reached for his jacket, hanging on the hook on the outside door, and then hesitated. 'I'm sorry, Mum.'

'What for?'

'It's me who drove him tae kill himsel'.'

271

'Who says he killed himsel'?' Ewan wanted to know. 'There was no suicide note – the police asked about that. It could have been an accident, like they say. We don't know yet.'

Victor shook his head. 'Can ye see our dad takin' the trouble tae sit down an' write a suicide note? An' why else would he take the gun intae the barn?'

'Mebbe he found Old Saul in pain an' decided tae put him out o' his misery.'

'Get real, Ewan! The dog wasnae shot – I checked. Dad killed himsel' because I broke his heart. It's my fault.'

'Don't be daft!' Jess's voice was suddenly strong and her face, which seemed during the day to have fallen in on itself, tightened with anger. 'Are you sayin' that yer father was so weak it took just you tae make him put an end tae his life? Never! The man's been losin' heart for the past four or five years, we all know that. We all watched it happen. You'd every right tae go yer own way. Sellin' the field tae builders was a mistake,' she conceded, 'but that alone wouldnae have driven him tae take his own life.'

'So you think it was an accident?' Ewan asked.

'No! Bert knew how tae handle shotguns while he was still at school. It's my belief that he killed himsel' because findin' Old Saul dead was the final straw. That dog was the last reminder left tae him o' better days. An' Victor's right – my Bert wouldnae waste time writin' letters once he'd made up his mind tae go.' Jess glared at her two sons, then finished with, 'That was never an accident – and even if it was, nothin''s goin' tae bring him back tae us, is it? Now go home tae Jeanette, Victor, an' we'll see ye in the mornin'. Ewan, I'm off tae my bed. I'll leave you tae lock up.'

Before going to his own bed Ewan had one final task to do. Fetching a spade and some sacking he went to the barn where

272

Old Saul now lay alone. For a moment he thought of washing the animal's coat clean, then decided it was fitting that a part of his father went to the grave with his favourite working dog.

Over the years a spinney in the corner of one of the fields not too far from the house had become a graveyard for the McNair cats and dogs. Ewan wrapped the body in sacking and carried it there, laying it down gently. When the grave was ready he put the spade aside and laid the old dog in its final resting place, then filled in the grave and firmed the soil down with the back of the spade.

After all was done to his satisfaction he stood for a while in the darkening night, his eyes fixed on the bare patch among the grass, remembering the day when he was in primary school and the minister, a severe elderly man, had told his class that animals couldn't go to heaven because they didn't have souls. Ewan, who shared every day of his life with animals, had protested angrily, earning a stinging reprimand afterwards from the teacher. Years later he had asked Naomi for her view on the subject and was cheered when she said firmly, 'As far as I'm concerned any living thing on this planet must have a soul. We're all here by the grace of God, aren't we? Why should animals lack souls when humans have them? Think how dull the afterlife would be without birds singing and fish leaping and dogs racing around and cats to stroke.'

Remembering her words, Ewan said a brief prayer then took a moment to recall the times he had shared with Saul, and how the dog had enriched his life.

At last, reluctantly, he left the grave and headed home. He was bone-weary and there was a lot to be done the next day. Just as he was slipping into sleep he realised that when his father's finger had tightened on the shotgun trigger Bert hadn't just killed himself – he had also killed any hope Ewan had of marrying Alison.

273

He had meant it when he told his mother that he didn't want to see Alison slaving from morning to night on the farm. He knew from what he had already seen that she could and would learn to be a farmer's wife, but he had determined that before asking her to marry him he would make sure he could offer her a better future than constant toil with never a penny to spare for herself or even for Jamie. But now his father and Victor were both lost to Tarbethill the farm's future depended solely on him. For his mother's sake he must do his best to hold the place together. And he could only manage that by sacrificing his own hopes and dreams. He had no other choice.

Looking back, Ewan McNair could never make sense of August 2007. While other years, months and even weeks and days in his life were clear as crystal the three or four weeks following his father's death resembled photographs he had seen of tornadoes – great black whirling clouds of smoke and dust, strong enough to pick up buildings, animals and people and carry them off. Single events – his sister's arrival, the tears she shed that eventually broke down Jess's dry-eyed acceptance and freed her to weep with her daughter, the inquest and its verdict of suicide, the guilt that stooped Victor's shoulders and gave his eyes a haunted look and the funeral service in a packed church – could be glimpsed occasionally within the massive whirling cloud, only to disappear as swiftly as they came.

He himself was like a robot going about the farm, doing what must be done with no time or desire to think about what was happening. Men from the surrounding farms came to assist him and Wilf with the work and Victor was there most of the time. Even so Ewan hurled himself into the task of trying to run the place single-handed, working from dawn till dusk.

'Ye'll work yersel' intae the ground,' his mother fretted, and when he didn't answer, said, 'Ewan, is it no' bad enough that I've lost yer father? I don't want tae lose you as well.'

'You won't,' he said tersely. 'I'm fine.'

Whenever possible Alison was at the farm, helping Jess. She usually brought Jamie with her because Jess loved having the little boy around. He was the only person at that time who could bring a smile to her lips and a light to her eyes. Alison too worried over Ewan and one day when he didn't appear for his midday meal she took some food to where he was working alone in one of the fields and made him take time to eat.

'Ewan, folk want to help you, and you need to let them.'

'What d'ye mean?'

'You're not really giving them the chance to take on some of your work; it's as if you're determined to show us all that you can manage without us.'

He refused to meet her gaze. 'I don't have any other choice, do I? Sooner or later I'm goin' tae have tae run the whole farm on my own with only Wilf and my mother tae help. Where's the sense in getting used tae the extra help we have just now? Everyone round here helps their neighbours after a death, but it can't last. Victor's got his own life tae go back tae, and the other farmers, too. If I ease up on the work while they're here it'll only make it harder for me when they go.' He took a massive bite out of a thick cheese sandwich.

'I'm not saying you should leave everything to others. I'm saying you need to take time while you can to start making plans for the future. There's a lot to think about.'

He chewed, swallowed, took a gulp of tea from the Thermos, then growled, 'I can't waste time thinking. All that matters is keepin' this place goin' for my dad's sake – an' that's what I'm doin'.'

'Ewan, face facts. If you want to hold onto Tarbethill land, you and your mother need to sit down and make decisions. There has to be changes.'

'I'm no' interested in changes. I'm goin' tae run this farm the way my dad ran it.'

'Your dad had two sons, then one son and Wilf, and even then it was difficult. You've only got Wilf and he's not a young man. You don't need to be afraid of change,' Alison persisted, 'because you're young and change will come more easily to you than to your father. Look what you've done already, setting up the wormery and doing up the cottage as a summer let.'

'The wormery won't pay its keep for a good while and the cottage won't bring much in.'

'I know that. But don't you see that they're both a start – a change of direction? There are other things that can be done to keep Tarbethill going and make life easier for you and your mother at the same time. I've got ideas for the place and I want to help, Ewan – if you'll let me.'

'You're a city woman, no' a farmer.'

'I *was* a city woman but now I'm a villager. I can learn about farming – I want to! Lots of women from towns and cities have become farmers' wives.'

Ewan's stare suddenly hardened into a glare. 'You've got enough tae do carin' for wee Jamie an' helpin' your parents in the pub without takin' on any other burdens,' he said, scrambling to his feet. 'And I've neither the time or the money tae take on the responsibility of a wife, let alone a fam'ly. Thanks for bringin' the food, but there was no need. I wasnae that hungry.'

'Ewan . . .' she said, but he was already striding away from her, the set of his broad shoulders warning her off making any attempt to follow him.

She began to screw the cup back onto the Thermos and found the tears in her eyes made it so difficult it took three tries before she succeeded. He had left one of the sandwiches uneaten, and she wrapped it carefully in its paper and laid it on top of the nearby wall in the hope that he might return for it once she was out of the way.

Ewan himself was near to tears of despair and exhaustion as he strode across the field. Alison's willingness to stand by him, being there to help him and Jess make plans for the farm's future, and her suggestion that they could still marry when he knew it was too late and he could never include her in his life, had been more than he could bear.

He had been deepening a ditch along the bottom of a field. When he reached the spot he seized the spade and started digging furiously, ignoring his tired muscles.

For the first time in his life he envied Victor, who had managed to escape from family responsibilities while there was still time.

Amy returned home at the end of August, summoned back to America by a friend in need.

'I'd been lookin' forward to takin' you and Stella back with me for Thanksgivin',' she said as she packed, hurling everything casually into her large suitcase. 'But there you are — Muriel was there for me when Gordon died, and now it's my turn to be there for her. P'raps the two of you can come over and visit with me some time.'

'Perhaps.' Clarissa was helping with the packing by removing everything tossed into the case, folding it, and setting it aside for re-packing.

'I'm goin' to miss this place.'

'You'll come back, surely.'

'Would that be okay with you?'

'Of course it would, any time.'

'I'm suddenly in urgent nee
Marcy said as she packed
checkout. 'I miss those nice
at Ingrid's. And there's Jenn
Fancy a couple of drinks a

'There's a football match
home to keep an eye on th

'Good, I'll phone Jenny.

'Could I invite Carrie?' H
nose up. 'Bernie's away at
he's bringing the twins back
they return to school, so she'
conversion. She told me yest
bored and I'm sure she'd ju
you and Jenny properly.'

'Oh, why not? I suppose
to know her better.'

'Great! I'll tell her,' Heler
It was one of those anno

'Then I will,' Amy said[...]
you somethin', Clarissa.'

'What's that?'

'You're a long time dea[...]

things such as talkative neighbours holding her back and discovering that the skirt and blouse she planned to wear that evening needed ironing got in Helen's way, and it wasn't until the family had been fed, the dishes washed, Duncan settled in front of the television set and the children engaged in games that weren't potentially lethal that Helen remembered she hadn't told Carrie about the meeting in the pub.

She almost jumped into her ironed clothes, applied lipstick, ran a comb through her hair, grabbed her bag and hurried round to the cottage by the river, arriving there at a quarter to seven.

To her astonishment a vision answered her knock at the door. Carrie wore a long skirt and low-cut jacket in shimmering turquoise, her face was immaculately made-up, her hair a shining cap. Jewels sparkled on her ears, fingers, wrists and around her throat, and her high-heeled strappy shoes were also turquoise with diamante straps.

'Oh – Helen! I thought it was my taxi.' Carrie seemed as taken aback as Helen.

'I came to ask if you were free to join me, Marcy and Jenny for a drink in the pub, but it looks as though you've got other plans.'

'What a shame! I'd have loved to be with you all, but an old school friend who lives in Kirkcudbright's invited me for dinner,' Carrie said hurriedly, adding on a relieved note, 'and here comes my taxi.'

She turned back into the house to pick up a small overnight bag, explaining, as she saw Helen eyeing it, 'Once she gets talking the time just flies by so I'll probably end up staying overnight.'

'Another time, then? Meeting for a drink, I mean.'

'Absolutely. Sorry about the rush but I'm already running late.' Carrie forced the old-fashioned door key into her small bag and moved past Helen to the waiting taxi, calling back, 'Have a nice evening.'

'I thought she was lonely with Bernie away,' Marcy said when Helen explained why Carrie wasn't going to join them.

'So she said, but apparently she has friends in Kirkcudbright.'

'That's all right, then. Actually, it's nicer with just the three of us. I don't see Carrie taking Ingrid's place – at least, not for a while. Anyone fancy a glass of red?' Jenny asked.

They had a lot of catching up to do as well as Jenny's wedding plans to discuss, so Carrie was swept from Helen's mind until she had said goodbye to the other two and was walking home. It was then that questions began to come into her mind: why had Carrie dressed so elaborately for dinner with an old school friend? Why stay the night if she was only going to Kirkcudbright, not that far from Prior's Ford? Why had she looked so taken aback when she saw Helen standing on her doorstep?

And the most puzzling question of all – why say she was visiting an old school friend, when Helen knew for a fact she was the only friend from Carrie's primary-school days, and that Carrie's family had gone from Prior's Ford to Berwick on Tweed?

Carrie wasn't telling the truth about her past – but for the life of her, Helen couldn't understand why.

It had been so long since she had last seen Alastair other than in passing that Clarissa was startled to find him on her doorstep. So startled that she stared at him, not knowing what to say.

'Are you busy?'

'I was just doing some baking. Come on in. Is the kitchen all right? I'm about to put some scones into the oven,' she explained as he followed her along the hall. 'Coffee?'

281

'Thanks. I'll make it if you want to get on with your baking.'

While he saw to the coffee, moving about the kitchen with the practised ease of someone used to being there, Clarissa returned to the task of cutting out the scones, brushing them with milk, lining them up on the baking tray and then rolling the left-over dough out in order to repeat the process.

By the time the scones were in the oven the coffee was almost ready. 'Would you like to sit out in the garden?' Clarissa suggested, but Alastair shook his head.

'Not particularly.' He scooped up the leftover scraps of dough and popped them into his mouth, something she had seen him do so often in the days when he had been a frequent and welcome visitor. Now, thanks to the poison-pen letter writer, those relaxed occasions were gone. She wondered, watching him dust flour from his fingertips, if they could ever return.

'We'll go into the living room then; it's too hot in here with the oven on,' Clarissa said. 'I've had a letter from Amy; she wants me and Stella Hesslet to spend Thanksgiving with her,' she said a few minutes later as she handed him his coffee.

'Oh?'

'The truth is she wants Stella to go. She thinks America would help get Stella out of her shell and she'd be more likely to agree if I went with her.'

'Perhaps Amy should stop interfering and accept the fact that Stella Hesslet might enjoy living in a shell.'

'That doesn't sound like you at all. I thought you liked Amy.'

'I do, I'm just tired of her meddling.'

Understanding dawned. 'Did she speak to you about those silly letters?'

'Of course she did – how could she resist?'

'What did she say?'

'Probably much the same as she said to you.'

'For goodness' sake, Alastair, those letters were just a piece of malicious nonsense and it all stopped after Naomi made it public in her sermon. Whoever was behind them must have come to their senses when it all came out into the open.'

'If you seriously believe that, why are you still keeping me at arm's length?'

'I'm not.'

'Clarissa, you're not very good at hiding your thoughts. It's one of the things I—' Alastair stopped short and then said carefully, 'One of the things I've always liked about you because it means you're a very honest person. You used to smile when you saw me on your doorstep, but today you looked positively frightened. You even glanced out at the road to make sure nobody saw you invite me in.' He drew a deep breath, then reverted to the tactics Amy had used on him. 'You can't forget what those letters said because they've made you face the truth – that you and I have been more than just friends for quite a while.'

'That's nonsense!' She put her cup down carefully, feeling heat rush to her cheeks. 'It's – ridiculous! Impossible!'

'It's not, Clarissa. Not for me, and I suspect – I hope, to be honest – not for you either.'

'How could we possibly . . .' She couldn't even say it.

'How could we be more than just friends? How could we, a man and a woman, possibly be in love with each other? It came naturally to me as I watched you pull yourself out of the black hole you were in the day I found you sitting in that field in the rain. I thought at the time you'd lost your wits, but seeing you start to rebuild your life was so – so inspiring. I'd never admired anyone as much in my entire life as I admired you. I fell in love with your courage and then I fell in love with you. I knew it for sure when you went travelling. You've no idea how much I missed you,' Alastair said, 'how much it hurt to know you were so far away. I counted the days from one letter to the next. I was terrified in case you changed your mind and decided not to come back to Prior's Ford – and to me.'

'Alastair, please just stop this!'

'I'm tired of keeping quiet, Clarissa. I've had girlfriends, but I've never ever cared for any of them the way I care for you.'

'I'm old enough to be your mother!'

'True, but that doesn't bother me at all. Why should it? You're you and I'm me – we're both just people and age doesn't come into it. Try thinking about putting your happiness first, instead of fretting about formalities. And before it occurs to you, as it probably will,' he added with a sudden grin, 'let me assure you that I'm not suffering from an Oedipus complex. I love my mum, she's great, but I've got no desire whatsoever to replace her with you. I could strangle that letter writer for spoiling what we had before. But, maddening though she is, Amy's interference has at least given me the chance to say I love you, Clarissa Ramsay, and I want nothing more than to spend the rest of my life with you.'

'Alastair . . .'

'Okay, let's be brutal and face the fact that it might well be the rest of *your* life rather than mine, but that doesn't matter. All that matters is you and me being together. So now it's your turn to tell me how you feel about me.'

'How can I possibly *love* someone in his thirties?'

'Thirty-seven isn't that young. If it helps, I'll be forty in less than three years.'

'You'll still be twenty-two years younger than I am!'

'I am so annoyed with my parents for not having had me a lot sooner. I've got an idea – you stop having birthdays and

284

then I'll be able to catch up. If it helps, I take back everything I said about wanting us to spend the rest of our lives together,' Alastair offered. 'I'll settle for us just spending as long as we want together. If either of us decides at any time to opt out then that's that. Sound fair?'

'I can't deal with this. Could you just go, Alastair? Now?'

'Only if I have to. D'you know something? Telling someone that you love them is fantastic! Just saying those four words, "I love you, Clarissa", was incredibly liberating. It must be the way people who find the courage to say, "My name is George and I'm an alcoholic" feel afterwards. I want to say it to you every night before we go to sleep and every morning when we wake up together. I want to devote myself to making you as happy as you've made me.'

'I can't. We can't!' She covered her face with her hands.

'If you don't love me that would be okay too, as long as it's true. And if it *is* true, it should be easy to say.' He waited for a while before letting his breath out in a long sigh of relief. 'I'm so glad to know you can't say that either. All right, I'll go. But it really does feel wonderful to be able to say something you really mean. I hope you can enjoy that feeling soon.'

Clarissa stayed where she was, fingers spread over her face, the palms of her hands pressed tightly against her mouth. She heard the living-room door and then the front door close quietly behind him and still she sat, unmoving, until the smell of burning scones stole through from the kitchen and reached her nose.

As she scraped the blackened lumps into the bin with trembling hands she realised she had to get away from Prior's Ford as soon as possible – perhaps for good, but certainly for long enough to give herself time to think. This, she realised sadly, was the second time she had run away from

285

the village. After her round-the-world trip she had returned to settle down in Willow Cottage, happier than she had been for a long time – thanks largely to Alastair. Now, because of him, she was running away again, but it was the only thing to do. The thought of meeting him in the village now there was such a huge gulf between them was unbearable. She had refused to say she loved him – but she hadn't been able to say she didn't love him, even to herself.

Unable to face the prospect of a holiday on her own with nothing else to think about but Alastair, waiting for a reply, she decided to spend some time with her stepchildren.

'At last,' Steven said warmly when he met her at the railway station. 'I was beginning to wonder if we would ever winkle you out of that village.'

'You know you're always welcome to visit me.'

'We know, and it's a great place to stay, but it's nice to see you coming to us. I'd hate you to think we're not family just because Father's not around any more.'

'I'd never think that. So how are Christopher and Alexandra?'

'Chris's still as busy as ever. He's been made a partner in his practice,' Steven said proudly.

'You said in an email. That's wonderful! Things going well for you too?'

'Business is steady so I can't complain.' Steven was manager of a building society and his partner Christopher was a vet.

'And your sister?'

'Ah! There's the car, at the end of that row.' They had reached the station car park, and Steven put his free hand beneath her elbow to guide her in the right direction. 'There's a new man in Alex's life.'

'Really?'

'Really. We've even met him and he seems a decent fellow. You'll no doubt be meeting him too. He thinks highly of Alex.'

'I'm not surprised.' Alexandra Ramsay was both beautiful and intelligent. 'What does this man do?'

'He's a university lecturer, something to do with science. Physics, I believe. Not stuffy, though, or intimidating. And not afraid of Alex. I don't think she'll scare this one off.' Steven put Clarissa's suitcase into the boot of the car.

'Good. I can't wait to meet him.'

'I have a feeling,' Steven said as he started the engine, 'that Alex burned her fingers a bit a couple of years ago – she never said, but I suspect a man was involved in it somewhere. That was the time she went to Prior's Ford for a while and got involved in cataloguing stuff for the local laird.'

'Oh yes – that was when I was travelling. She stayed at my house with Ginny Whitelaw. Did I tell you about the way Ginny's been helping to restore the Linn Hall gardens? I visited the estate when it was open during the summer, and it's looking really good already. You and Christopher must come and see it next year.'

Clarissa stayed for an enjoyable three nights at Steven and Chris's comfortable, relaxing flat and would have been happy to spend the rest of her week there, but felt obliged to spend her final two nights in Alexandra's smart terraced house.

To her surprise she found that Alexandra, who took after her father and wasn't nearly as easy to get on with as her brother, seemed less intimidating and easier to like than before. It may have been that the very nice university professor who clearly thought the world of her had opened up a softer side to her nature, but Clarissa suspected that she herself had become more able to cope with her stepdaughter. Since being widowed and finding the courage to go travelling on her own before settling down in Prior's Ford she had rediscovered herself and gained in confidence.

That, she realised with an inner twinge, was mainly down to Alastair. Try as she might, she couldn't go for more than an hour without thinking of him – wondering what he was doing at that moment, if he was thinking of her, and if so, *what* was he thinking about her?

When Alexandra asked casually during a tour round the shops before going to a theatre matinee, 'How's Alastair?' she gave a guilty start because he had been in her mind.

'Alastair?'

'That painter who lives just outside the village. I thought the two of you were friendly.'

'Oh, yes – he's fine. You saw quite a lot of him when you were in Prior's Ford that time, didn't you?'

'Yes, I did. We had some good talks,' Alexandra said casually. 'I like his balanced view of life. How are those people in the big house?'

'The Ralston-Kerrs? They're doing well. They were very impressed by the cataloguing you did for them while you stayed in the village. Apparently it helped a lot. I was saying to Steven and Chris that you should all come up north in the summer to see the changes in the estate.'

'That would be nice.' Alexandra glanced at her watch. 'Time to head for the theatre.'

34

Marcy Copleton and Sam Brennan were usually the first villagers to be up and about in order to open the store in time for the newspapers to arrive.

'Look at that sky – it's going to be another beautiful day,' Marcy said happily as they left Rowan Cottage and walked together across the village green.

'Good – we might get a lot of summer visitors in the store.'

'Sometimes I feel it would be lovely to be able to throw the alarm clock across the room and turn over and go back to sleep instead of having to get up early every morning. But on a day like this, with nobody else but us and the birds around, it's my favourite time.'

'It's never mine,' Sam grunted. 'Before we know it the papers have to be sorted and deliveries organised and then the kids start coming in on their way to school—'

'And spend money – you love the sound of the cash register, don't you?' she teased him.

'Well, there is that. I hate having to try to keep ahead of things every morning.'

She slipped her arm through his. 'Oh, Sam, my love, don't be such an old curmudgeon. Take a leaf out of my book and learn to enjoy the moment.'

'Can't afford the time,' he responded. They crossed the road towards the store. 'Someone's stuck a sheet of paper on the window.' He hurried ahead of her and pulled the Sellotaped paper free. 'What the . . .?'

'What is it?'

'Read it for yourself.' He thrust the sheet at her. Marcy scanned it swiftly and then went back to the top of the page and read it again, more slowly this time.

'This is really nasty!'

'Why put it on our door?'

'To make sure that everyone passing by or coming in sees it. I wonder if there are any other copies?' Marcy said, looking across the green. 'Isn't that a sheet of paper stuck on the pub door?'

As Sam turned, the door of the Neurotic Cuckoo opened and Joe Fisher emerged, carrying a long-spouted watering can. He yawned widely and then, spotting them, waved before starting to water the hanging flower baskets.

'I'm sure it's a notice like this one,' Marcy said. 'If there's one on his door as well, there must be others.' The faint sound of an approaching engine reached her ears. 'That's the paper delivery coming. Sam, you open up. I'm going to get that notice off the pub door before Joe spots it, then look for more.'

'I can't do everything myself!'

'You'll have to. We can't leave stuff like this around to be read. Here – put that out of sight.' Marcy pushed the sheet of paper into his hand and sped off across the green towards the pub.

She arrived back about twenty minutes later with a fistful of papers.

290

'You took your time!' Sam was irritably sorting out newspapers and magazines.

'They were everywhere! Stuck to the bus stop, on the butcher's window and both the Gift Horse windows, as well as the end wall of the almshouses. Even on the church door – and at the school and the village hall. I'm afraid Joe Fisher got to the notice on the pub door just before I did, but he's a decent man and he promised not to mention it to anyone. I'm dying for a cup of tea. I hope you put the kettle on.'

'Of course I did. It helped pass the time until you got back. I made some pancakes to go with it and whipped up a few jars of raspberry jam as well.'

'Don't be so sarky. You do the tea and I'll finish the papers,' Marcy offered. 'What's the time? I reckon Helen'll be up and about soon.'

'What's Helen got to do with anything?'

'Carrie Alston's a friend of hers. She might agree to let the poor woman know what's going on.'

'My advice is to keep well out of it and say nothing.'

'We can't do that. D'you think this is the work of whoever wrote those poison-pen letters before?'

'I doubt it. The letters were posted to people and this stuff's meant for everyone to see,' Sam was saying when Jimmy McDonald arrived to start on his delivery round.

'Mornin' Sam – Marcy. Look what I found.' He flourished a typed sheet of paper and then backed off nervously as Marcy pounced and snatched it from his hand.

'Where did you get that?'

'It was Sellotaped to the lamp post at the end of our street. It says that that Mrs Alston who's moved into old Doris Thatcher's cottage wants work as a businessman's escort.' Jimmy looked from one to the other. 'What's a businessman's escort?

Sounds more like a car than a job. P'raps I've read it wrong and she's selling her car?'

'Hold the fort, Sam, I'll be back as soon as I can,' Marcy said and was gone, clutching the paper she had taken from Jimmy, before Sam could stop her.

'Oh, darn it! Did you have to let her see that notice? Now look what you've done.'

'How was I to know she's interested in cars?' Jimmy asked, aggrieved.

The closer Helen got to Carrie Alston's cottage the more she longed to be able to turn tail and flee back home.

'I don't know Carrie all that well,' she had protested to Marcy. 'I haven't had any contact with her since we were in primary school together. She's become an entirely different person since then.'

'So have you. You write such sensible advice in the Lucinda Keen page. It would be kinder for you to tell her what's going on than anyone else in the village.'

It was ironic, Helen thought as she forced herself to open the garden gate and walk up the path to the front door, that she had only managed to start being an agony aunt by imagining that all the letters had been written by the timid Carrie she had once known. 'And now look what I've got to do – all because of a pair of wet knickers,' she thought in despair as she forced a reluctant finger on to the bell push.

Musical chimes sounded within the cottage but to her delight there was no response. Reprieved, she turned and was scuttling back to the gate when a voice said, 'Oh, it's you, Helen,' and she turned to see Carrie rounding the side of the house, a coffee cup in one hand.

'I was just having a look at the area where the new kitchen's going to be built and I thought I heard the doorbell. How

292

lovely to see you! Come on in and have some coffee – or should we be wicked and have something stronger?' Even though it was still quite early she looked fresh as a daisy in a black and white shirt over dark green trousers, her face fully made-up and with not a hair out of place.

'Coffee would be lovely,' lied Helen, wishing she had thought of having a glass of something stronger before leaving her own house.

She had neatly folded the sheet of paper given to her by Marcy and tucked it into her jacket pocket, but when she brought it out while Carrie was fetching the coffee she discovered it was all crushed. She must have been clutching it on the walk from her own house. She began to smooth out the creases then gave a guilty start as Carrie asked brightly from the door, 'What have you got there?'

'It's – is your husband in?'

'He and the girls left for Edinburgh early this morning. They suddenly insisted they wanted to go back to their mother's, thank heavens, and if he doesn't see them off on the train in person goodness only knows what the brats would get up to. The last time we trusted them to travel on their own they deliberately missed the train and went shopping on Bernie's credit card. He was beside himself with worry when the headmistress phoned to ask why they hadn't turned up, then he almost had a stroke when he got his credit card bill and realised how much they'd spent.'

'Oh dear. Carrie, I'm afraid that I—'

'I can't wait to get him to myself again,' Carrie prattled on as she poured coffee for them both. 'I don't know why all the fairy stories are about wicked stepmothers instead of wicked stepchildren. I wish I was a writer like you – I must tell you all about the ghastly twins one day, then you can write a novel about me and make lots of money.'

'Carrie . . .' Helen tried to find the right words, failed, and thrust the still crumpled sheet of paper at her hostess in exchange for her coffee. Carrie took it, read it, and then asked evenly, 'Where did you get this?'

'Marcy Copleton and Sam Brennan found it on the door of the village store when they opened up this morning. There were others, scattered all round the place. Marcy tore down all the notices she could find, but she may have missed some. I'm so sorry, Carrie!' The other woman remained silent, staring down at the paper in her hand. 'We had a rash of poison-pen letters a while ago, but they seem to have stopped. Now this! You've only just come back and I can't think who would have wanted to do such a thing to you.'

'Can't you? Who else could it be but Maureen and Rhona, the little . . .' The rest of the sentence described Carrie's step-daughters in a torrent of words that made Helen wince. 'No wonder they were in such a hurry to get back to their mother, and no wonder they were so sweet to me before they left,' Carrie stormed on. 'They even brought us breakfast in bed this morning. They both went upstairs early last night – claimed they were tired. They must have crept down again when we were asleep to print these on my laptop and then scatter them around the place. Just wait till their father finds out, he'll be furious!'

'Are you sure it was the twins?'

'I *know* it's them. They must have found my business diary – they're always snooping where they shouldn't. But this time they've gone too far! For a start, I'm going to make sure their allowances stop here and now. Let their mother support them from her alimony money for once! Bernie's always been far too generous to them. Now it's time to remind him if it wasn't for me doing this' – the paper was waved at Helen – 'he wouldn't *have* the money to lavish on his darling little daughters!'

'You mean – it's true?'

'Of course it's true. How else do you think we could afford to buy this place and pay for all the alterations? Not that that'll happen now because once word gets round – and no doubt it's being spread all over the place as we speak – there's no question of us being able to enjoy our holiday home in Prior's Ford.'

'That evening I invited you to the Cuckoo for a drink and you said you were having dinner with an old school friend, were you . . .?'

'Of course. A last-minute booking by a regular client. A nice man,' Carrie said with a reminiscent smile. 'And very generous!'

'But – I thought you and Bernie owned a successful business.'

'Yes, we do,' Carrie said impatiently. 'And we could live very comfortably on what it makes if it weren't for those horrible brats and their money-mad mother bleeding the poor man dry. It's the money I make working as an escort that lets us manage to have a decent lifestyle for ourselves.'

'But aren't there other ways to make extra money?'

'Like cleaning other people's houses?' Carrie sneered. 'That's what my mother did when I was a kid and believe me, Helen, I decided at an early age I was never going down that road. We should all use the talents we have, and as I've worked very hard to develop mine it made sense to exploit them. If it wasn't for my business skills and my second career, Bernie and his business would have foundered years ago. And he knows it.'

'But don't you feel . . . ?'

'Proud of myself? Yes, I do. I'm a self-made woman and I'm also very selective. Only the best and the wealthiest clients for me. I've even managed to bring in some very lucrative deals for the company as well. Oh, don't look so prudish, Helen!'

'Bernie knows about this – this other thing that you do?'

'He's known from the start. We never keep secrets from each other, that's the basis of our perfect marriage. As far as Bernie and I are concerned there's a big difference between love and business – and what I do with other men is strictly business. We love each other very much; that's why we're going to have to leave Prior's Ford. I've no intention of changing my lifestyle to please prune-faces like Ivy McGowan. Talking of Ivy, think how much I'll have enriched her sad little life. More coffee?'

'No, thank you.'

Carrie poured more for herself. 'Dear old Poison Ivy's going to revel in delicious gossip about how she always knew Carrie Wilson would end up as a bad lot! Now then . . .' She set the full cup of coffee down, tore the sheet of paper into strips, dropped them on the floor, and took the small notebook and gold pen she had used to list guests for her house-warming party from her bag. 'I'm going to have to phone Bernie and tell him not to bother coming back here when he's seen his brats off on the train, cancel the builders, phone the estate agent and tell him to put this place back on the market, pack our clothes, arrange for a removal van to collect the furniture we've installed . . .'

'Then she said how nice it had been to meet up with me again, and we must keep in touch by email, and I left her writing her list,' Helen said half an hour later in the Gift Horse.

'You poor thing, having to break news like that to her.'

'Actually, Jenny, it was much harder for me than for her. She behaved as though it was just a passing inconvenience. I looked in on Marcy on my way here, she's nipping over for a coffee if she can find the time.'

The door opened to admit some customers. 'You go and start making the coffee. I could do with a cup and so could you, by the looks of you,' Jenny said before turning to the newcomers. 'Good morning, isn't it a lovely day?'

By the time the coffee was made and the customers had departed, bearing their purchases, Marcy had arrived.

'But only for two minutes because I've already stretched Sam's patience to breaking point today. Thanks, Helen.' She grabbed the proffered cup and took a mouthful of coffee. 'That tastes good! I've come to tell you that I didn't manage to find all the leaflets – the store's buzzing with the news about Carrie. Ivy McGowan and Moira Melrose are in their element. What on earth's been going on? Make it quick.'

'Carrie and Bernie are leaving the village. In a nutshell, Carrie's been moonlighting as a high-class escort to keep their business afloat. It seems that Bernie's weird twins found out and scattered leaflets all over the village as a farewell gift to her before clearing off to stay with their mother, out of harm's way.'

'But that's awful! How could her husband let her do such a thing?'

'Easily, apparently. She says that as far as they're concerned it's a sensible way to raise money and it has nothing to do with their marriage, which is very happy. She sees it as a way of making the best use of her – talents. And so, apparently, does he. She's even managed to coax some of her clients to buy the furniture they make.'

'That sounds to me like an appalling attitude. But now I can tell you,' Jenny said, 'that when Andrew met her he was sure he'd seen her before, having dinner in a Dumfries hotel with a man – not Bernie. It must have been a client. If they're leaving, what's going to happen to Doris's cottage now?'

'Goodness knows.' Marcy drained her cup and set it down.

'I must go before Sam arrives with the intention of dragging me back to the store by my hair. I can't honestly say I would blame him, poor love.'

'I'll come with you – I've got some shopping to do,' Helen said.

As they reached the door it was thrown open and Ivy McGowan marched in, shopping bag in hand.

'The whole village's in a right to-do about that Carrie Wilson,' she announced with satisfaction. 'Did I not tell you she was a sly wee besom when she lived here with her parents? I always smell trouble when it's in the air and I knew that lassie hadn't changed, even if she does doll herself up and put on airs and graces now. A wolf in sheep's clothing, that's what she is – a proper wolf in sheep's clothing! Goodness only knows what she might have got up to if she hadnae been found out in time – opened a bawdy-house right here in the village for all we know.'

'If Carrie had decided to open her own bawdy-house in Prior's Ford, at least we'd have had the satisfaction of knowing it was a high-class establishment,' Marcy said as she and Helen escaped, leaving Jenny to cope with the old woman. 'They do say that something good often comes out of something bad, and it must be true. I haven't seen Ivy look so pleased since poor Doris Thatcher died.'

35

Jenny and Andrew were married on a perfect September day when vain summer was lingering to take yet another final bow while patient autumn waited in the wings, content to know its moment was very close. Gardens were still filled with colour and the village looked its best.

Ingrid and Freya managed to pay a flying visit to Scotland for the occasion; Ella stayed behind as she had joined a female football team and had an important game coming up. Ingrid insisted on Jenny and Maggie staying at her house on the night before the wedding.

'What's the point in that?' Jenny had wanted to know. 'We've been living together for years so we don't need any of that nonsense about the groom not seeing the bride before the ceremony.'

'I know, but you need to have your hen party, don't you? If you and Maggie stay here the girls can have a reunion and Marcy and Helen can join us. It'll be like old times. Oh, Jenny, how I miss those old times!'

'We all do. When are you coming back to Prior's Ford for good?'

A shadow fell across Ingrid's face. 'I don't know. My father's not getting any better as time goes by and there's no way my mother could manage without us. Peter's taken to the hotel business really well, bless him, and the girls have settled in at school. But let's not worry about the future now – let's just look forward to your happy day. And we must have that hen party because I want to catch up on all the village news. Letters and emails aren't the same as being together with a glass or two of wine!'

So Jenny gave in, and the four of them talked far into the night while Freya, Maggie and their friends enjoyed a noisy reunion in Freya's bedroom.

'Who's going to give you away, Jenny?' Ingrid asked.

'Nobody. Naomi says it's not necessary nowadays, and I don't have any family at the wedding, so I decided against it. It's just me and Maggie.'

'Who needs family when you've got friends?' Marcy shrugged.

'I'll drink to that,' Helen agreed.

The next morning they all went in two cars to a hairdressing salon in Kirkcudbright, then to a restaurant for lunch before returning to Ingrid's to get ready for the wedding.

Ingrid was in her element. 'This,' she announced as she took Jenny's dress off its hanger, 'is how a wedding should be – with everyone involved. Jenny, I wish now we had thought of inviting you and Andrew to honeymoon at our hotel in Norway, then we could have spent longer together.'

'I think that might have been a step too far.' Helen giggled. 'After all, it's their honeymoon.'

'As Jenny herself said, she and Andrew have already been living together for years. Maggie and Calum could have come as well.'

'We've settled for a few days in Wales, and we were going

to take Maggie and Calum with us, but Maggie put her foot down.'

'I should think so,' Maggie called from the next room, where Freya was helping her get ready. 'Who would want to go on someone else's honeymoon? Yugh!'

'So they're staying with Naomi,' Jenny finished before slipping the dress carefully over her head. 'What do you think?'

'Wait until the whole outfit's on,' Marcy suggested.

When it was, they all surveyed her for so long in silence that Jenny began to feel a twinge of anxiety. 'Tell me!'

'It's – perfect,' Helen said tremulously, and the others nodded.

'Really? Maggie helped me to choose it.'

'Then good for Maggie,' Marcy said as Jenny turned and surveyed herself in Ingrid's full-length mirror. She had chosen a dress in pale green silk, fitted to the hip then opening into a full skirt. Over it she wore a cream-coloured light jacket with a draped shawl collar. Her high-heeled shoes matched the dress and her hat was cream and wide-brimmed with a band of pale green tulle.

'It does look nice, doesn't it?'

'It's going to knock Andrew out,' Helen assured her as Freya led Maggie in. There was another burst of oohs and aahs, and the girl blushed with pleasure. Her simple, short-sleeved cream dress was patterned here and there with large violet flowers. The skirt flared at the hem and she carried a small posy of cream and violet flowers.

When the bride and bridesmaid emerged from the house to walk the short distance to the church there were more oohs and aahs from the women waiting by the gate, and a burst of applause.

The churchyard was thronged with people and Andrew and Calum, both smart in new suits and with shoes gleaming in the sunlight, stood at the church door, talking to Naomi. Inside the church Gilbert McBain played the organ, the music a pleasant background to the buzz of conversation.

When Jenny was spotted everyone stopped talking and turned towards her, falling back to either side so that she and Maggie and their friends found themselves walking through an aisle of people. Suddenly Jenny's stomach was full of butterflies. She clutched her small posy of pale yellow roses tightly and for a few seconds wished everything had been allowed to stay the way it was, with the village believing that she and Andrew were already married.

Then Andrew turned towards her, and when she saw the look on his face the butterflies vanished and she knew that, without realising it, she had been waiting all her life for this day, this man, and this occasion.

'You look . . .' he began to say, then had to stop and clear his throat before he could finish, 'beautiful!'

'Doesn't she just,' Naomi agreed, beaming. 'And hasn't God sent you a perfect day for a wedding? If that isn't approval I don't know what is. Andrew – Calum – we'd better get inside to let Gilbert know we're about to start. Jenny, you and Maggie wait out here until everyone's gone in, then watch for my signal to start walking down the aisle.'

'Right. Calum' – Jenny caught her son's hand and drew him aside for a moment – 'you look fantastic – so grown up!'

'You look okay yourself, Mum,' he said gruffly.

'Yes, Calum, you're actually quite dishy,' Jenny heard Maggie murmur.

Calum's ears went bright red. 'Oh, shut up!' he said, and hurried after his father while Maggie grinned at Jenny.

'I knew that would rattle his cage!'

'You've really taken to being a big sister, haven't you?' Jenny asked as the last of the guests filed past them into the church, each with a smile and a murmured good wish.

'It's not hard when the kid brother's half decent.' Maggie shrugged. They followed the last of the wedding guests into the foyer and reached the inner door. 'Wow, look at that!'

Jenny looked, and gasped. The church was not only filled to the back pews, it was also glowing with colour from masses of flowers all round the altar and along the walls of the two side passages. It looked as though every gardener in the village had wanted to contribute to her wedding day.

The quiet organ music ceased and Naomi signalled to them before nodding to Gilbert. As he started to play 'Here Comes the Bride', Jenny stepped forward, with Maggie following. Andrew turned and smiled at her, and she felt as though she was walking through a flower garden filled with peace and with love. A broad, delighted smile spread across her face as she walked towards the altar and Andrew.

Marcy was right. Who needed family when the world held wonderful friends with so much love to give?

Clarissa enjoyed the time spent with her stepchildren more than she had expected, but as always it was good to return to her own house and her own things. On her first morning back she checked the kitchen cupboards and made a list, then took it and her shopping basket to the village store. To her relief, she didn't meet Alastair. She still didn't know what to say to him when next they met.

'Nice holiday?' Jinty McDonald asked as they queued together at the checkout.

'Very nice, thanks. I enjoyed catching up with all my step-daughter's and stepson's activities, but it's always good to get back home.'

'Nothing like it. The village's settling down for the winter now that the holiday season's over. It's good to see the way the falcons and the Scarecrow Festivals have brought people into the place, but nice to get it back to ourselves again, I always think. Shame that you missed Jenny and Andrew Forsyth's wedding, it was a wonderful day for everyone. And have you heard that Alastair's leaving us?'

Clarissa felt as though someone had just punched her hard in the chest. 'Alastair Marshall?'

'Mmm. Landed himself a job in Glasgow. It all happened suddenly; he's off in a couple of days' time. The place won't seem the same without our Alastair around,' Jinty said casually, unaware of the chaos she had created.

Returning home, Clarissa picked up the phone to call Alastair, then put it down again. She unpacked her shopping and put it away neatly, moving like an automaton, then went out again.

Some forty-five minutes later she parked the car in the village of Kippford, one of her favourite spots on the Solway Firth. The tide was out and only the boats moored in the deepest part of the firth were still afloat. On the opposite side of the firth a small green boat lay aground on the mudflats; behind it, grass sloped up towards cosily rounded bushes and trees just beginning to show the first signs of changing into their beautiful autumn colours.

The water was like glass and the flats, she noticed, had been sculpted into runnels and whorls by the action of the water. A flock of birds clustered together on a patch of water and the sky above was blue with only a powder puff of cloud here and there. The entire scene was one of stillness and peace. It had a calming effect and gradually the storm raging in her head began to ease, giving her, at last, the chance to think rationally, and to weigh up the pros and cons of the dilemma she was in.

She stayed where she was, her eyes on the peaceful scene, and for the first time in ages allowed her mind free rein, holding back the 'buts' and 'what ifs' that had been tormenting her for many weeks. When she felt able she started up the engine and drove past the row of cottages, some white-painted and others with the beautiful pale grey local stone sparkling in the sun, all sitting behind small, well cared for front gardens.

As she headed for Prior's Ford the sky began to cloud over and by the time she had parked the car in a lay-by near the old ruins that gave the village its name, a drizzle had started. Clarissa set off on foot down the lane and when she reached the stile where she and Alastair had first met, the rain was falling in earnest, soaking her hair.

Smoke rose from the farm cottage's chimney and the door, usually open, was closed against the increasingly heavy rain. She knocked and the door was opened a moment later. Alastair, taken by surprise, stared down at her.

'Don't go,' said Clarissa.

Read on for a sample of the
next book in the Prior's Ford series,
Mystery in Prior's Ford

1

'I must be getting old,' Marcy Copleton announced. 'I hate change, and too many changes have been happening in this village recently.'

'Oh, come on – it's exciting,' Helen Campbell argued as she hoisted her basket onto the counter, 'I enjoy seeing new people around the place, and the Gift Horse turning into Colour Carousel.'

'That's because you've got plenty to write about in the Prior's Ford column of the *Dumfries News*. And as for Colour Carousel, you're surely not saying that you don't miss Ingrid and the Gift Horse and the coffees we used to enjoy there.'

'Of course I miss her, and Peter and the girls, but Anja's like a breath of fresh air,' Helen was saying when the store's door opened and Anja Jacobsen swept in, her sky blue top, crimson cropped trousers and blonde hair, short and standing out in spikes all over her head, filling the village store with colour and vitality.

'Hello, I am looking for chocolate biscuits.' Even her voice, with its sing-song accent, lit up the air around her. 'Jenny has been working hard all morning, and she needs sustenance.'

'Chocolate digestives are her favourite. Second top shelf, right over there. How are things coming along?'

'Very well. We'll be all finished for the opening next Wednesday,' Anja assured them as she put the packet of biscuits on the counter. 'Done and dusty, as you say.'

'Dusted,' Helen corrected her without thinking.

'That too,' Anja assured her, producing payment for the biscuits from a tiny scarlet soft-leather purse slung like a pendant from a silver chain about her neck.

'That's pretty. Where did you buy it?' Helen wanted to know.

'This? I made it.'

'Are you planning to sell purses like that in the shop?'

'No, but if you want one I can make it for you.'

'I have two daughters, Gemma and Irene. Could they each have one?'

'Of course. In different colours?'

'Yes, please. You choose them.'

'It's as good as done,' Anja assured her, scooping the biscuits up. 'Goodbye!'

'Doesn't just seeing that girl give your spirits a lift?'

'I suppose so,' Marcy admitted. 'But I still miss Ingrid.'

'We all do.' Ingrid MacKenzie had lived for years in the village with her husband Peter and their two daughters, Freya and Ella. She owned and ran a gift shop called the Gift Horse with the assistance of Jenny Forsyth, and all four women were close friends. A year earlier, the MacKenzies had left for Ingrid's home in Norway when her father developed Alzheimer's and his wife was unable to cope with the family hotel on her own.

Ingrid's original plan was to find a new manager for the hotel and then return to Dumfries and Galloway, but that had not as yet been possible, so she and Peter had decided to stay on indefinitely. As Ingrid's niece Anja had recently qualified as an interior designer and had two ambitions – to travel and to set up her own business – Ingrid and Peter had offered her their Prior's Ford home and the chance to turn the Gift Horse, which Jenny had been struggling to run on her own, into Colour Carousel. Jenny was in full agreement.

'It's not the same without you,' she said when Ingrid phoned to ask her opinion. 'I'm happier as an assistant rather than a manager.'

'You are such a good friend! Anja's excited about the chance to start her own business, and to visit Scotland. And we'll be back – eventually. I miss you all. Hug Helen and Marcy for me, and ask them to give you my hug,' Ingrid said.

'The thing is, there have been so many changes since the MacKenzies went away,' Marcy reverted back to the original topic as she helped Helen to pack her purchases. 'People have started moving in to that new housing estate across from the farm . . .'

'Which should please Sam.'

'Oh, it does,' Marcy's voice was dry, and Helen chuckled. Sam Brennan, Marcy's partner and owner of the village store, liked nothing more than the sound of money dropping into the till. 'Which reminds me,' Marcy went on, 'that's twenty-one pounds and thirty pence, please.' Then, as Helen began to fish around in the depths of her shoulder bag, 'it's the village's character I'm concerned about. I've always liked knowing every face that came in the door. I even miss Ivy's sharp tongue, and I never thought I would say that!'

'Sometimes I wish some clever person could invent tiny helium balloons to fasten to the contents of handbags so that they float to the top when you need them,' Helen fretted, and then, producing the large shabby purse she had used for more years than she could recall, 'At last! I miss Ivy more than I thought I would, too,' she went on as she began to count out notes and change. 'Poor old soul. She was so determined to outlive Doris Thatcher, and so pleased when Doris passed away, leaving her the oldest inhabitant. And within a year she was gone too. I was certain that she would get her telegram from the Queen, and I'm sure she was as well, but she turned out to be six years short. We don't even have an oldest inhabitant any more.'

'We must have. We just don't know who it is.'

'Sometimes,' Helen said as she tucked her change into the purse, replaced it in her shoulder bag and gathered up her shopping, 'I feel as though it might be me.'

'So, how's your love life comin' along?'

Clarissa Ramsay winced. 'Amy, that's no question to ask of a mature woman in her fifties.'

'Forget the mature, and forget the fifties.' Even though Amy Rose was at home in America her voice travelled the miles with ease; it was as though she were standing in the hall with Clarissa. 'You're a woman, and love strikes at any age – as you well know. Come on, how are you and Alastair managin' with all that distance between you?'

'I've seen him since I last spoke to you,' Clarissa admitted. 'I spent a week in Glasgow, and it was lovely to see him. He's enjoying working in that art gallery.'

'You stayed with him?'

'Amy, he shares a small flat with a work colleague. I booked into a hotel.'

'On your own?' Amy's voice rose a good half-octave.

'Yes on my own. It's . . . difficult with Alastair being so much younger than I am.'

'Oh, tosh! I bet he doesn't agree with you on that,' Amy

312

retorted, and then, taking Clarissa's silence for agreement, she went on, 'Look here, Clarissa, you've finally admitted that you're mad about the boy – remember that song? I still love it – and he's clearly mad about you, so for goodness' sake will the two of you do something about it? If you wait until he comes back to the village it'll only be worse because then you'll have to face everyone. If the two of you are a real couple by the time that happens, it'll make the facin' a lot easier because you can do it together.'

'Maybe you're right, but—'

'You're darned right, I'm right. Listen,' Amy said, 'One of the reasons I was phonin' was to say that I fancy another trip to Scotland. Are you up for it?'

'That would be lovely. You know that you'll always be welcome here.'

'Good, that's settled. I'm all booked up to arrive in three weeks' time, on August third. Don't bother to meet me, I'll buy myself a run-around automobile, same as last time. Why don't you arrange a week's holiday for you and Alastair around about the tenth to give you the chance to get to know each other properly without anyone else around?'

'But—'

'Get a cottage, or a tent. I'll hold the fort while you're gone. It'll be great to catch up with what's goin' on in Prior's Ford. Can't wait,' Amy said, and hung up, leaving Clarissa to gape at the receiver in her hand.

It wasn't possible, she told herself once she had remembered to close her mouth and put the receiver back on its rest. She and Alastair couldn't just . . . she felt her face grow hot at the thought, while butterflies began to flutter around her stomach.

She had allowed herself to get into the most terrible mess. A short while after she and Keith, the man she had married in her late forties, retired to Prior's Ford he had died suddenly, leaving her alone and among strangers. The discovery, while going through his papers, that Keith had been unfaithful to her throughout their marriage, and with her closest friend, had been too much. She had wandered from the house and was found by Alastair Marshall, an artist in his thirties, sitting on a stile in the pouring rain, soaked to the skin. He had rescued and befriended her, and helped her to gain the strength of mind to rediscover herself. Ridiculous though it was, they had fallen in love with each other.

Amy, on a visit to Clarissa the previous year, had forced the two of them to accept the truth they were trying to deny, but by that time Alastair had accepted a job with an art gallery in Glasgow.

They missed each other badly, phoned almost every day, and Clarissa had been to Glasgow two or three times. It had been wonderful, spending the evenings and weekends together and wandering around the city alone when he was working, so happy that she couldn't stop smiling. But she was still afraid to make the final commitment. Alastair had begged her to book a double room, but she had refused.

'I'm . . . you might not—'

'Clarissa, I love you for the person you are, and for your mind, and your warmth. I want you, all of you, not some brainless bimbo with a beautiful body. I will never ever let you down. I just want us to belong to each other, completely. What else can I say?'

She wanted him too. She longed for him, but to her the age difference was still a barrier. Perhaps, she thought as she went into the kitchen to put on the kettle, Amy had the right idea. Perhaps they should rent a cottage in some quiet place where nobody knew them. It would take all her courage, but they couldn't continue the way they were. Her middle-aged

314

body might repel him, but if she kept refusing to take the final step she would probably lose him anyway.

Eventually, if all went well between them, she and Alastair would have to present themselves to everyone as a couple, and she winced at the prospect, then tried to take comfort in the thought that at least they would be facing the music together.

She had no idea, as she made a calming cup of coffee, that Prior's Ford would, quite soon, have a lot more to talk about than an affair between an elderly retired teacher and a young artist.

SECRETS IN PRIOR'S FORD

Eve Houston

There is consternation among the villagers of pretty Scottish borders town, Prior's Ford, when a firm expresses interest in re-opening an old granite quarry. Almost overnight neighbours and friends fall out, with some welcoming the work the quarry will bring while others are ready to fight to preserve the village's peace.

Publican Glen organises a protest group – but when a local newspaper takes an interest in him and the story, he starts to feel very nervous indeed. And when Jenny Forsyth attends a protest meeting she is shocked to discover the quarry surveyor is an unwelcome face from her past.

Clarissa Ramsay, newly widowed, is too preoccupied to care much about the threat facing the village. She's discovered her husband Keith had a secret life. . .

While up at Linn Hall, the impoverished Ralston-Kerrs, struggling to keep the estate that is their ancestral heritage from going under, find that the quarry re-opening represents a test of loyalty to the village that regards them as its lairds.

978-0-7515-3961-5

DRAMA COMES TO PRIOR'S FORD

Eve Houston

Actress Meredith Whitelaw, axed from a popular television
soap, has descended upon Prior's Ford to 'rest' – but instead
she creates havoc for the local dramatic society.

Clarissa Ramsay, travelling the world, keeps in contact with her
friend Alastair Marshall, who finds himself missing her more with
each letter that arrives. Then Clarissa's aloof stepdaughter Alexandra
bursts into his life, in search of refuge and consolation.

Unexpected news for Lewis Ralston-Kerr causes alarm and
apprehension to his parents, busy refurbishing their tumbledown
manor house. And Jenny Forsyth and her husband Andrew
discover, when Jenny's long-lost stepdaughter Maggie moves
in, that the sweet little toddler has become a difficult
teenager with a grudge to settle . . .

978-0-7515-3962-2

TROUBLE IN PRIOR'S FORD

Eve Houston

Taking advantage of recent tourist interest, the residents of
Prior's Ford plan a summer festival. But someone is determined to
sabotage the event, and it takes all the villagers' detective skills
to stop the vandals in their tracks.

Meanwhile, at Tarbethill Farm things are going from bad to
worse. In dire financial straits, Victor, the eldest son, is tempted
by a developer's offer on their land. But if his father finds
out it promises to tear the family apart.

At the big house, Lewis remains absolutely besotted by his baby
daughter, while his family still secretly wonders if she really is his.
And as Molly starts to take advantage of Lewis's good nature, can
Ginny bear to keep silent about her feelings for him?

978-0-7515-4207-3

THE DAMASK DAYS
Evelyn Hood

Christian Knox is a girl who dreams – of a life beyond
that of a Paisley housewife, of a world of learning beyond
her Ladies' School, of possibilities her father dismisses as 'daft ideas'.
But Christian is determined and when her father refuses to finance
her education further she resolves to pay for it herself, by working as
a tambourer, embroidering freelance for local textile manufacturers.
Soon she's managing a group of Tambouring women on behalf
of Paisley's biggest weavers, among them Angus Fraser, a
man old enough to be her father but wise enough
to appreciate her talents.

Plunged into the fascinating world of Scotland's fledgling
textile industry, Christian soon finds her combination of Lowland
resolve and female flair begins to make its mark. And, in the shape
of her greatest, most fought-for inspiration, the Paisley Shawl, it
is a mark to be remembered for generations to come . . .

978-0-7515-4506-7

THIS TIME NEXT YEAR
Evelyn Hood

Young widow Lessie Hamilton is shocked and upset
to realise she is sharing her tenement landing with a prostitute.
But when Anna McCauley begs Lessie to help disguise the fact
that one of her clients has passed away in her bed, she agrees.
Soft-hearted and desperate to buy medicine for her sick
toddler, she accepts the twenty shillings Anna gives
her, promising one day to repay the money.

But keeping her promise is not easy, and from that day
forward the fates of Lessie and her younger brother, Davie,
are inextricably intertwined with Anna's and the family
of her deceased client . . .

978-0-7515-4516-6

A HANDFUL OF HAPPINESS

Evelyn Hood

Like so many in Clydeside's dockland tenements, Jenny Gillespie has suffered her share of troubles during the Great War. Firstly, her fiancé Robert Archer leaves her for England, a new job and another woman. Then, with her brother missing in action, she is forced to put the demands of her relentless family before the prospect of a new beginning at a Glasgow department store.

Jenny's job in the tracing office of Dalkieth's shipyard is difficult enough. But then her former fiancé returns as both a qualified naval engineer and her new boss. Robert wants to rekindle their relationship, and whilst the thought of leaving her cramped tenement home is tempting, Jenny knows that she cannot afford to trust him. It is only when she receives an unexpected proposal of marriage that Jenny, perhaps, has the chance to grasp the handful of happiness she longs for . . .

978-0-7515-4511-1

Other bestselling titles available by mail:

☐ Secrets in Prior's Ford   Eve Houston   £7.99
☐ Drama Comes to Prior's Ford   Eve Houston   £7.99
☐ Trouble in Prior's Ford   Eve Houston   £7.99
☐ The Damask Days   Evelyn Hood   £7.99
☐ This Time Next Year   Evelyn Hood   £7.99
☐ A Handful of Happiness   Evelyn Hood   £7.99

The prices shown above are correct at time of going to press. However, the publishers reserve the right to increase prices on covers from those previously advertised, without further notice.

sphere

Please allow for postage and packing: **Free UK delivery.**
Europe; add 25% of retail price; Rest of World; 45% of retail price.

To order any of the above or any other Sphere titles, please call our credit card orderline or fill in this coupon and send/fax it to:

Sphere, P.O. Box 121, Kettering, Northants NN14 4ZQ
Fax: 01832 733076   Tel: 01832 737526
Email: aspenhouse@FSBDial.co.uk

☐ I enclose a UK bank cheque made payable to Sphere for £ . . . .
☐ Please charge £ . . . . . . to my Visa, Delta, Maestro.

Expiry Date ☐☐☐☐   Maestro Issue No. ☐☐

NAME (BLOCK LETTERS please) . . . .

ADDRESS . . . .

. . . .

. . . .

Postcode . . . . Telephone . . . .

Signature . . . .

Please allow 28 days for delivery within the UK. Offer subject to price and availability.